KILL SEASON

A JAKE CASHEN NOVEL

DECLAN JAMES

ONE

He walked with sure, strong steps as he told his boy how to kill. He picked a prime spot for him in the northeast portion of the property. Flatlands. Deer would pass through here on their way to the stream in the valley. Father and son meant to pick them off. Where was the sport in that?

"Keep your nose out of your phone," the father said.

"Dad, I know," the boy said, though he was almost a man. Same posture as the father. Wide stance. He carried his twelve-gauge slung over his shoulder.

"Just keep quiet. No squirming around. You make too much noise and they'll stay clear. Know where your scent is moving with the wind. Aim small, miss small."

"I know," the son said, his tone clipped. The kind of attitude that should have earned him a slap in the mouth.

"Those your favorite words today?" the father asked, his tone light. He laughed at his own joke.

"Yeah," the father said. "I guess you do know. Trust me. Someday you'll have the pleasure of annoying your own son just like I am."

"Go on, Dad," the boy said. "Before you're the one who scares the deer away."

The father put a hand on his son's shoulder, squeezing it.

Perfect specimens. Both of them. They had the same long legs. The same angle to their shoulders. Athletes, for sure. Wrestlers, probably. This was Blackhand Hills after all. They'd driven up in a black pick-up truck with Stanley High School stickers on the windshield.

"I'll head back your way just before lunch," the father said. "If neither of us shoots anything."

"We better shoot something," the son said. "I'm tired of looking at an empty freezer."

"Me too," the father said. He was smiling as he turned away from the boy. The boy slipped into his deer blind at the base of a large oak tree. It was another prime spot. Far from state land, they shouldn't have any interference from the "Orange Army" lining up just two miles south of here. No. These were legacy hunters. The father had probably hunted this same acreage since he was old enough to hold his own gun. Skilled. He had that look about him. That strut.

The killer steadied the weapon, eyes glued to the scope. Seeing everything. Every detail of the father's orange vest. His calloused hands as he held his shotgun, easy, natural, like it was an extension of his arm.

He had a swagger about him as he walked uphill toward his own blind set-up just one hundred and fifty yards away.

The killer refocused the scope on the boy. Not a boy. Not really. Sixteen maybe? Seventeen? Nearing his physical prime. Young. Hungry. A young buck himself. Cock-sure and arrogant, probably. The killer knew the type. Thought he would live forever. Big man. Expected girls to fall at his feet. Probably never looked past their bodies. Nothing but sex objects to this kid, surely. They were all like that.

The killer aimed. From this vantage point, it would be almost too easy. One shot, straight through the base of the kid's skull. Lights out. Gone. No more girls to torment. Or weaker boys. Yeah. He probably did that too. Removing him from the gene pool would be a favor.

But the father. He was bigger. Maybe not stronger, but more seasoned. Surely the more skilled hunter of the two of them.

The silverback. The alpha. If the two of them got into a physical fight as some fathers and sons do, no doubt the father still had the psychological advantage if not the same brute strength as the boy. They likely hadn't yet reached that point in their relationship where the son would overtake his old man. Not yet. In a year or two maybe. But the killer would never let that happen. Their relationship would end today.

Yes. The father was still the alpha. The apex predator.

The prey.

Lowering the scope, the killer quietly retreated. Taking slow, deliberate steps, the killer stayed downwind of the father, cutting a wide swath, knowing exactly where the father was going.

The killer could take plenty of time. Be patient. Just like the father as he climbed into his own blind and settled in. Waiting. Watching. Always ready.

Oh yes. The father thought he was the most lethal threat out here.

The killer's blood started to thrum, coursing with adrenaline. The father whispered to himself. The killer couldn't quite make it out, but had heard this so many times before. A prayer. A mantra. Some call to the hunting gods. Oh, he'd get an answer. Just not the one he expected.

The father waited. The man sat in his camp chair, checked his weapon, lifted his head and smelled the wind. All the time in the world. He thinks he has all the time in the world. A shot rang out to the northeast.

The boy.

Rage coursed through the killer. The father started to rise, angling himself toward the distant sound of the shot. The father pumped his fist. Proud. So proud. He'd trained his son to take an innocent life.

The wind picked up and there was movement in the trees just to the northwest. The boy was still east of the father. The killer watched as the father kept looking that way. Did he truly hope the boy shot first? How big of him if he did.

"Not today," the killer whispered. "You'll kill nothing else."

Just then, a buck traipsed through the clearing. The killer tensed. He was beautiful. A six-point. Anger rose as the killer watched.

"Coward," the killer thought. The deer was too young. Probably hadn't even had a chance to breed yet. The father likely wouldn't care. He only cared about his empty freezer. A freezer he could easily fill at the local grocery store. He'd tell himself he was a conservationist as he shot and gutted that magnificent animal.

"Not today," the killer whispered. Then the father did something the killer didn't expect. He made a gesture; lowering his shotgun, he waved a hand.

The buck's ears pricked. He was looking past the father. He was looking straight at the killer. A heartbeat later, the buck darted away out of view.

Now. It had to be now. The killer sighted the father once more. The man sat so very still. Oblivious to what was really happening around him. Probably giving himself a mental pat on the back for the mercy he showed that buck.

The killer would show him a different kind of mercy. And no mercy at all.

The killer picked a spot just above the father-hunter's right ear. The shot would blind him in an instant, slicing through his optic nerve. He wouldn't feel anything. And that would be his mercy.

The killer squeezed the trigger. The shot rang clear and true. The killer kept the rifle steady after, still watching it all unfold through the scope.

The father jerked backward, going rigid as stone. Then he slumped to the ground, dead before he hit the leaves. The killer watched as blood began to trickle from the wound, painting the leaves that cushioned the father's fall.

The killer studied him. Committing every detail to memory. A memory to be retrieved later. A masterpiece. It would be art.

He died with his eyes open. Many of them did. His right hand still gripped tight around his shotgun even in death. Interesting.

The killer focused on that. The way the man's hands turned quickly white as the blood began to drain from his body. His left hand twitched for just a moment. An involuntary muscle spasm. The man was already gone, but the electrical activity in his brain slowly shorted out.

His hand. His left hand. The middle finger began to curl inward, as if clutching the ground one last time. It was then the killer noticed the ring.

A class ring? It had a large, blue stone in the center. With the high-powered scope, the killer could see every fine detail etched into the sterling silver. No, not a class ring. Even better.

The image through the scope wavered as excitement shot through the killer. A wrestler. Yes. The killer could make out the tiny male figure in a wrestler's stance on the side of the ring. Across the top, the ring read "State Champ 2001."

The killer put a hand up, muffling the laughter that threatened to erupt.

A champion. The alpha of alphas. Oh, today had been a very good day.

Time was running out though. The killer focused once more on the father's face. There was no fear in his glassy eyes. No pain either. It had been a perfect kill, after all.

"I could take the ring," the killer thought. A true trophy. But that would be folly. There would be tracks. Footprints. Perhaps even DNA as the killer shed tiny flecks of skin or hair. And the boy would come soon.

Even now, the father's cell phone began to buzz. It must have fallen from his pocket as he slumped to the ground. It landed face up beside him. Through the scope, the killer could read the caller ID.

Travis.

The boy's name? He would have been close enough to hear the rifle shot. It wouldn't sound like the twelve-gauge his father hunted with. But maybe the boy wasn't sophisticated enough to understand the difference.

It would be something to watch. The boy might be the one to find his father. If the killer waited just a little bit more, there'd be a chance for a second kill. Take them both today. Father and son. Hunters. Hunted.

The thought of it made the killer's blood sing. It got harder to hold the rifle steady.

No. Not today. It wasn't part of the plan. The minute the killer deviated from the plan would spell doom.

The father's phone rang again. Travis. Travis. Travis.

He was coming. It would be enough that the son would find the masterpiece. The killer's gift to the world. For today it was enough.

But there would be others ...

TWO

Twenty pairs of disapproving eyes settled on Detective Jake Cashen during the morning roll call. Then half of them turned to grins as they got the full effect of Jake's ringtone. He'd broken a rule.

"Phones on silent, Detective," Lieutenant John Beverly said, peering at Jake over the top of his glasses. "Breakfast is on you tomorrow morning."

Jake fumbled for his phone as the strains of Wagner's "Ride of the Valkyries" reached peak volume. Laughter went through the other cops in the room. It was Gemma calling. His sister. They all knew her well. They also knew she didn't usually call unless there was some fire Jake needed to put out.

He clicked the volume button on his phone and slipped it back into his pocket.

"Anyway," Beverly said. "As I was saying. I want extra patrols out at Blackhand Park. We're getting lots of complaints about underage drunks out there. Let's not let that place turn into another Grover Courtyard."

In the late eighties and early nineties. Grover Courtyard had been a Worthington County hotspot where local bands came to play. By the time Jake graduated from high school, it had turned into a drug dealer's paradise.

"Arlene Bloom is at it again," Beverly continued, running down the most notable crime reports from in and around the county. Arlene Bloom was known as a frequent flier. She lived in a trailer park in Galway Township and thought 911 was appropriate for whatever neighbor disputes or parenting issues she was having on any given day.

"Neighbor said she brandished a pistol at him yesterday," Beverly said. "Said she had her laundry hanging on a line for over a week and he complained about it. Next day he caught a raccoon in a live trap after two nights of it rummaging through his garbage."

"Oh lord," Jake said. "Corky."

"Yep," Beverly confirmed. Arlene Bloom kept the thing as a pet. Just last year, Jake had gone out to her trailer and found him sitting at her kitchen table eating breakfast cereal.

"She'll kill him," Deputy Chris Denning said. "She treats that raccoon better than her actual kid."

"Well," Beverly said. "I'd like it if we made an appearance out there. Calm them both down before this thing escalates. Cashen, you've built a rapport. Take a drive, will you?"

"What?" Jake said. "A rapport?"

"She asked for you specifically," Beverly said. This got another round of snickers from the group. Jake knew the more he protested, the worse Beverly might make this particular turd bag of an assignment.

His phone vibrated again. He stole a glance at the screen. Gemma. Again.

"Seriously," Lieutenant Beverly said. "Something you wanna share with the class, Cashen?"

"All good, Lieutenant," Jake said. Though he knew it wasn't. His sister knew he was at work. She also knew mornings were the worst time to call. Usually Gemma's emergencies consisted of leaky pipes, the latest verbal abuse from their cantankerous grandfather, or something to do with one of the cars. He'd invoked the story of "The Boy Who Cried Wolf" to her a zillion times, to no avail.

"Well," Beverly said. "That's about all I got. Except it's opening day for gun season. Expect the usual level of trespassing complaints and general asshattery on state land. DNR is stretched pretty thin so let's back them up where we can."

"So are we," Sergeant Jeff Hammer said. He wasn't wrong.

"We're all on the same team," Beverly said.

"Their team is better paid," Deputy Denning said.

This got a round of laughter and generalized griping from the group. Jake's phone started buzzing again. He was kicking himself for not leaving the thing at his desk like he usually did during roll call. It was like his sister had a sixth sense about that too.

"That is all," Lieutenant Beverly said, wrapping up yet another meeting they all knew could have been an email. Beverly gathered his notes and dismissed the shift to start their day.

"Jake," Beverly called. "You mind staying after class?"

This earned Jake a couple of catcalls and more laughter. Jake didn't mind. It would give him a refreshing respite from the phone call he knew he'd soon have to return.

"You bet," he said. He waited for the room to clear before approaching Beverly at the lectern.

"Everything okay at home?" Beverly asked.

"Who knows," Jake answered. "I'm sure she'll call again."

As lieutenants went, John Beverly was a decent one. Didn't micromanage. Tried his level best to get his people what they needed. And he knew how to stay out of the way. Jake knew that was in large part to the credit of Sheriff Meg Landry. She'd inherited the gig after former Sheriff O'Neal died suddenly of a heart attack. Though Landry had never set out to be sheriff, she was doing a heck of a good job at it. She'd been the one to pin Jake's detective badge on him last year, seeing something in him he'd tried damn hard to push away.

But here he was, a year later, one of only two detectives handling crimes against persons in the whole county.

"About Ed Zender," Beverly said, referring to the *other* detective in the crimes against persons division. Though even the term "division" was loose. They were two guys with side-by-side cubicles in a twelve-by-twelve-foot office on the second floor.

"I just got off the phone with him," Beverly said. "He's gonna be laid up for a few days yet. Doc's referring him to a spinal surgeon."

"Oh geez," Jake said. Ed Zender had thrown his back out bowling last week, the culmination of close to thirty years on the job carrying a heavy gun belt and service weapon at his side. Jake knew his days were numbered on that score too.

"Is he in the hospital now or at home?" Jake asked.

"Hospital," Beverly responded. "They've got him in traction."

"I'll try and pop in," Jake said.

"I was hoping you'd say that," Beverly said. "I know he'd sure appreciate it. I'm sorry to say, the burden of all this is going to fall on you, workload wise. We don't have the manpower or the budget to bring anybody else up to detective right now. I talked to Majewski though. If there's any slack he can pick up while Ed's gone, feel free to press him into service."

"I will," Jake said. He felt bad for Ed, but the truth was, the man had been more or less just punching a timecard for years. Ed Zender could be an okay guy, but a lousy detective.

"And if you need to work overtime on anything," Beverly said, "I'll make sure to get it approved."

"I appreciate that," Jake said. "Let's just hope for a quiet couple of weeks." The second he said it, Jake regretted it. He'd committed the worst of all jinxes. Even Beverly's eyes went wide.

Jake's phone buzzed yet again. Beverly patted him on the shoulder. "You better get that. The last thing I'd wanna be on is your sister's bad side."

Jake smiled. He and Beverly started to walk out of the room together.

"Hey," Beverly said. "On that score. Not her bad side, I mean. But about your sister. Is she seeing anyone lately?"

Jake stopped short. Last time he checked, John Beverly was very married, not to mention a good fifteen years older than Gemma.

"Not for me," Beverly said, his face going white. "No. No. It's just speaking of the DNR. I'm friendly with one of the wardens. Good guy. Anyway, he was asking about her. We bowl together."

Jake laughed. "You like this guy?"

Before Jake could say anything else, he and Beverly turned the corner and ran smack into Darcy Noble, head dispatcher.

"Jake," Darcy said. It took a moment for Jake's brain to catch up with what his eyes were seeing. Darcy was crying. No. Not just crying. Sobbing. She'd broken out in hives.

Beverly reacted first. He put a hand out to steady her.

"Jake," she said again, heaving out her words. "A c-call. I took a call."

"What is it?" Jake said. His nerve endings went on high alert. He'd never seen Darcy like this. Ever. She had always been cool and calm as she carried out her duties.

"There's been some kind of accident," she said.

The buzzing phone in Jake's back pocket took on new meaning. Gemma. He knew. Deep in his bones, he knew. This time, there really was a wolf.

Beverly held on to Darcy's shoulders, keeping her upright as she struggled to find the words.

"Out on Grace Church Road," Darcy said. "The Palmer farm. An accident. It's bad, Jake."

The morning's events replayed in Jake's mind. They were like floating puzzle pieces slamming into place. Grace Church Road. The Palmer farm. It was a sixty-acre tract of land in Lublin Township, not far from his grandpa's place. Prime buck country. He'd hunted it himself so many times with his boyhood friend,

Ben Wayne. It was opening day. Gemma kept calling. Now, her son Ryan was best friends with Ben's son Travis.

Travis. Ryan. My God. In slow motion, Jake reached for his still ringing phone in his back pocket.

"Where's Ryan?" Jake heard himself say. In front of him, Darcy's face registered Jake's words. She shook her head vigorously.

"No," she whispered. "Jake, it's not Ryan."

In his ear, Gemma was sobbing.

"It's Ben, Jake," Darcy said. "It's Ben. It's Ben."

THREE

The Palmer farm was eight miles to the east. It had been in Nelson Palmer's family for a hundred and fifty years. A hundred years ago, Ben Wayne's great-grandfather met Nelson's great-something grandfather in a bar and struck up a conversation. Both families had worked for the Arden Clay Mill since the first day old John Paul Arden broke ground on it. They were friends. Mill brothers. When Ben's great-grandfather started scouting land to hunt with his son, Grandpa Nelson was only too happy to help him out.

He had sixty acres adjacent to the farm. Some of the best hunting ground in southern Ohio, let alone Worthington County. A private honey hole that had boasted at least three state-record trophy bucks over the years.

When Jake pulled into the simple two-track path off Grace Church Road, his stomach churned as he saw the flashing blues of the patrol cars first on scene.

He hadn't wanted to believe it. In the ten minutes it took him to get here from downtown Stanley, he thought maybe it was a mistake. Maybe it wasn't the Palmer woods after all. There was state land just up the road that would be teeming with new hunters this morning. Surely one of those idiots had made a terrible mistake. It couldn't be here. Not here.

Jake parked behind one of the cruisers and straightened his tie. A third cruiser was parked further into the woods, its back door wide open. There was someone seated in it wearing camo pants and a pair of hiking boots. Stiffening his back, Jake walked up.

A purple-faced Travis Wayne sat in the cruiser, furiously tapping his boot against the ground. Deputy Tom Stuckey had his hands on Travis's shoulders, forcing him to stay in the back of the car.

"Travis?" Jake said. The boy's eyes were almost swollen shut. For an instant, Jake thought he'd been hit. He quickly realized Travis's tears had done that. A river of snot ran down his nose. On the ground just outside the vehicle, Jake noticed a pile of vomit.

"Travis," Jake said again. "Stay with me, son."

Travis met Jake's eyes. The horror in them ripped Jake's guts out. He swallowed hard. There were lights up ahead, deeper into the woods.

"Uncle Jake," Travis croaked. "My dad …"

"Hang tight," Jake said. "I'll come back to talk to you. Stay with us, okay? Just hang tight."

Travis started to cry again. Jake made eye contact with Deputy Stuckey. He gave him a slow, deliberate nod. Stuckey understood. He was to keep the boy safe. Keep him right where he sat.

Steeling himself for what was to come, Jake trudged into the woods.

Voices drew him at first. Then, the unmistakable metallic tang of fresh blood hit his nose.

Two more deputies stood on the side of the path. They kept a ready stance, hands on hips, waiting for Jake.

"Detective," Deputy Rathburn said. She was new. Only on the force for a year. Her partner, Deputy Matt Bundy, had maybe ten years on. He knew Ben and Jake both. He'd been a freshman when they were seniors. A good practice wrestler, but he never won a wrestle-off his entire high school career.

"Jake," Bundy said. "It's ..."

Jake put a hand up. He couldn't hear it. He had to see it for himself. Jake walked past Bundy and Rathburn, following the scent of blood.

He was there. The body rested in a fetal position at the base of a large oak tree. His camp chair sat upright, pointed toward the thickest part of the woods. Beside it was a Yeti tumbler. The coffee within it would still be hot.

He wasn't Jake. This wasn't Ben, his friend from preschool on. His hunting buddy. His teammate. This was a victim. And he was Detective Cashen now. It's all he could ever be for Ben Wayne again.

"His boy heard a gunshot," Deputy Bundy said. "Texted him right after, thinking he'd shot something. Travis said he'd heard a buck go through here a couple of minutes beforehand. When five minutes or so went by and Ben didn't answer his texts, the kid thought it was off and came back up here. Said he thought Ben was sleeping at first."

Jake got closer. The victim had a bullet wound through his right temple, perfectly midline from his ear to his eye. The entry wound. Jake looked over his right shoulder. There was a clearing maybe twenty yards to the south. He looked back. Though he wouldn't touch Ben, he knew the exit wound must have gone through the left side of his head. What was left of Ben Wayne's brains were splattered all over the base of the tree.

"He found him," Jake said. "Travis found him."

"Yes, sir," Deputy Rathburn said. "He said he shot at a ten-point from where he was seated about a quarter mile to the northeast. A bit later, he heard a second shot from where his father was set up. That's when he started texting."

"A quarter mile is such a long way," Bundy said. "Travis swears he was aiming east of him. He swears it but ..."

"Who else was out here?" Jake asked.

"What?" Bundy said, his voice cracking. From the corner of his eye, he saw Matt Bundy double over and grab his knees.

"I can't believe it," Matt said. Deputy Rathburn put a hand on her partner's back.

"I just saw him," Bundy said. "He was picking up lunch at the Vedge Wedge. I teased him about it. He ..."

"I need you to tape this area off," Jake said. "I want a fifty-by-fifty area blocked off from the body on all sides. No one goes in or out. You understand?"

Matt slowly pulled himself upright.

"I'm gonna call for three more deputies. But I want you both to get started. Get me names. Anyone else who had permission to hunt out here today. I want the license plates of every vehicle you see parked along the side of the road for a mile square. Anyone parked at the farms too. I want the woods walked too. A mile square. But nobody within that fifty-by-fifty tape. Got it? Not until you see me or Mark Ramirez from BCI. We clear?"

"Jake," Bundy said. "Ben's ..."

"We clear?" Jake shouted.

"Of course," Rathburn said.

"Yes," Bundy said.

"Then get moving," Jake said. "Get the tape from your kit. Rathburn? Start a crime scene log. Nobody comes in or out without you writing it down."

Bundy and Rathburn shared a look, but started moving back up the trail toward the road. It gave Jake the last moments alone with Ben Wayne that he would ever have.

It was quick. It had to be quick. Ben would have heard Travis's shot. His body was facing northeast. He would have turned toward it. Jake saw Ben's cell phone laying on the ground beside him. Not in his pocket. Not in the side compartment snapped to the camp chair where Ben usually kept it.

He'd taken it out. From here, Jake could see he'd clicked it to silent mode.

His eyes. Ben's eyes. Sightless and milky, Jake knew the path of the bullet had passed right behind them. Lights out.

A quick death. But Jake was under no illusion Ben had felt no pain.

Jake felt numb. Nothingness. His mind blank but for the checklist he'd already started.

Have to get the Bureau of Criminal Investigation guys down immediately.

Have to search Travis's phone. He'd get consent.

Trail cameras. He knew Nelson Palmer had some. Jake would need to pull the cards. Christ. Did the Palmers even know what happened yet?

Jake closed his eyes and said a Hail Mary. He hadn't planned it. It just came to him out of nowhere. He made the Sign of the Cross and started back up the trail. Rathburn and Bundy were already making their way back, yellow police tape in hand.

Jake said nothing as he passed them. He went straight for the parked cruiser at the entrance to the trail. Travis still sat in the back, his shoulders quaking.

Jake put a hand on Deputy Stuckey's arm, gently pulling him aside. Stuckey made way for Jake.

Pulling his slacks up at the knee, Jake squatted down so he was eye level with Travis Wayne.

Just a kid. A baby. That's what everyone would say. Not Jake. He shared something with Travis now that few people would ever understand. It happened to Jake much sooner, of course. He'd only been seven years old. Thirty years ago on the morning his childhood ended.

So maybe Travis had an advantage in that. His mother, Ben's wife and high school sweetheart, Abby, died five years ago from breast cancer. Now, Travis was a true orphan. A man by force if not by choice. And he was only sixteen.

"He wouldn't answer me, Uncle Jake," Travis said. "I should have gone down sooner. I thought he'd start yelling at me for making noise. I told him I didn't want his help. I told him ..."

"Travis," Jake said. "Do you know who else was in the area? Did you see anybody? Talk to anybody? Your dad likes to get breakfast at Charlie's. Did you do that today?"

Travis shook his head. "It was just us," he said. "We were running late. Ryan ... Ryan was supposed to come out with us. We went to pick him up and his mom wouldn't let him come to the door. He's s-sick or something."

The air in Jake's lungs felt like it had turned to tar. Ryan. His seventeen-year-old nephew. Of course he would have made plans to hunt with Ben and Travis. With Ed Zender on medical leave, Jake had to work. Otherwise they would have hunted Grandpa Max's land together.

God. Ryan. Gemma. She'd been hysterical for the few seconds Jake had her on the phone this morning. He couldn't understand anything she was saying. He'd hung up with her as soon as Darcy broke the news about the 911 call.

"But there was nobody else," Travis said. "I swear. It was just us. I didn't shoot his way. I didn't. I didn't. I didn't. I hit a buck. It ran off to the north. I was going to get my dad to help me track it."

"It's okay," Jake said, realizing half of Travis's hysteria was the fear that his errant bullet had done this.

"Travis," Jake said. "Look at me. This wasn't your fault. You hear me? You understand what I'm saying? You didn't do this. You aren't responsible. Say it back to me."

His lips quivering, Travis whispered the words. "I didn't do it."

"That's right," Jake said. Another unmarked cruiser pulled up. Lieutenant Beverly stepped out. Good. He'd make sure Jake got all the resources he needed. From Beverly's passenger side, another officer emerged. This one from the DNR. They'd want to talk to Travis too. The back door opened and Jake's sister Gemma stepped out. For a moment, Jake's temper flared. What was Gemma doing here? Then, he knew. With Ben gone, and Ryan his best friend, Gemma was probably Travis's emergency contact.

"I've got to do my job now, Travis," Jake said. "Gemma's going to take care of you. You listen to her. Okay?"

Jake rose and went to Gemma. She was done crying. She'd applied extra makeup around her eyes, trying to hide the certain blotches and puffiness.

"Take him to your place," Jake said. "Don't let him go home."

"Jake," Gemma choked out. "It's real? He's gone? Ben's gone?"

"Yes," Jake said. "I can't get into details yet. You understand? You'll take care of him? He needs you. I ... need you."

Something came over his sister. She squared her shoulders. Her eyes went hard. It was a look he'd seen on her a thousand times. She'd been just twelve when their parents died. It was Gemma who had found them. Gemma who had first seen the horror of it. Just like Travis.

Gemma was a survivor. A warrior. A mother.

"I've got this," she said. And Jake knew she had. They stood there like that. Eye to eye. Big sister. Younger brother. Each of them knew there would be time to feel this later.

Gemma put a quick hand on Jake's sleeve, then brushed past him to get to sixteen-year-old Travis Wayne. He was one of her babies now.

Jake went to Beverly. "What's the word, Jake?" Beverly said. "You know Officer Scott Kowalski?"

"Thanks for coming out," Jake said. "But there won't be anything to do."

"I understand we have a hunting accident ..." Kowalski said.

"No," Jake said. "Not a hunting accident. This was an execution."

FOUR

The rain held off all day. But as Jake made his way up the gravel driveway leading to the two-bedroom cabin he called home, it began to drizzle. He sat in front of the house for a moment, watching as droplets fell, quickly obscuring his view from the windshield.

He'd left a pair of work boots on the porch steps. The bottoms were caked with mud. Jake stepped out of the car and headed up the walk.

The front door was never locked. There was no need for it up here. You couldn't see the cabin from the road. You couldn't see the trails that snaked back through the woods that stretched for two hundred acres. You couldn't see the big house at the highest point in those woods where his grandfather lived. Where his great-grandfather had lived and died.

Jake changed out of his suit and pulled on a pair of jeans and a flannel shirt. It was still raining when he stepped outside and slipped on his muddy work boots. He took the trail leading around the house, heading uphill to a small clearing where he'd dug a firepit on Grandpa's orders.

An ax was planted in the center of a large tree stump, firewood stacked beside it. Jake had completed building two out of four of the solid oak benches Grandpa wanted around the pit. The other two were laying in pieces, waiting for Jake to get a spare weekend to finish.

Jake closed his fingers around the handle of the ax. Then he closed his eyes.

He was seven years old. He and Ben Wayne were catching frogs in the bog behind Ben's house. His mother was inside making Sloppy Joes for them. Ben's favorite.

Ben squatted near the water, his skinny legs covered in mud. His Chuck Taylors might have been white at some point, but now they were gray, the untied laces frayed as Ben squat-walked further into the weeds, looking a lot like a frog himself.

"I'm telling!" a squeaky voice shouted from behind them, scaring a fat bullfrog from its hiding place. The frog leapt in front of Ben, splashing him with mud.

"You're not supposed to go in there!" Ben's little sister shouted. She was just four. Even skinnier than Ben. She had knock-kneed sticks for legs, inspiring the nickname Jake invented for her.

"Dang it, Birdie," seven-year-old Jake had said. "You're scarin' 'em all away!"

"You're not s'pose to go in there," Birdie said, adamant. She had crooked pigtails and a face full of freckles. "Mom said there's leeches. They'll 'tach to your balls!"

"Yeah?" Ben said. He turned, quick as a snake, and tossed a heavy, wet clump of mud right at Birdie's feet. A few brown droplets

splashed the front of her purple dress. She stuck her tongue out at her older brother then ran up toward the house, screaming "Mom!" the whole way.

"Brat," Ben said, wiping his mud-caked hands on the front of his shirt. Birdie was right. Ben was going to catch holy hell when Mrs. Wayne saw him. She was probably going to take a hose to both of them before she'd let them back in the house.

"Come on," Jake said. "Let's go wash off in the creek before your mom sees us. And maybe check your balls for leeches."

Ben's eyes widened. The blood drained from his face. Jake couldn't stop laughing. Only Ben had ventured that far out into the bog. He ran ahead of Jake and jumped straight into the creek, wiping off the front of his pants.

"Ben!" Mrs. Wayne had called. "Jake!" She hadn't sounded angry though. She sounded worried. She came running to the creek, carrying Birdie in her arms. Ben kept right on splashing in the water. But Jake stopped cold. He knew something was wrong. Judith Wayne's face was streaked with tears. Jake remembered thinking it was the first time he'd ever seen a grown-up cry. She would be there, keeping an arm around Jake as his grandfather came and told him the news that would change his life forever.

"They're gone," Grandpa would say. "Both your parents, Jake. They've gone to heaven and it's time for you to come home."

It was Ben who had asked how you get to heaven. Jake didn't speak a word for almost ten days after that.

The rain let up. Jake found the ax in his hands. He didn't remember pulling it out of the stump.

"Ben," he whispered. "Dammit. Ben."

Rage poured through him. It wasn't Ben's sightless eyes he saw in his mind. No. It was seven-year-old Ben's face, staring at him as Jake was told his mother and father were dead.

"No!" Jake shouted, a guttural cry that echoed through the woods. Jake brought the ax down on the closest bench, the one he'd finished first. He smashed it to pieces, swinging over and over again until an electric shock ran straight up his arm, making his bad shoulder explode in pain.

He kept right on swinging. Smashing. Pulverizing the wood. He cracked open the palm of his right hand. Blood trickled down his wrist as the rain began to come down in sheets.

Jake lost time. Space. He only cared about the weight of the ax in his hand. The numbness through his shoulder. The pain settling low in his back. The satisfying crunch as he sent splinters flying in all directions.

"Jake!"

His grandfather's voice finally cut through like a thunderclap. His gnarled hand, still strong as oak itself, clamped down on Jake's good shoulder.

"Jake," Grandpa Max shouted again. "Come in from the rain, boy. You'll catch your death of cold."

But Jake didn't feel the cold. Grandpa jerked the ax out of his hand, replanting it in the stump. It was then Jake noticed the rain had changed over to snowflakes. Then it wasn't his own health he worried about. At seventy-nine and mostly blind, Max Cashen had no business being out here at all. When he turned back to the trail, Jake followed him.

Grandpa had a walking stick. He used it to keep himself steady as he trudged downhill. The old man didn't need his failing eyes to know the way.

They reached the cabin together. Jake threw a blanket around his grandpa as he kicked off his muddy work boots. Max took a seat on the couch, then coughed into his fist.

"You should have stayed inside," Jake said.

"Grab me a beer," Grandpa said. "Grab one for yourself."

"I don't want a beer," Jake said. It wasn't what he meant. It was that beer wasn't strong enough.

Grandpa, as always, knew Jake's mind. He hoisted himself off the couch and went to the kitchen. He pulled down a bottle of Polish vodka from the freezer and poured shots for each of them, measuring it with sightless skilled precision into two paper cups. He downed his quickly and handed the other to Jake.

"Take it," he said.

Jake did.

"He's dead, Gramps," Jake said. The liquor warmed him. Grandpa took his cup and poured Jake another.

"I know," Grandpa said. "Came over on the police scanner."

"I told you not to listen to that thing," Jake said. "Get rid of it."

"It wasn't an accident, was it?" Grandpa said. He put the bottle of vodka back in the freezer and slammed the door shut.

"No," Jake said.

"Nobody else is supposed to be back there," Grandpa said. "Nelson doesn't let anyone else back there. Not even his own grandson. That boy turned out to be an idiot. Shoots at anything brown. Nelson ran him off a couple of seasons ago. Told him to stick to state land like the rest of the dimwits."

"Ryan was supposed to be with him," Jake said.

"He wasn't," Grandpa said.

"Travis," Jake said. Then he couldn't say another word. The rage crept in. The vodka might as well have been water. He felt the blood rush to his head. Jake turned, heading toward the bedroom. He raised his fist and put it through the nearest wall.

Grandpa was there. He threw his arms around Jake and pulled him back with surprising strength.

"You gotta let it go," Grandpa said. "You gotta push it down. Way down."

"What if I can't?" Jake said. When he closed his eyes, he saw Ben, muddied, holding a gray toad in the palm of his hand. Laughing as the thing leapt and landed on the top of his head.

Grandpa grabbed him by the shoulders, shaking him hard. "You're telling me someone murdered Ben. You're sure?"

"Yes," Jake said.

"This wasn't some stray shot. God. Not Travis."

"No!" Jake said.

"Okay then. So then it's you. Your job. You gotta find who did this, Jake. There's nobody else. That boy? Travis? That's what he needs you to do. You know damn well if Ben were here, he'd tell you to make sure. Travis won't survive if you don't find whoever killed his father. You have to make sure he goes down for it, Jake."

"I should have gone with them," Jake said. "I worked today instead. We're down a detective. I should have gone with them."

"No," Grandpa said. "It doesn't work like that. You wanna feel sorry for yourself? There will be time for that later. Right now, there's work to be done. Isn't that right?"

Jake clung to his grandfather. He gripped his elbows. The two men pressed their foreheads together.

"You make sure," Grandpa said. "You hear me? You make sure. You know how it's gotta be. There's no room for your emotions. No room for memories and what ifs. You know I don't like it. I'd have rather you'd been a lawyer. An accountant. Hell, sometimes I wonder if you'd have just been better off working at the mill. But that's not you. This is. This thing you do. You're better at it than anyone else. Aren't you?"

Jake took a breath. He straightened. He let go of the old man. He stood before him, arms at his sides, shoulders back.

"Yeah, Gramps. Yeah."

"All right then. So you have another drink if you need it. Punch the goddamn wall again if you want. Tonight. Then tomorrow, you find this asshole. You make sure. You do it all the right way. For Ben. For Travis. For you. You understand?"

Jake clenched his jaw so hard he started to see stars. He was here, Ben. Jake could feel him. Grandpa was right. There was no one else. Certainly not Ed Zender. Not the Bureau. Not Sheriff Landry. There was just him. This case. This time.

Grandpa saw it come over Jake. Something in his eyes had changed. Grandpa nodded then patted Jake on the shoulder. He would feel the pain from the ax there later. He would feel the pain in his fist later. He would feel the pain of Ben's death.

Later.

FIVE

Dr. Ethan Stone stood at the end of a metal examining table. Behind him, Ben Wayne's body lay, covered up to his neck with a plastic sheet. He didn't look real. He was a bloodless wax figure, his pearl eyes fixed open, staring at the buzzing fluorescent lights of the examining room.

"Thanks for handling this so quickly," Jake said. Sheriff Landy stood beside him. She didn't normally come to things like this. She made up some thin excuse but Jake knew what really bothered her. She was worried about him. Knew how close Jake was to the victim. It was kind of her, perhaps, but Jake felt nothing right now. Only cold, clear purpose.

"Tell me what you can," Jake said.

"Well," Dr. Stone said. He was ancient. Seventy-five years old, he'd served as Worthington County's chief medical examiner since before Jake was born. He'd started his career as an army doctor, serving two tours in Vietnam at the bitter end of it. He didn't have to. Eligible for multiple deferments, Ethan Stone chose to go.

"Bullet entered just above his left ear. Through and through. He wouldn't have felt much, Jake. Probably nothing at all. Just ... lights out."

Jake walked to the head of the examining table. Dr. Stone took a gloved hand and turned Ben's head, showing the entry wound through the left temple. It was a small hole. No more than a few millimeters. You could have fit a pencil through it.

It was the right side of Ben's head that had the real damage. The bullet had exploded out, blowing tissue and bone as far as twenty feet. There was very little left.

"My God," Landry said. "His son found him."

She knew the answer. Meg Landry had a daughter about the same age as Travis. Jake knew the sheriff was seeing through a mother's eyes now. He had no time for it.

"You still don't have a bullet?" Dr. Stone asked.

"Not so far," Jake said.

"It could be anywhere," Stone said. "If there's much left of it at all."

"Can you tell anything though? From the wound?" Landry asked.

"Oh sure," Stone said. "There's no doubt in my mind. This wound was made from a high-velocity rifle. This was no shotgun. Not a handgun either, Jake, you get what I'm saying?"

"What do you mean?" Landry asked. She was a good boss. The best Jake had ever had. It hadn't been easy for her to take over after Sheriff O'Neal died of a heart attack. She was a woman. This was a small town not used to women in traditionally male roles. Plus, she'd spent very little time as a "real" cop. She'd been in admin most of her career. A role at which she excelled.

"He means there's no way this was a hunting accident," Jake said. "No hunter would have been out there with a weapon like that. Ben was murdered."

"I've seen wounds like this before," Dr. Stone said. "Plenty. Too many. In dead soldiers, Jake."

Jake nodded.

"This was a kill shot," Stone said. "I'm talking sniper. Couldn't testify to it. It's not based on anything in my forensic examination. It's just what I've seen. Between you and me, I'm sure I'm right, Jake."

"The killer would have had a scope," Jake said.

"Most definitely," Stone said.

"He was hunted," Landry said. "My God. That's what you're saying, isn't it?"

"We can't assume anything yet," Jake said.

Dr. Stone reached for the zipper on the plastic body bag, then slowly pulled it up.

Oddly, Jake hadn't felt anything looking at Ben's wounds close up. But the sound of that zipper sent a current up Jake's spine. He took a breath and stepped back.

"I've still got to wait for toxicology to come back," Stone said.

"He wasn't on anything," Jake said. "Ben would never go out on a hunt like that. Especially not with his boy."

"I'm sure you're right," Stone said. "Ben was a responsible hunter. But I can't finalize my report until I get all the labs back. I can tell you he didn't have any alcohol in his system."

"I appreciate that," Jake said.

"I'm sorry, Jake," Dr. Stone said. "I know you boys were close. This is a damn shame. A damn shame."

"I appreciate that," Jake said once more.

"I'll email my preliminary report by the end of the day," Stone said. "Anything else you need, you know you'll have it. I'm putting a rush on those labs. Not that I think it'll make much difference to your investigation. It's just … well … it's one thing I can do."

"Thanks," Landry said.

Jake gave Dr. Stone a curt nod, then walked out of the examination room.

"Jake," Landry said. "Anything you need. You know that, right?"

"I do," he said. "Right now, I just need to get back out to the scene. BCI should be finishing up. I'm hoping they found bullet fragments. Then I've got to head over to talk to Travis again."

She put an arm on his shoulder, her face lined with worry. Jake went rigid. Her care. Her concern. He couldn't let it in. He couldn't let anything else in but the job.

"I have to go," Jake said. He brushed past Meg Landry and headed back to the crime scene.

Jake pulled in behind Mark Ramirez's white crime scene van. Ramirez worked out of the Richland office of Ohio's Bureau of Criminal Investigations. Jake waved to the two Worthington County deputies set up on either side of the Grace Church Road entrance to Nelson Palmer's property.

It was cold today. The weather guy was calling for the first real accumulation of snow later tonight along with freezing rain through the morning. Two local schools had already called off for tomorrow. Stanley High School was one of them.

Jake made his way back into the woods. He'd been back here so many times, he could have found his way blindfolded. Ramirez was just coming out. Speaking into his cell phone, he put a finger up, acknowledging Jake.

"Thanks," Ramirez said to whoever was on the line. "I'll send it over to you after I'm done here." Then Ramirez clicked off and offered Jake a hand to shake.

"We're just about wrapped up here," Ramirez said. "Sorry about this one, Jake. I understand you and the victim were close."

"What can you tell me?" Jake asked, ignoring the comment.

Ramirez pursed his lips. "Not as much as I'd like," he answered. "Not a single casing. No bullet fragments either. Splatter pattern near that oak tree there tells me the kill shot came from the southeast. But you already knew that from the positioning of the body."

"Can you tell from how far away?" Jake asked.

Ramirez shook his head. "I can't. I can tell you the victim never fired his gun. He was caught completely off guard."

"What about tire tracks?" Jake asked.

"We were able to match one fresh set coming in from the road. They matched the victim's F-150. He had two different models on his truck. The odds of it being anyone else's ..."

"Is non-existent," Jake said. "So my killer came in here on foot."

"Looks that way," Ramirez said. "But I don't have a single footprint. The ground's too firm. Too much brush and fallen leaves. Same issue with trying to find bullet fragments. These are deep woods. Whatever clues there might be have just been swallowed up. And with the snow they're calling for …"

"Nelson Palmer has trail cams," Jake said. "Actually, Ben set them up. As far as I know, the Waynes were the only family Nelson ever gave permission to hunt out here. He was very strict with who came in or out of here."

"I talked to him," Ramirez said. "He told me the same. The cameras all face north. The nearest one was about ten yards from your victim's deer blind. I've got one shot of him walking out in front of it with his son. Then it caught him coming back by himself. But then he walked beyond it. Nothing else on that camera but deer and a couple of fat raccoons, Jake."

Jake nodded. It was what he expected to hear.

"It's frustrating," Ramirez said. "Without ballistics, I can't be sure what kind of weapon did this, but my gut's telling me it wasn't any kind of shotgun. Not a hunting accident."

"There weren't any other hunters out here besides Ben and his boy Travis," Jake said.

"And he was in the wrong direction for a stray bullet," Ramirez said. "You talk to your M.E.?"

"Just came from there," Jake said. "Dr. Stone couldn't tell me much more than you have. He's got a theory though. Not one he can go on record with."

"He's one of the best," Ramirez said. "I'd for sure trust whatever that old geezer has to say."

Jake nodded. "I wouldn't call him that in his presence. Ethan Stone could still kick both of our asses if he wanted to."

"Don't doubt it," Ramirez said. "What's he say?"

"Says the kill shot came from a high velocity rifle. He thinks it was a sniper hit."

"He'd know," Ramirez said.

"That's what he said," Jake agreed. "Said he's only ever seen that kind of wound in soldiers."

Ramirez shook his head. "God, Jake. I'm so sorry. I wish I could give you more answers."

"You've given me enough," Jake said. "I'm starting to at least understand what this wasn't, Mark."

Ramirez put his hands on his hips, spreading his jacket wide. "An accident," he said.

"Right," Jake said. "Mark, I need you."

"Whatever I can do," he said. "You know that."

"Be careful," Jake said. "You might not like what I'm asking. But I need you to sniff around. See if you can find any other similar crime scenes or victims like this. Cold cases. Unsolved murders where the victim got taken out with a sniper rifle. No other clues as to how they came or went."

"You got it," Mark said. "I can't think of any off the top of my head, but I'll do a deep dive."

"Thanks," Jake said. He didn't know whether to hope Ramirez came up with something or not. But his gut was telling him this wasn't random. Ben Wayne wasn't just the victim of bad luck. And he knew Ben Wayne as well as anyone. He had no enemies.

"Let me get back to the office," Ramirez said. "Give me a couple of days to make some calls and run some stuff through the system. I'll get back to you as soon as I can."

"Thank you."

"What about the boy?" Ramirez asked. "He's gotta be in shock. But are you sure he didn't see anything?"

"I'm heading over to formally interview him now," Jake said, aware how flat his voice must have sounded. Ramirez was liable to think Jake was in shock as well. He wasn't though. Not even close.

"When you talk to him. I checked in with Scott Kowalski."

"The DNR guy?" Jake asked.

"Yes," Ramirez answered. "He went out to the kid's blind. Figured out where he shot his buck. It was the total opposite from your victim's direction. Kowalski said the buck didn't go thirty yards. Perfect shot. Kowalski took the buck home and skinned and butchered it himself late last night. He's a good dude."

"Wow. Thanks for telling me. I'll let Travis know."

"Figured it might give him some peace of mind, anyway. I'm sure his mother's gotta be pretty shook up too," Ramirez said.

"No mother," Jake answered. "She passed away a few years back. The kid is staying with my sister at the moment. Her boy and Travis Wayne are tight."

"Oh geez," Ramirez said. "I had no idea. The hits just keep on coming with this one, don't they? I'm so sorry. I swear. I'll do what I can. Give me a few days. I'll call you as soon as I come up with anything."

"Appreciate it," Jake said, shaking Mark Ramirez's hand once more. Then he turned and walked out of the woods. He knew he would have to spend the rest of his day trying to help Travis Wayne remember every detail about the day he lost his father.

Six

Gemma met him in her driveway as Jake pulled up. His sister paced, picking at her acrylic nails. She wore her hair in a loose ponytail and no makeup. Jake couldn't remember the last time he'd seen her like this. She looked younger this way. Vulnerable. Pretty. He knew she wouldn't cry in front of anyone else but him and not even that today.

"They're both inside," Gemma said. She went to Jake, throwing her arms around him. She squeezed him tight. He put an arm around her waist and smoothed her hair back with the other hand.

"How you holding up?" he asked.

"Not great. Travis won't eat."

"He's cutting weight," Jake said. "First tournament's in two weeks."

"You can't be serious. He can't be thinking about wrestling."

"It might be what gets him through, Gemma. He's going to need his team more than ever."

"Oh, they're constantly in and out," she said. "I had to turn three of them away because I knew you were coming. They're inside."

"You said they," Jake said. "Who's inside?"

"Oh," Gemma said, picking at her nail again. "Erica got here a couple of hours ago. She took a military flight from Fort Lewis. I sent Ryan to pick her up from the airport."

"Birdie's here?" Jake asked. He hadn't seen Ben's little sister since they graduated from high school twenty years ago.

"Yeah," Gemma said. "She's anxious to talk to you too."

Jake nodded. He followed Gemma into the house. He found Ryan in the kitchen making himself a sandwich.

"Ryan, where's Travis?" Jake asked. When he saw his uncle, Ryan fell apart. His shoulders dropped and he barreled into Jake, clinging to him for support.

"It's okay," Jake said as Ryan softly cried. It occurred to Jake it might be the first time he'd allowed himself to.

"I don't know what to say to him," Ryan whispered. "What do you say to him?"

"You don't have to say anything," Jake said. "You just have to be there. You just have to keep being his friend."

"He found him," Ryan said. "He keeps saying it's his fault."

"I'll talk to him," Jake said. "That's why I'm here. Just keep it together as much as you can. Keep the team together."

Ryan pulled away, nodding. He wiped his eyes with the back of his hand. Gemma came in behind him and put her arms around her son.

"Come on, Ry," she said. "Uncle Jake needs to spend some time with Travis. He's got to do his job today."

"Get that walk shoveled for your mom," Jake said. "I think it's finally stopped snowing."

Ryan nodded and let Gemma pull him away. Over her shoulder, Gemma pointed toward the back of the house. "They're in the basement," she said. "I've got Trav set up in the spare room down there."

"Thanks," Jake said. He waited until Gemma and Ryan went into the garage. Then he steeled himself and headed down the basement steps.

He found Travis Wayne sitting on Gemma's old recliner, his knees drawn up, his chin resting on them.

"Hey, Trav," Jake said. The television was on. One of the classic sports channels was replaying an Ohio State, Michigan game. Desmond Howard had just made his legendary 93-yard punt return, scoring for Michigan and securing his Heisman win.

Travis reached over and clicked it off with the remote. Slowly, the boy rose to his feet.

Jake didn't ask him if he was okay. He didn't say he was sorry. He didn't say any of the empty but well-meaning things he'd probably already heard a thousand times in the last twenty-four hours. Instead, he just crossed the room and met Travis where he was, taking a seat on the couch opposite him.

"Hey, Coach," Travis said, his voice hoarse. For the past year, Jake had acted as the assistant wrestling coach for Stanley High School. Travis was about to start his sophomore year at 120. The kid was good. Maybe even better than his dad had been. It hit Jake like a blow to the solar plexus as he realized for the first time that Ben would never get to see it.

"Gemma said you had some questions for me," Travis said.

"I do," Jake said, hardening himself against the "never woulds."

"Jake?"

She came around the corner, holding two water bottles in her hand.

"You remember my Aunt Erica?" Travis asked.

Birdie, Jake thought. It's all he'd ever called her. Jake rose to his feet to meet her. Birdie was tall, like Ben had been. Almost Jake's height in her steel-toed combat boots. She hadn't changed out of her army fatigues she'd worn on the plane. Jake recognized the double bars on her sleeve that marked her as a Captain.

"My God, Birdie," Jake said, finding a smile. "You're all grown up!"

She was. She had the same shade of wheat-blonde hair as Ben's. The same blue eyes and straight nose. She searched Jake's face, blinking rapidly, no doubt to stave off her own tears.

"Jake," she said, gasping out the word. Then Birdie came to him. She pulled Jake into a bone-crushing hug. She was thin, but Jake felt the outline of hard muscles. The skinny, knock-kneed little girl he kept in his mind was gone. She was solid. Strong. A woman.

"I'm sorry," Jake said, giving into the things people say. The things he'd avoided saying to Travis.

"I'm glad you're here," she said.

"I wish it was under better circumstances," he said. "But I've got to ask Travis a few questions."

"I understand," she said. "Gemma said you were on your way. You're a detective now."

"I am," he said.

"You don't mind if I sit in?" Birdie said, all business. She didn't direct the question to Travis. Jake realized it was rhetorical. Travis was a minor. He was here on police business.

"Of course," he said. Then again. "Of course."

Jake pulled out his notepad and took a seat back on the couch. Birdie stayed standing, taking a wide stance with her hands behind her back. She looked more official than he did.

"Travis," Jake said. "I know this is rough. But I need you to try and remember as much as you can about yesterday morning."

Travis nodded. "It was normal. It was just ... normal. We were up a little after four. We had breakfast at Charlie's."

Charlie's Diner was a little greasy spoon about two miles east of Nelson Palmer's farm. A lot of the hunters in the area frequented the place as a ritual on opening day for gun season. Charlie served a lucky breakfast he called the Hunter's Omelet. It was really just a western omelet with tabasco sauce, ham, bacon, sausage, onion, green peppers, tomatoes, and thick cheddar cheese. Charlie added a side of home fries and the worst coffee Jake had ever tasted.

"Do you know what time you got to Charlie's?" Jake asked.

"Five," Travis said. "We had our breakfast. We were out of there by five thirty."

"Do you remember who else was in the diner?" Jake asked. "Who you talked to?"

Travis shook his head. "Just the regulars. Charlie was there. Nick and Bob McGee. The Baranskis. Dave and Mike Overmeyer. That was it. We sat at the counter, ate our food. Then we were off."

Jake knew Charlie didn't even have a proper wait staff. He'd just cook the food, call it out, and relied on his regular customers to just come behind the counter and grab it. Everyone bussed their own tables too. For forty years, Charlie Dowd had served the same breakfast and charged the same fare. Two bucks.

"Nobody new," Jake said.

"No," Travis said. "It was just a normal morning. Dad was excited. He bought a new twelve-gauge last month from Barney. He gave me his old one. We shot at the range a week ago."

"Okay," Jake said. "Do you remember seeing anyone out at Nelson's? Any other trucks?"

"No, Coach," Travis said. "It was just me and my dad. We pulled into the two-track and got going. He helped me set up on the northeast part of the property. I was in the valley area where those two creeks meet up."

Jake had hunted the same spot a few times himself. It was the prime location on all of Nelson Palmer's sixty-acre tract of woods. Just about every deer in the county would move right through it.

"Dad was about fifteen acres southwest of me," Travis said. "We were in our blinds by six, waiting for the sun to come up. Dad told me to call him if I saw anything. It was quick. I don't think it was fifteen minutes before I saw a big buck come through. He was a monster, Coach. Mr. Palmer had seen him on his trail cam late last summer. I took a shot. Got him clean. Right in the heart. He went down about thirty or so yards from me. I nearly pissed my pants. I texted my dad like he wanted me to. Told him I was on my way to him so we could drag the sucker out."

Jake already knew Ben never answered that text. Now that Travis was talking, his words came out in a river. Unbroken. The boy barely took a breath.

"I was walking along the creek. I think I got maybe a hundred yards then I heard another shot."

Birdie stood beside her nephew, still as a statue.

"What did you do then?" Jake asked.

"I froze," Travis said. "I thought it was my dad at first. I waited maybe thirty seconds, then tried calling him again. He didn't answer. I stayed along the creek bed then kept on heading southwest back toward him. Then ... I found him. My dad was lying on the ground. His rifle was still in his hand. That's when I knew. I knew it wasn't his shot at all."

Travis didn't break down. He went stony silent. Jake reached out and put a hand on his knee.

"And you never saw anyone else? Didn't hear anyone else?"

Travis shook his head.

"I know it wasn't my shot, Coach. I know it wasn't." Travis met his eyes. "My deer was right in front of me. I never got to drag it out. After I got to my dad ..."

"It's okay," Jake said. "A DNR officer went and got your deer out. It was right where you said. Perfect shot. He butchered it for you if you want it."

Travis squeezed his eyes shut, holding back fresh tears.

"Trav, is there anything else you can remember about the shot you heard?"

"I've been thinking about that a lot," Travis said. "Coach, I can't stop hearing it. And that's the thing. It was off."

"What do you mean off?" This time, Birdie asked the question.

"I mean, it didn't sound like a shotgun. Not that heavy, boom. It was like a crack."

Jake met Birdie's eyes. The last he'd heard, she was an Army M.P.. He had no doubt she understood what Travis's words might mean.

"Trav," Jake said. "I'm going to talk to Nelson Palmer more, but as far as you know, was he having any issues with trespassers? Did you or your dad see any signs of anyone else who might have been on the property lately?"

Travis shook his head. "Nothing. Everybody knows we're the only ones he gives permission to hunt those woods."

It was true.

"Ben told me Nelson's daughters never go out there," Birdie said. "He said he's got two son-in-laws who don't hunt."

"They live in Columbus or somewhere," Travis added. "I've never even met them."

Jake closed his notebook. "That's what I've always understood too. Thanks, Travis. This is helpful. If you think of anything else, you just call me. If you need anything, you call me. Day or night. You know that, right?"

Travis nodded.

"You have a minute for me?" Birdie asked. Her brow knit, she locked eyes with Jake.

"Sure," he said. "I've gotta head back to the office, Travis. But I meant what I said."

"I'll be okay," Travis said. But Jake wondered if that were true.

He and Birdie headed upstairs together. Ryan was still out shoveling snow. Gemma was in the kitchen. She must have seen something in Jake and Birdie's expressions. The moment they came up, she made some excuse and went back out into the garage.

"Jake," Birdie said. "This isn't right. This wasn't some accident. Somebody murdered my brother. That's what you're thinking, isn't it?"

"Birdie," Jake said. "I don't know anything yet."

"That's crap," she snapped. "That was a rifle Travis heard."

"We don't know that yet," Jake lied.

"Yes, you do! Ben was wearing hunter's orange. Nobody else was supposed to be back in those woods. Travis knows the difference between a rifle and a shotgun. You have to tell me what you know."

"Birdie," Jake said. "You have to trust me to do my job."

"Don't Birdie me. My name is Erica. And this is what I do too, Jake," Birdie said. She pointed to the stripes on her sleeve.

"Not today," he said. "I don't need you going off half-cocked. I'm going to figure out what happened. That's a promise. Ben was my friend."

"Which means maybe you're too close to it," she said.

"Birdie," he said, gritting his teeth.

"Don't," she said, her tears finally coming. "Ben's the only other person who ever called me that. Thanks to you."

"I'm sorry." And he was. He hadn't meant to make her even more sad by using the name.

She put up a hand. Jake wanted to say more, but he had no idea what. He didn't get the chance. His phone buzzed. Jake put up a finger, then walked to the other side of the room to answer it.

"Detective Cashen? This is Deputy Rathburn."

"Hey, Mary," Jake said. "What've you got for me?"

"I'm not sure," Rathburn said. "But I'm over at Barney's Guns. I think maybe you're going to want to come out here. Barney's got something I think you're going to want to hear."

Birdie stood there, staring at him. Jake hoped Rathburn's voice didn't carry enough for her to hear. With cold determination on her face, Jake figured she'd probably try to tag along.

He clicked off with Deputy Rathburn. "I've got to go," he said.

"You'll tell me what's going on?" she asked.

"When I can," he said. "That's going to have to be enough."

Birdie nodded. But Jake's gut told him it wouldn't be.

SEVEN

B arney's Guns was the last store in an abandoned strip mall off County Road Twelve. Family-owned since 1973, Barney Jr., as the locals called him, was really named Curtis Barnaby and he wasn't a junior at all.

Barney Jr. had graduated four years before Jake in high school. He'd been the heavyweight for one year, before blowing his knee out on a ski trip Coach Frank Borowski had forbidden him from going on. Ever since, the Barnabys had hated everything to do with Stanley High School as if it was the coach's fault.

Barney's had a giant "In Guns We Trust" sign taped to the front window. For all his bluster, Jake had always found Curtis to be a fairly affable guy who donated huge sums of money to the local Veterans Center and church soup kitchen.

"Hey, Curtis," Jake said as he walked in the store. Curtis stood behind the counter, arms folded. He had tribal tattoos snaking up his meaty arms. He wore his hair long, tied in a ponytail down his back. Deputy Rathburn leaned over the counter, her eye on a tactical twelve-gauge shotgun. She straightened as Jake came to her side.

"Detective," she said. "Thanks for coming out so quickly."

"Whatcha got for me?" Jake asked.

"Barney?" Rathburn said. "Would you mind telling Detective Cashen what you told me?"

Curtis smiled wide. "Detective Cashen. Nice work, Jake. Hope that came with a fat pay raise."

"I still work for the county, Curtis."

"Sure," Curtis said. "I know how you guys do. You'll retire at forty-five with a double pension then go rake it in working for the DNR counting fish or some such."

Jake rolled his eyes. Curtis was a blowhard. Jake knew he didn't mean anything by it and also that Curtis would give him the shirt off his back.

"Sorry to hear about Wayne," Curtis said, his smile fading. "I always liked that kid. He came in here last year with his boy. I sold him that new twelve-gauge. Did he have it with him?"

"I think so," Jake said.

Curtis shook his head, tearing up. "I just saw him a couple of days ago. He was talking about how Travis hadn't shot a buck in a couple of years so he was hoping he'd end his dry spell."

"Curtis," Jake said. "What is it you wanted to tell me?"

"Well, your deputy here was asking whether anyone new had come in. Who I've been selling high velocity rifles to. There haven't been many. None actually. Nobody really has a need for that stuff around here. Except for Louie Jaffe."

"Louie Jaffe?" Jake said.

"Yeah," Curtis said. "You know him. 'Member we used to call him Crazy Louie? That old guy who lives in the crappy green house out on County Road Seven. Next to the Detweiler farm. You know. Used to set off M-80s to scare the squirrels off his woodpile. 'Member he burned his barn down that way?"

"Crazy Louie?" Jake repeated. He hadn't heard that name in years. "He's still alive? Geez. I thought he was like a hundred when we were kids."

"Right?" Curtis said. "He was probably forty-five when we were middle schoolers, Jake. Don't that make you feel old?"

"I guess," Jake said. "Wow."

"Anyway," Curtis continued. "Last year or so, Louie's been in here buying up 7 millimeters. He's got a Classic Browning BAR. I didn't sell it to him. He said he got it at some gun show near Toledo."

Rathburn met Jake's gaze. She gave him a nearly imperceptible head shake. He read it as her assurance that she hadn't told Curtis the M.E.'s suspicions about the weapon used to kill Ben. It had been a topic at roll call this morning. He shot her a quick wink to tell her he understood.

"So anyway," Curtis said. "Lately, Louie's in here just about every week buying up more rounds. He cleaned me out, actually. So I asked him what the hell he's doing with it. You know, kinda joking. Just making polite conversation. Well, Louie got pretty butt hurt the last time. Started ranting and raving about the Second Amendment. Like I'm the guy he needs to be spouting off to. He got in my face. Turned all purple. Called me some names I won't repeat. I ended up throwing him out of the store last week. He's off his nut, Jake.

That's all I'm saying. I don't know if he had anything to do with what happened to Ben. But he's well armed and losing his marbles. I've actually been meaning to come in and talk to you about it."

"Was there anything specific he was railing about?" Jake said. "Or just the Constitution in general?"

"I couldn't even follow half of what he was saying. But he's all bent outta shape about those developers coming into Arch Hill and tearing up the woods. That subdivision that's going in. That ain't even anywhere near his place. You know he tried suing the county over it."

"He sues the county every year over something," Jake said.

"My sister works in the clerk's office," Deputy Rathburn said. "He handwrites all his pleadings on coffee-stained notebook paper. He won't listen when she tells him that's against the court rules and she can't accept it. He's been banned from the courthouse a couple of times."

"I quit listening after he called me names," Curtis said. "Then he goes after my old man. He's not even here to defend himself. Anyway, like I said, I threw him out of the store and told him not to come back until he remembered his manners. I'm not saying he's some kinda murderer."

"I get it, Curtis," Jake said. "I appreciate that. You keeping your ear to the ground is really helpful. Keep it up."

Cutis puffed his chest out and smiled. "You bet," he said. Jake knew he was as good as his word. He also knew the downside to Curtis's new purpose would likely be a barrage of phone calls on random Worthington County happenings over the next few months.

Jake let Curtis show him a new batch of Glock handguns then made a polite exit. Rathburn waited outside for him, next to her cruiser.

"I know it might not sound like much," she said. "Curtis likes to feel important."

"No," Jake said. "It's good. He hears things. That was a good instinct, coming in and talking to him."

"Well, there's more," she said. "I didn't want to say anything in front of him. But he's not the only one worried about Louie Jaffe."

"What have you heard?" Jake asked.

"I did what you asked. We talked to all the adjacent landowners near Palmer's farm. Jaffe isn't exactly adjacent, but it's the same area. So, but I got to thinking. Palmer isn't the only one who lets people hunt on his private land. Anyway, I went and talked to the Detweilers too. They haven't noticed anyone on their property who shouldn't be. But they were complaining about Jaffe too. Said he's been shooting off that rifle all hours of the day. It's been scaring their dogs. Their neighbors to the south had the same complaint. You know the O'Keefe farm?"

"Sure," Jake said.

"Well, Willie O'Keefe apparently got roped into confronting Jaffe about the noise."

"Let me guess," Jake said. "Jaffe didn't take it well."

"He did not," Rathburn said. She took her notepad out of her breast pocket. "Willie said Jaffe came around the corner brandishing his rifle. Pointed it right at Willie's head. Then he fired a round in the air and said the next one would be right through Willie's temple."

Jake went rigid. The image of Ben Wayne's head on the M.E.'s table flashed through his mind.

"Great," Jake said. "Looks like I need to have my own conversation with Louie Jaffe."

"Yeah," Rathburn said. "I was going to. But I wanted to clear it with you first. Plus, I don't know. I kinda get the impression maybe Louie would treat a female cop even worse than Willie O'Keefe."

"You might be right," Jake said. "And I don't want you or anyone else going out there without backup. Does O'Keefe want to file a report?"

"No," Rathburn said. "I asked him that. O'Keefe seems to think Jaffe's harmless."

"You're kidding?"

"That's what I said," Rathburn said. "Only Jaffe's been pulling that kind of crap as long as anyone can remember."

"For sure," Jake said. "Hell, he ran a bunch of us off his property when we were maybe twelve. It used to be a rite of passage running up to Crazy Louie's house, touching it, then running back before he came out."

"That's what Willie O'Keefe said too," Rathburn admitted. "Only, this high-powered rifle is new. His excessive target practice off his back porch is new. You heard what Curtis said."

"Louie cleaned him out," Jake said.

"There was one other thing," Rathburn said. She flipped through her notes. "There were a group of kids who went up to Jaffe's place last week. I think this rite of passage you're talking about is alive and well. Anyway, O'Keefe's friends with one of the dads. Uh ... Zielinski's the name. His boy, Jonah, told him

Louie ran him and a couple of his friends off. Scared the crap out of them, I guess. The boy kind of clammed up when his dad pressed him for more details. O'Keefe said the dad came to him asking whether he should go up there and talk to Louie. They both just decided to leave it alone for now. Anyway, whatever happened, it's getting some chatter on social media."

"What?"

"I don't know where they're posting. I'll see what I can find out for you. But there are tons of rumors going around town about Jaffe and whether he's involved in this."

"This is good work, Rathburn. I appreciate you taking the initiative. I don't know that I would have immediately thought to canvas the other farms in the county. Keep it up. If it's an ambition of yours, you'll make a great detective someday."

Mary Rathburn beamed. A blush crept into her cheeks. Lord, Jake thought. She was so new. Still so fresh-faced at twenty-three years old. She probably could have passed for twelve. She'd make a great addition to the vice squad. She still needed a little seasoning, but he made a mental note to ask her about it in another year.

"You learn anything else from your canvassing?" Jake asked.

"Not really," she said. "None of the landowners within a mile of Palmer's farm have seen anything unusual. Not the day Ben Wayne died, not in the weeks leading up to it. The guy who owns the property due west of Palmer's said he had some issues with some teenagers using the back forty of his property for a party spot. He found some beer cans and vape pipes at the end of last summer. He put up some no trespassing signs and a trail cam and that pretty much resolved it. But that's it. People around here tend to respect the rules."

Jake nodded. "Palmer hasn't let anyone on his property but the Waynes ever."

"He told me that," Rathburn confirmed. "He's pretty torn up. Blames himself."

"For what?"

"Just that it happened on his land. He's a mess, Detective. He was talking about selling everything off for good and moving closer to his daughters. Or getting a place in Florida like his wife's been asking for years."

Jake couldn't blame him. Though he wouldn't let himself think too far, the thought of ever setting foot on Palmer's land again turned his stomach.

"Well," Jake said. "Thanks again. This was really excellent detective work today."

Rathburn nodded. "I know you're close with the family. If you see Erica, can you give her my condolences. I suppose I'll see her at the funeral. It's just ... I'm not sure I'll know what to say."

"You know Bird ... um ... Erica Wayne?"

Rathburn nodded. "She used to babysit for me and my little brother."

It was hard for Jake to imagine skinny, knock-kneed Birdie Wayne being in charge of anyone else as a kid.

"I'll tell her," Jake said, smiling. With that, it was time to head home. Gemma wanted him over for dinner. For Travis. For Ryan. Jake wasn't sure if he could face it.

EIGHT

"How's the family holding up?" Sheriff Landry asked. She wanted Jake to meet her in her office first thing in the morning. He sat in front of her desk, Lieutenant John Beverly sat beside him.

"They're in shock still," Jake said. "Travis is angry. He punched two holes in my sister's basement wall last night. He's lucky he didn't break his hand." As he said it, Jake flexed the fingers of his own right hand. They were still stiff from him doing the exact same thing back at the cabin. He kept that detail to himself.

It had been quite the scene at last night's family dinner. Unbeknownst to both Gemma and Birdie, Travis had gotten into Gemma's liquor cabinet and downed several shots of gin. Not long after the hole punching, Jake had him in the backyard, letting him puke his guts out.

"That poor kid," Beverly said. "My kid's dating one of his teammates. I hear they're over with him round the clock."

"They've been great," Jake said.

"I understand the sister is on leave from the army?"

"She's stationed at Fort Lewis up in Washington State," Jake said. He'd made small talk with Birdie last night, trying to dodge her pointed questions about the status of his investigation. "She's an M.P."

"I got a call from her this morning," Beverly said. "She's asking a lot of questions. She's worried maybe you're too close to this one, Jake."

Jake stiffened. So this wasn't just a status report Sheriff Landry wanted. And Birdie had apparently been dissatisfied enough with what he'd told her last night to try to go over his head. He gripped the sides of the chair and tried to make his breath even.

"Look," Jake said. "Birdie ... Erica Wayne and I go way back. I've known her since she was pretty much in diapers. I'll tell you what I told her. Yeah. I loved Ben. This is tearing me up as much as anyone else. But I've got this under control. I can separate my emotions from my job. You put me in this job because you knew how good I was at it. Has that changed?"

"No," Landry said, her tone sharp. "Not at all. I just want to make sure that you don't forget to reach out for help if you need it. The department can provide a grief counselor. Take advantage of your Employee Assistance Program. You pay union dues for that."

"I don't need EAP," Jake said. "If I find I need something, you'll be the first to know."

"I don't care!" A shout came from the hallway. Beverly was on his feet.

"Son of a ..." Beverly said. "I told that tool I'd meet him in my office."

Landry's door opened a crack. Jane, her civilian clerk, poked her head in. "I'm sorry, Sheriff. Mr. Brouchard kind of barged in. He says the mayor sent him."

Landry rolled her eyes. "Let him in. We might as well kill as many birds with one stone as we can."

Jake rose to leave. One of the benefits of his job was that he could leave the politics to Sheriff Landry. He preferred to talk to prosecutor Tim Brouchard only when he had to.

"Oh no," Landry said. "Don't think you're making a clean getaway just yet, Cashen. Sit."

The door opened all the way and Tim Brouchard pushed through it.

"Good," he said, surveying the room. "Glad you're all here. It'll save me the trouble of hunting you all down. I want to know what's going on with the Wayne murder."

Jake clenched his fists.

"Tim," Landry said. "We haven't even definitively ruled it a homicide yet. It's premature to ..."

"Oh yeah?" Brouchard said. He was a tall, pot-bellied man with thick black hair and wide-set eyes. At fifty-six, he also found himself a trophy wife twenty years his junior. Anya Brouchard just happened to be Jake's former high school girlfriend. He tried not to think about the two of them together. He still couldn't figure out what Anya saw in him.

Brouchard pulled out his phone, scrolled through it, then slapped the thing on Meg Landry's desk.

"You've already lost control of the thing," he said.

Jake got to the phone first. He picked it up and tried to make sense of whatever Tim Brouchard was on about. It was a Facebook page called *The Dark Side of Blackhand Hills*. It was your basic nightmare of a community social media page. As a rule, Jake stayed away from social media. He scrolled upward. One post stuck out, written in all caps.

WHAT ARE THE WORTHINGTON COUNTY/KEYSTONE COPS TRYING TO HIDE? IF THEY WON'T FIND OUT WHO KILLED BEN WAYNE, WE WILL.

"What the actual hell," Jake muttered.

"Exactly," Brouchard said. "The thing's gone viral. I got a bunch of internet sleuths jamming my office up with phone calls and emails demanding answers. These trolls are out there interviewing witnesses."

"Who?" Landry and Jake said it together.

"They were out at Charlie's Diner yesterday, harassing all of his customers. They showed up at the DNR checkpoint, talking to different hunters as they were coming in with their tags. I got a call from Bob Wendell, the butcher. Couple of these pencil necks even staked out his shop to talk to guys as they were bringing their deer in for processing. He said they were chasing down some wild rumor that Ben Wayne's body got sent through Wendell's meat grinder and sold off in one-pound packages."

"Oh my God," Landry said.

Jake seethed. "Kids," he said. "Dumb kids."

"It was just some recent Stanley High School grad who started that page," Beverly said. "It's nothing. They'll get fired up about whether their neighbor's pulled a burn permit. Or God forbid, somebody makes a turnaround in one of their driveways. It's nothing. Give it a day or two and they'll be back to worrying about lost pets."

"You have a suspect," Brouchard said. He phrased it as a statement, not a question.

"Not yet," Jake said. He handed Brouchard's phone back to him.

"Well, these yahoos seem to think you do. Did you know Louie Jaffe's been taking shots at kids again? They say he was seen walking the trails by Palmer's farm."

Jake rose to his feet. "I'll get out and talk to Louie this week."

"If you can find him," Brouchard said. "He's in the wind, Jake. Couple of these dipshits went out there to try and confront him. They're lucky he didn't blow their brains out. He wasn't there, thank God."

"Wasn't there?" Beverly said. "Louie barely leaves his property these days."

"How in the world did these Facebook people know you were planning to talk to Louie?" Landry asked. "How did they know he was even a suspect?"

"He's not a suspect," Jake said. "Not officially. I just had a conversation with Curtis Barnaby. He's been in buying up high-powered rifle ammo. It doesn't necessarily mean anything."

"It means Barney Jr. or somebody else in that gun shop's got a big mouth," Brouchard said. "This is unacceptable. I cannot have this case tried on social media. This is big buck country. I can't have our hunters feeling unsafe out there. We've got enough trouble with the garden variety protestors these days. They're all over the place. You need to lock this down and lock it down quick."

"You need to calm yourself," Jake said.

"You didn't even know about this, Detective," Brouchard said, pointing to his phone. "You don't have control of your own investigation two days out of the gate."

"I know how to do my job," Jake said. "You better just make sure you know how to do yours. When the time comes to make an arrest, you can be sure I'll hand you an airtight case. What happens after that is up to you. I'll be watching."

Jake got within an inch of Tim Brouchard. He was taller, though Brouchard was far wider. The man was sweating. His breath smelled like stale onions.

"Enough," Landry said. "Both of you. So we got some social media attention. Big deal. My people know what they're doing, Tim. You can quit thumping your chest. We all know when the next election is."

Brouchard took two steps back. "And I'm not the only one up for it," Brouchard said. "Remember that, Meg. I was born and raised in this county. You weren't. You'd do well to keep me on your side."

"That a threat?" Jake shouted.

"Enough!" Landry said again. "We're done here, Tim. Go back to your office and let my people get to work. You're the lawyer. Isn't there anything you can do to get that online group shut down? Charge them with obstruction of justice or something. Scare some sense into them."

"I'm looking into it," he said.

"Great," Landry said. "See Detective Markham in computer crimes on your way out. She might have some ideas on how to help you. Don't forget we're all on the same side here."

Brouchard straightened his suit jacket. He glared at Jake one more time before turning on his heel and storming back out the door.

"What in the hell was all that about?" Beverly asked.

"Cover," Jake said. "He's going to go down there and tell his lackeys and our local yokel news that he's thrown his weight around up here."

"It's not his lackeys I'm worried about," Landry said. "Tim Brouchard needs the mayor and county commissioners on his side. Jake, as I recall, you don't have a big cheering section there."

Jake's maternal uncle Rob Arden sat on the board of commissioners. He and his in-laws hated all Cashens on account of his dead mother marrying one of them.

"Great," Jake said. "Maybe I need to pay a visit to good old Uncle Rob."

"Don't," Landry said. "You let me handle the commissioners. Just focus on what you have to do. And for the love of God, find Louie Jaffe before he hurts someone. Or someone hurts him."

Jake nodded. "Next on my list. But first I've got to go bury my friend."

NINE

As Jake walked into Nowak's Funeral Home, he came face to face with a 16x20 poster of eighteen-year-old Ben Wayne in a singlet and wrestling stance. Shock speared through his heart. He hadn't expected it. He should have. Young Ben. Fierce. Lanky. Fire in his eyes. Beside that poster was another Jake hadn't looked at in nearly twenty years. Another blow-up of his State Champ wrestling team. His own teenage face stared back at him.

"Jake," a choked voice greeted him. Two seconds later, he was enveloped in a bone-crushing bear hug from Jolly, the former team heavyweight.

"Hey, Jolly," Jake said, catching him around the arms just before he would have turned Jake's spine to powder.

"I can't believe it," Jolly said. "I just can't."

"I know. I know."

Jake had no hope of making it to the front of the room anytime soon. They were all here. All thirteen remaining men from the starting lineup. The fourteenth man's ashes were somewhere in the front of the room. Jake's team. Ben's. They had been their captains.

"Do you know what happened?" one man asked. "He didn't do this to himself, did he?"

"We heard they gutted him. Is that true?" another said.

"Stop," Jake said. "Just … stop."

"They're saying online it was these tree huggers from up north," came another voice.

"Look," Jake said. "I'm sorry. I can't talk about the case. For now, I'll just say quit reading crap online. When there's something to say, it'll be me saying it. Okay?"

Jake spent a few more minutes reminiscing with the guys. They all wanted to recount the glory days. How Ben had been the one to hold the team together. How Jake had been the one to kick their asses when they needed it.

He heard. But he couldn't listen. Couldn't let their words sink below the surface. Not now. Not yet. Finally, Jake managed to break away and make his way toward the front of the room where Birdie and Ben's parents were.

Lance Harvey followed him. Next to Ben, Lance had been Jake's closest friend in high school and on the team. While the others had needed Jake to say something, to listen to their stories, Lance had hung back, waiting.

"Sorry about that," Lance said. "I told all of them to give you air when you got here."

"It's okay," Jake said. A line had formed. He could just see the top of Birdie Wayne's head as she shook hands and hugged every mourner coming through the line.

"Have you seen Erica yet?" Lance said. "I hadn't seen her since just after high school. Almost didn't recognize her. She's something."

"She's going to have to be," Jake said.

"Yeah. Ben's folks aren't doing so great. They're pretty frail. Erica asked me to pick them up at the airport. I don't think Ben's mom really knows what's going on."

Judith Wayne had been diagnosed with Alzheimer's at just sixty. Four years on, her disease was rapidly progressing. Ben's father had beat cancer only to suffer a stroke last year that left him mostly paralyzed on his left side.

"I think that family is cursed," Lance said, echoing Jake's thoughts. When Abby Wayne, Ben's wife, died a few years ago, it seemed like they'd suffered through ever worsening tragedies.

"Lance," Jake said when he knew they were out of earshot of anyone else. "You spent more time with Ben in the last few years. Can you think of anyone who might have wanted to hurt him?"

Lance shook his head. "No. That's the thing. I've been racking my brain over it, Jake. Everyone loves Ben. Same as in high school. He was one of the best guys I know."

"You two had lunch a couple of times a week. Was he dating anybody? Bring anyone new into his life?"

Lance shook his head. "No. It's been five years since he lost Abby. You weren't here when it happened. It almost destroyed him. I'm serious. He scared the hell out of us. But slowly, he started coming back to life, you know? I'd say the last two years he's been doing great. You coming back to town was good for him too. But as far as dating? Forget it. We've all tried to fix him up. He wouldn't hear of it. He was still in a place where he felt like he'd be cheating on Abby. He told me once maybe he'd think about it after Travis was off to college or started on his own life. I told him Travis wanted him to be happy. Anyway, no. Ben wasn't seeing anyone."

"You don't think maybe he just wasn't admitting it to anyone?"

"No," Lance said. "No way. I'm telling you. He wasn't ready."

"All right. All right," Jake said.

"Jake," Lance said. "You sure this wasn't ... you know ... I mean, Travis was out there ..."

"No," Jake said. "That I can tell you. The bullet that killed Ben didn't come from Travis."

"Jake!"

A soft voice came from his right. Jake turned. Anya Strong beamed beside him, tears making her eyes shine. No. Not Strong. She was Anya Brouchard now. She came to him, hesitant, her eyes darting from him to Lance. Lance came in for a hug. Anya went up on her tiptoes and kissed Lance's cheek.

"Good to see you," Lance said. "Man, why do you always smell so good?"

Anya's bright laughter was a welcome distraction from the piped-in organ music. She broke from Lance and went to Jake.

"I'm so sorry," Anya said, her voice breaking. No, Jake thought. Not now. Not here. A million years ago, this girl had been the only one he'd let himself be vulnerable to. The only one who knew that he was thinking about his parents ... both of them ... when he hoisted that State Championship trophy up with Ben twenty years ago.

"I know," Jake said. He hugged her, but kept his back stiff. She folded into him. Lance was right. She did always smell good. Honeysuckle and roses.

"Are you okay?" Anya said, mouthing the words. There was a time she could tell what he was thinking with just a look. And he could do the same with her. His first love. Forged from the tragedies they both shared. He had lost his parents to violence. She had lost her sister. Now, today, they were surrounded by a similar loss.

"I'm glad you came," Jake said, dodging her question. Even now, he couldn't lie to her. No. He was not okay. But that wasn't the point.

"Good to see you, Jake," Tim Brouchard said, though he made no eye contact with Jake. Instead, he put a possessive hand on his wife's back. Over her head, he smiled and nodded at well-wishers. God, Jake thought. Even here. Even now, Tim Brouchard was campaigning. Anger turned his stomach. He wanted to throw Brouchard straight into a wall. The urge even had a taste. Metallic. Like blood.

"I need to see Ben's folks," Jake said to Anya, doing his best to ignore Tim.

"Of course," she said. "I put together a luncheon for after. Over at the Elks Lodge. Please try and come. I know everyone would love to talk to you. You know, away from here."

Jake nodded, but knew he'd never go. Anya likely knew it too. Jake turned. As Tim drew Anya away and back into the crowd, three men came through to Jake. Virgil Adamski, Chuck Thompson, and Bill Nutter. The Wise Men. They belonged to a group of retired cops who met at Papa's Diner downtown every Tuesday morning.

Virgil got to him first. "Hey, Jake," he said, nodding toward Lance. "So sorry about Ben."

"Anything you can share with us?" Nutter whispered. "We've heard ..."

"No," Jake said, abruptly. "There's nothing I can share. And even if I could, not today. Not here."

"I didn't mean ..."

Jake had a recent history with these men. It wasn't good. His urge to punch something kept growing.

"Jake!"

Gemma had weaved her way through the crowd as if she could sense her brother's shifting mood. Every once in a while, Jake was caught by how striking his sister really was. Today, Gemma had foregone half the makeup she usually wore. She pulled her blond hair back in a conservative bun and wore a jet-black suit. Beside him, Lance made an audible intake of air. His protective brother instincts flaring, Jake shot him a look.

"Jake," Gemma said again. "Ben's dad wants to see you. I'm going to have to take him back to the house soon. Judith is getting agitated and it's just all too much for them."

"Go on," Lance said. "I'll handle the rear guard." Adamski, Thompson, and Nutter took their cue and moved further into the crowd.

"Thanks," Jake said. "Lance, there's something else."

"Anything."

"Just keep your eyes open today. If you see anybody who shouldn't be here. Anyone we don't know."

Lance nodded. "Of course."

Jake thanked him, and headed through the thickest part of the crowd with his sister. The line of people hoping to pay their respects stretched all the way down the block and snaked around behind Duffy's Bike Shop on Fourth Street.

Jake hadn't seen Judith and Rudy Wayne in probably fifteen years. His breath caught when he finally did. Rudy was roughly ten years older than Jake's own father would have been if he'd lived. That put him in his mid-sixties. But the man in front of him looked closer to ninety. He was wheelchair bound, his left arm shriveled to a husk. When he made eye contact with Jake, his left eye was milky-white.

"He can't really speak anymore," Gemma whispered in Jake's ear.

It didn't matter. Jake understood what was in Rudy Wayne's mind as he leaned down to gently give the man a hug.

"I'm sorry," Jake said. Though Rudy Wayne's left arm hung useless at his side, his right one gripped Jake hard. Rudy managed one word.

"Promise!"

Jake stepped back. He gave the older man a stiff nod.

Ben's mother sat in a winged chair behind Rudy. She had a smile on her face as she watched the procession. There was no casket. Birdie had decided to have Ben cremated. It was the right choice. But another portrait of him sat on an easel beside his mother. It was taken a few years ago on a beach. A happier Ben stood with an arm around a bright-faced Abby Wayne. Young. Pretty. Healthy. Now, both gone.

"Thanks for being here," Birdie said. She looked tired. Jake put a hand on Rudy's shoulder and rose.

"How's Trav?"

Birdie shrugged. "He hasn't broken anything in the last two days. We locked up the beer and liquor. I'm taking him back to the house after I get my mom and dad squared away. Ben left things kind of a mess."

"The house?"

"The house. Everything," she said. "He didn't have a will. I can't believe it. After Abby died, he swore to me he'd take care of all that. As it stands right now, Travis gets everything, of course. As he should. But Ben didn't name anyone to handle all of it. Travis needs a guardian. My parents are in no condition for any of that. Dad's insisting he wants to go back to Fort Myers."

Jake knew the elder Waynes moved down there over a decade ago. They'd found an assisted living facility where they lived in a condo together with round-the-clock care for Judith.

"How long is your leave?" Jake asked.

"I get two weeks," she said. "But I'm working with my CO to get more time."

"I'm so sorry. You've got a lot on your plate."

She shook her head. The two of them had managed to move away from the main crowd. Gemma started handling the receiving line, leaning down to whisper in Rudy's ear as each mourner made their way through.

"I'm so angry at him," Birdie said. "I know it doesn't make any sense. But I am. Does that make me awful?"

"I think it makes you human," Jake said. "There's no manual for this, Birdie. We're all just doing the best we can."

Her attention left Jake. She froze, eyes widening.

"You son of a bitch," she whispered under her breath. Jake watched as Birdie's face turned red, then purple.

"Birdie?"

"You son of bitch!" she yelled. Then Birdie launched herself through the crowd. She flung herself at a skinny white kid, maybe eighteen or nineteen years old. He had a cell phone in his hand. With horror, Jake realized the kid had been recording with it.

"Birdie!"

She snatched the phone out of the kid's hand. Before Jake could reach her, Birdie had him in a headlock and pushed him back toward the wall.

"Birdie!" Jake shouted. He put a hand on her arm. Her grip was like steel. "Erica!"

"You're one of them, aren't you?" she hissed. "You and your little internet vultures."

"Nothing to see here, folks!" Gemma called out behind them. From the corner of his eye, Jake saw his teammates muscle their way to the front of the room en masse. They quickly formed a wall in front of Jake and Birdie. Three men broke through it. Virgil Adamski. Bill Nutter. Chuck Thompson. The Wise Men.

"Birdie," Jake said. "Let the kid go. He can't breathe. You're gonna kill him."

"Good," she said. "You hear that, you ghoul? Good!"

But she loosened her grip.

"You saw it," the kid said to Jake. "She assaulted me. You saw it. You have to arrest her. I'm pressing charges."

"No, you're not," Jake said through gritted teeth. He picked up the kid's phone from the ground. The lock screen hadn't yet been triggered. Jake went to the kid's camera roll.

"That's an invasion of my privacy!" he yelled.

"You were recording me, you asshole," Jake said. Sure enough. The last video he'd recorded was of Jake and Birdie during their hushed conversation. Before that, he'd been taking photos and videos of everyone in the crowd.

"I'm doing *your* job," he said. "And I know my rights under the First Amendment. We have freedom of the press."

"He runs that online group," Lance called out. "Dark Side of Blackhand Hills or whatever it's called."

"I know my rights!" the kid called out. "All of you. Take out your phones. They can't stop you. They can't silence us! If you'd do your job, we wouldn't have to!"

Red rage poured through Jake's veins. Behind him, he could hear Judith Wayne start to cry. The sound of it broke something inside of Jake. He curled his fist and grabbed the kid.

"You son of a ..."

"Jake!" Bill Nutter launched himself forward. He grabbed Jake's arm. Adamski and Thompson moved in. The three of them circled the kid. Adamski got in Jake's ear.

"Not here, son. Not now. You let us take care of this."

Jake let out a breath. The storm quieted inside him just a little. But every eye in the room was on him.

"We'll take care of it," Nutter said.

"Fine," Jake said to the kid, pocketing his phone. "You can pick up your phone from the station tomorrow. You know who I am. Ask for me. Birdie?"

Her face still flushed, Birdie finally stepped back. Virgil Adamski held the kid's arm in a vice grip. He, Thompson, and Nutter went shoulder to shoulder, backing the kid up until he had no choice but to exit the room and head for the parking lot.

"I can't be here anymore." It was Travis who spoke. Jake's heart fell. The boy had witnessed the whole thing.

"I don't think I can either," Birdie said.

"You go," Gemma said. "I've got this."

Jake whispered to Birdie. "You sure you locked up all the liquor? I think we both could use a drink."

Birdie let out a breath, then linked her arm with Jake's. As his former teammates moved to flank the rest of the Wayne family, Jake got Birdie the hell out of there.

TEN

By the next morning, the story of Jake and Erica Wayne's run-in with a member of the Dark Side of Blackhand Hills had gone viral. Their social media page had gone from just under three hundred followers to over ten thousand. Every keyboard warrior in the tri-state area had some wild theory about what happened to Ben Wayne. Jake sat in Meg Landry's office as she paced in front of her desk.

"You just had to muscle that kid," she said.

"Sheriff, I was not about to let a bunch of soulless basement dwellers spread grief porn all over the internet. That kid had his phone in Erica Wayne's face. He was recording Ben's parents. You can take my badge if you want to. I'm not going to apologize."

"Don't be so dramatic," she said. "Nobody's taking your badge. I just wish ..." She sat down hard in her chair. "I don't know what I wish."

He smiled. "You wish you'd have been there to see it."

"Yes," she said. "Ghoulish weasels. But these theories they're spreading online are getting out of hand. Most of them are absolutely ridiculous. Aliens. Bigfoot. Some military coup. But there are a couple that could cause trouble. Did you see somebody thinks maybe you need to have a harder look at Nelson Palmer's kids? They're saying Palmer recently changed his will to leave all his land to Ben's family. Is there any truth to that?"

"No," Jake said. "None. Plus the Palmers are sick about this whole thing. They loved Ben too. He was family to them. I'm more worried about Louie Jaffe, to be honest."

"That's the other thing I wanted to talk to you about," she said. "I got a call last night. On my personal cell. You know Pat Stuckey?"

"I know he's got a machine shop in Lublin Township," he said.

"Well, he's also got a daughter who's friends with mine. Paige and Cara Stuckey are in the same grade and in choir together. He got my number off the parent volunteer list. Anyway, Stuckey has a younger boy, Caleb. Pat said Caleb and a couple of his friends had a run-in with Jaffe a few days ago. They claim they were walking alongside the road by Jaffe's house and he started shooting at them. One of the boys says it was a rifle, not a shotgun."

"Jaffe's been scaring kids off his property for decades," Jake said. "It was a rite of passage to see how close you could get to him."

"Did you know about this?" she asked.

"I heard a rumor. Nothing concrete. Deputy Rathburn heard some scuttlebutt from one of the neighbors out there. I'll look into it. Stuckey shouldn't be calling you about that stuff. For sure not at home."

"He wasn't very amenable to the suggestion," Landry said. "Anyway, somebody's gotta talk to the old guy."

"I'll head out to talk to him now."

"Alone?"

"He knows me," Jake said. "Can't say he likes me much. But he knows who I am and knows what I do. He'll be home now. I'll take a couple deputies with me."

"Just be careful," she said. "What we know for sure about Jaffe is that he's well armed."

"I can handle him," Jake said. "Promise."

"I'd feel better if you took more muscle with you."

"And that's the surest bet to escalate things with Jaffe. Gonna need you to trust me on this one."

Landry leaned forward and put her hands flat on her desk. "I do. Just don't make me regret it. You don't have a warrant."

"I'm not planning to search anything unless I ask him and he consents. So far, Jaffe's only guilty of being good for Curtis Barnaby's business. Last time I checked that's not a crime."

Pursing her lips, Landry nodded. "Fine. You do this your way. Just don't take any chances you don't have to."

"I never do," Jake said. Landry gave him a raised brow, but didn't challenge his assertion. She dismissed him and Jake headed straight out to the parking lot.

Louie Jaffe's property was located five miles to the west of the Palmer farm in Navan Township. You couldn't see Jaffe's house from the road. He owned a twenty-acre tract of tillable farmland. Eighteen acres stretched out to the road. Jaffe's house and the small woods behind it made up the remaining two acres.

With the way it was set up, nobody could come in or out of Jaffe's place without him knowing.

Jake met the deputies parked in a single cruiser up by the road. He instructed them to hang back. He knew if he drove back there with too big a presence, Jaffe wasn't likely to even come to the porch.

"Just stay on channel four," Jake said. "I'll call for help if I need it. Or ... I don't know. You hear any shots fired, maybe haul ass back there, eh?"

Deputies Denning and Sailor gave him odd looks. Like they didn't know if he was serious or not. He let them stew as he drove up Jaffe's dirt road.

His house hadn't changed in more than thirty years. Jake wasn't proud of it now, but he was one of the kids who'd tried to prove his coolness by running up here on foot and touching Jaffe's front door. He'd been maybe ten years old. When Gemma found out, she'd dragged him out of bed in the middle of the night and made him confess his sins to Grandpa Max. Gemma would have been no more than fifteen at the time. As he recalled, Grandpa had made him haul fresh gravel up the length of his driveway for three Saturdays in ninety-degree heat after that.

Jaffe lived in a 1980s-era manufactured home with green siding and white shutters that had been hanging by a thread for twenty years or more. He had American flags draped over the porch, and a twenty-five-foot flagpole in the yard. Jaffe flew the Stars and Stripes, the Marine flag, and a POW-MIA flag. Jake would have felt better for his own chances with Jaffe if he'd flown a thin blue line flag along with the others, but Louie Jaffe had issues with civilian authority.

"Mr. Jaffe?" Jake called out. "It's Jake Cashen. I'd like to talk to you for a few minutes if you'll come on out and meet me."

Jake could see movement through the window. He rested his hand on the handle of his weapon, unsnapping it from his holster just in case. Though he knew if Louie Jaffe had a mind to blow his head off, he'd likely already be dead.

"Mr. Jaffe?" Jake called out again. The front door flew open, startling him. Jake took a ready stance.

"Relax," the old man said. "I saw you comin' a mile away. If I wanted to shoot at ya, you'd already be full of holes."

"You wouldn't be threatening me now, would you?"

Jaffe came fully outside. The man didn't have a bare patch of skin that wasn't crinkled. Like his skin was made of jerky. He had that look about him as if his body was made up of ninety percent whiskey instead of water. But Louie Jaffe still had a trim build with corded muscle and large, vascular biceps.

"What do you want?" he asked, though Jake figured he already knew.

"Mr. Jaffe, I need to ask you some questions."

"None of your bullshit," he said. "We aren't friends. This isn't a social call. You ask me what you want to know straight out. If I feel like answering, I will."

Jake thought for a moment. Meeting Louie Jaffe's wise eyes, he knew his usual interview strategy wouldn't work. So, he gave Jaffe exactly what he asked for.

"I'd like to know where you were on opening day between say four and six a.m."

"Your friend got killed," Jaffe said. "That Wayne kid. Rudy's boy."

"Yes."

"Some idiot trespasser probably clipped him. He was probably sitting there in his fancy blind with a cushioned chair and a heater, playing on his phone."

"It wasn't like that, Mr. Jaffe."

"Oh no?"

"And you haven't answered my question. Where were you on opening day?"

"Same place I always am. Sitting right out there in my woods. Bagged a ten-point myself in the first five minutes. A monster. I've been waiting all year to get after that one. Knew he'd be a good eater."

"You were here on your property? Did anyone see you?"

"Don't give nobody else permission to come out here. Suppose you already know that. You've lived around here long enough."

"Did you go anywhere else that day?"

"Sure. Went into town to get a twelve-pack at the Dollar Kart. The one out by your old man's."

"What time was that?"

"After eleven. I had nothing to do with what happened to Rudy's kid. As long as he was minding his own business and not creeping into mine, I had no beef with that kid at all."

"Where'd you shoot your deer?"

"Told you," he said. "Out back on my own property. I got my license. I got my tags. I follow the law, Detective."

"We've had some complaints, Jaffe," Jake said. "I understand you've been shooting targets out here."

"Then you also understand that's none of your business. No law against it. Not violating any noise ordinances out here. And if you thought I was, you'd have sent someone out here about it before all this. What you got is a bunch of dipshits wagging their tongues to get attention."

"You've been buying up a particular kind of ammo over at Barney's," Jake said.

"That against the law now?"

"No. I'm just curious."

"That's your problem. So I guess in addition to idiots, we got ourselves a big mouth in Curtis Jr."

"Mr. Jaffe, you're right about something. We do have a lot of big mouths in town. Some of them seem to think you've been gearing up for something. With all the shooting. Buying up high velocity ammunition ..."

"Last I checked that's still legal in this country. Now I've been polite. I've answered your questions. I understand you've got a job to do. I know that's a good thing. Something happened to me like that, I'd like to think you'd do your job to catch whatever son of a bitch did it."

"I would," Jake said. "You're correct. Did you have a couple of unwanted visitors out here recently? Some middle school boys?"

"Can't say as I recall," Jaffe said.

"Did you shoot at them?"

Jaffe smiled. "They impress all their pimply little friends with that story? Seems to me you and your zit-poppers used to do the same."

He was getting nowhere. "I'm just trying to follow up on a couple of complaints."

"You see that?" Jaffe said. He gestured toward the window on the south side of his house. It had a piece of cardboard taped over it.

"Little pecker heads came up here and threw rocks," Louie said.

"Which pecker heads?"

"I didn't ask for their ID," Louie said. "But one of 'em busted out that window the other day. He's lucky I didn't shoot his balls off for that."

"Did you shoot at them?"

"Would've been within my rights if I had. This is my castle and I'm allowed to defend it."

"You're not allowed to use deadly force over a busted-out window!"

"It starts with the window!" Louie said. "Let me make myself clear. I'm running out of patience. I'll defend myself. I'll defend my property. If people leave me alone, I'll leave them alone. If anyone else tries to mess with me ... if they come up here shooting at me or my place, they ain't getting out of here alive!"

"I'll ask you again. Did you shoot at anyone?"

"No! Now get on outta here. I'm done answering your questions."

"Mr. Jaffe. I'm just trying to follow up on a few complaints we've had ..."

"Bullshit," Jaffe said. "I had nothing to do with whatever happened to Rudy's kid. If you say it wasn't some dumbass shooting where he shouldn't have been, well, then I guess your job's that much more urgent. So I recommend you quit wasting my time and barking up my particular tree. You come back here with a warrant, well, then maybe I'll even let you look around. I'm pretty sure no judge in the county will sign off on one for ya. So I'm gonna head on back inside and keep minding my own business."

With that, Jaffe went back inside and slammed the door in Jake's face. Jake clenched his teeth, but he couldn't argue a single one of Louie Jaffe's points. He had nothing. Absolutely nothing here but a bitter old man who'd built the life he wanted to live for himself. He might be crazy. But in all the years Jaffe had lived out here, since he came home from Vietnam, any run-ins he'd had with other people or the law had happened right here on his front porch. It just made no sense at all to Jake why Jaffe would have left his property and trespassed on Nelson Palmer's.

Jake turned to go, his gut telling him Jaffe was exactly right. He'd just wasted both of their time. He texted Sheriff Landry to tell her as much, then promised to head out to talk to Pat Stuckey's boy.

Eleven

At twelve years old a piece, Caleb Stuckey, Kaden Price, and Jonah Zielinski had swaggers they hadn't earned. The three of them sat on a bench in the break room of Pat Stuckey's machine shop. Pat paid them each eight bucks an hour to sweep up and shovel snow. At three months older than the others, Jake soon figured out Caleb was the ringleader.

"You're not in trouble," Jake said. "Let's get that clear off the bat. I'd just like to hear your side of what happened between you and Mr. Jaffe."

"What's that old nut job saying?!" Caleb said. His feet barely touched the floor as they dangled off the bench.

"You don't need to worry about that," Jake said. "Just tell me what happened when you saw him."

"He tried to kill Jonah," Caleb said.

"How's that?"

"By shooting his head off," Caleb answered.

"Okay," Jake said. "Let's take this from the top. When did all this happen?"

"Last Tuesday," Jonah chimed in. "We went up to his house to see if Mr. Jaffe needed any help around the house. He's like a hundred, right? We're all trying to get service hours for school."

"These boys are in the Junior Honor Society," Pat said, as if that meant they couldn't also be telling tall tales.

"What happened?" Jake asked.

"He came out shooting!" Kaden said.

"You knocked?"

"'Course we knocked," Caleb said.

"And you're saying Louie just came out, gun in hand?"

"That's what we're saying," Caleb answered. "Told us we had a three count to start running the other way. Only he didn't even get to two. He started shooting. Bullet whizzed right by Jonah's ear. Isn't that right, Jonah? It put a hole in his coat."

"This coat?" Jake asked. Jonah was wearing a navy-blue puffer coat that was at least two sizes too big. Probably a hand-me-down from an older brother.

"Not this one," Jonah said. "I wasn't wearing it that day."

"Uh huh," Jake asked. "You wouldn't know anything about Louie Jaffe's front window getting broken, would you?"

"We offered to fix it," Kaden said. "Like Jonah said. We were looking for service hours."

"How did it get broken?" Jake asked.

"Beats me," Caleb said. "We just offered to fix it."

"Was that before or after he started shooting at you?"

"Before," Caleb said.

"But after he started counting to three?" Jake asked.

"They told you what happened!" Pat Stuckey said.

"I'm just trying to get a clear picture of the chain of events. These are pretty serious accusations, Mr. Stuckey."

"You calling these boys liars?"

"No, sir," Jake said. "I'm just trying to get the facts."

"The fact is," Kaden said. "Jaffe's nuts. We ain't even told you what happened the other day. What we saw."

"What was that?" Jake asked.

"We were just going door to door trying to see if anybody needed us to shovel their driveways or sidewalks. You know. After it snowed," Caleb said.

"They're good boys," Pat Stuckey said. "I taught 'em right."

"Where was this?" Jake asked.

"On Grace Church Road," Caleb answered. "It was like six thirty in the morning. Anyway, we saw Jaffe's old Jeep. The one with all the stickers all over it. It was parked by the side of the road. Right by old farmer Palmer's place."

"What day was this?" Jake asked.

"Opening day," Kaden chimed in. "The day Mr. Wayne got killed."

"You're telling me you saw Louie Jaffe's Jeep parked on the side of the road?"

"You have trouble hearing or something?" Caleb said. He got a smack in the back of the head from his old man for it. Jake shot him a hard glance.

"How do you know it was Jaffe's?" Jake asked.

"Cuz nobody else around town drives a beat-up old puke-green Jeep like that," Caleb answered. "Scared the piss out of us. We took off running on account of what happened the last time we saw that old nut job."

"And you're sure it was opening day?" Jake asked.

"We're sure," Jonah added.

"You know my deputies have been asking questions about that day. Trying to figure out who else might have been out in those woods. Why didn't you come forward before?"

"We just did," Caleb said. "Why didn't you come asking before this? It's Jaffe you might wanna talk to."

"I'll keep that in mind," Jake said.

"You got enough?" Pat Stuckey asked. "These boys need to get on back to work."

"I've got enough for now," Jake said. "I'm sure I'll have more questions later. Can I count on your cooperation?"

"You bet," Pat said. He shook Jake's hand and ordered the three boys back to work.

Jake headed back out to his car, fairly certain there wasn't a word of truth to anything these boys had just told him. For now, it was their word against Jaffe's. But rumors could have devastating consequences. Jake just prayed he could get to the bottom of this one before it blew up in his face.

TWELVE

Sunday night, Max Cashen decided it was time to make his special venison lasagna. He made the sauce from scratch, using tomatoes he'd canned from the garden a year ago fall. He didn't need his eyes to carefully spread each layer of cheeses, sauce, and ground venison from the eight-point Ryan had shot during bow season just a few short weeks ago. Years ago, when Grandma Ava was still alive, she would make the noodles using her ancient chrome industrial Kitchen-Aid mixer. Now, it was the one "cheat" Grandpa had. He let Gemma get noodles from one of her clients. They were homemade still, just not Ava's.

He insisted both Jake and Ryan take showers before sitting down to dinner. Jake went down to his cabin without complaint. Ryan complained plenty, but used the second-floor guest bath while Gemma checked her crockpot peach cobbler. That too was one of Grandpa's favorites. She made it with peaches canned from a local orchard, dumped in with two boxes of vanilla cake mix. Jake's job was to bring the ice cream. He got it from the Dollar Kart at the end of the road Grandpa couldn't go into anymore. But that was a story for another day.

Jake came back to the main house before Ryan got out of the shower. He'd worked hard in practice this morning. It might not be this year, but Jake knew he had the makings of a State Champ next year as a senior.

"How was Travis today?" Gemma asked as she replaced the lid on the crockpot. She smacked Grandpa's hand away when he tried to dip a finger in.

"You stay to your side of the kitchen," she warned Grandpa.

"He looked good," Jake said. "Still got some work to do on his conditioning. He's got a tough match coming up against St. Iz. That kid's going to be riding him all the way to his senior year. But Trav's a better wrestler. He's just gotta realize it."

"Jake," Gemma said, putting her spoon down. "I'm asking you how Travis looked."

Jake turned, facing his sister straight on. "And I'm telling you."

"Did you invite the kid and his aunt like I told you?" Grandpa said.

"Yes," Gemma answered. "Erica said Travis still has a couple of pounds to cut. She tried to talk him into coming anyway. He just wanted to take a nap. I think ..."

"Then leave him be," Grandpa said. "Boy knows what he needs. Doesn't need a couple of women cackling at him."

"I was not cackling," Gemma said.

Jake smiled and turned again before he let his sister see him laugh. She picked up her spoon and rapped him in the shoulder with it anyway.

"Ow!"

"Tell the boys to get in here," Grandpa said. "Lasagna's ready to be cut."

He shooed Gemma away when she tried to take the casserole dish from him. Grandpa placed it dead center on the kitchen table and grabbed the biggest, sharpest butcher knife he had from the block. He tended to talk with it. Jake grabbed Gemma and got her out of the danger zone.

"They're almost finished shoveling the driveway," she said.

Jake looked out the window. Ryan was critiquing his younger brother's technique. When Ryan turned his back, Jake caught Aiden sticking his tongue out at him.

"Careful," Jake called out the front door. "It'll freeze like that."

Aiden jumped. At seven, he was turning into a monster of an athlete himself. It was hard to tell at this age, but Jake thought he had the makings of a hell of a wrestler too. But he had a long way to go.

"He wants to do OHWAY this spring," Gemma said, reading Jake's thoughts.

"He's too young," Jake said. "He needs a break. He's gonna spend his whole summer playing baseball."

"The other dads are all ..."

"Don't care," Jake said. "You'll burn him out. This idea that kids that young need to push themselves twelve months out of the year ... it's not good for them. Let him play. Let him be a kid."

"Sit your asses down and eat this food!" Grandpa hollered. The door was still open. Aiden and Ryan set their shovels down where they stood and heeded their great-grandpa's command.

With expert precision, Grandpa sliced the lasagna, plated it, then slid four servings down the table.

Grandpa said a quick grace, then the boys started shoveling their lasagna down. Jake knew Ryan might regret it later in the week when he had to make weight. He'd have to work twice as hard at practice tomorrow.

"I get a pound before the next tournament," Ryan said to Jake, his mouth full.

Jake spread his hand wide. "Didn't say a word. You're seventeen. You should know what you need to do by now without me on your case."

"So," Grandpa said. "You wanna tell me what went down at Louie's place the other day? Hearing rumors you think he killed Ben."

"What?" Jake said. "I think no such thing. And you know better than to grill me about a case I'm investigating."

Gemma put her fork down. Jake noticed she hadn't touched her lasagna yet.

"What?" he asked.

Ryan and Gemma passed a look.

"What?" Jake asked again, more forcefully.

"Tell him," Gemma said.

Ryan shrugged. "It's just rumors. Like Grandpa said."

"Jake," Gemma said. "Is it true Louie Jaffe shot Jonah Zielinski the other day?"

Jake folded his hands on the table. "I think you two need to quit getting your information from social media."

"They were messing with him, weren't they?" Grandpa said. "Dammit, Jake. Louie's earned the right to be left alone. You're the reason those kids get ideas in their heads about him."

"Me?"

"Your generation," Grandpa said. "I know what you used to get up to. Running up there. Setting off cherry bombs in his front yard."

"I never did that," Jake said.

"Well, you kids used to trespass on his property. Told you not to but you did it anyway."

"Not since I was eleven years old, Gramps. And I didn't know kids were still doing that. You ever do it?" Jake directed his question to Ryan and Aiden. "Cuz if I catch wind that you were out there bothering that old man ..."

"No!" Ryan said. "I've never gone out there. And Aiden knows I'd kill him if he did. But some of those younger kids. Like Caleb Stuckey's little group ... they're bad news."

"What are you doing hanging out with a bunch of middle schoolers?" Gemma asked.

"I don't hang out with them," Ryan said. "Caleb's older brother is in my class though. He says Caleb's always getting himself in one mess or the other. But ... he said Caleb and his friends saw Louie out there the day Ben got killed. Is that true?"

"Ryan, you know I can't talk about that with you either."

"Why would Crazy Louie wanna hurt Travis's dad?" Aiden asked. "They said at school he's got a skull collection from the war. Chopped off the heads of the King Kongs."

"Viet Cong," Grandpa said, exasperated. "Not King Kong. And that's ridiculous. Don't believe everything you hear."

"Grandpa's right," Jake said. "Don't believe everything you hear. And don't go spreading it around either. We've got enough of that going on in town."

"Louie didn't kill anybody," Grandpa said.

"He did too!" Aiden protested. "They gave him medals for it!"

"He didn't murder anybody," Grandpa said.

"I don't like it," Gemma said, rising to clear Aidan and Ryan's plates. "They're all talking about it at school. On social media. It's all around Travis. It's ghoulish and upsetting. After what happened at poor Ben's funeral, you'd think that would have put a stop to it. It hasn't though, Jake. It's starting to scare me."

He rose and helped his sister clear the plates. As she stacked them on the counter, he rinsed them off and handed them back to her to load the dishwasher.

"He reads all of it," Gemma whispered.

"Who, Ryan?"

"Yes, Ryan," she said. "But Travis too. It's not healthy. I wish you'd have a talk with him."

"I have," Jake said. "He knows I'm doing everything I can to find out who did this."

"You really think it could be Louie?" She mouthed the name.

Jake looked over his shoulder. The boys had excused themselves and were putting their coats back on to finish the driveway. Grandpa had retired to his recliner in the front room.

"I doubt it," Jake said. "But I'm not ruling anyone out just yet."

"These boys," she said. "They spend all hours of the day and night online reading these conspiracy theories put out by that group. It's all a bunch of kooks and basement dwellers. Half the people on that page now don't even live in Worthington County. Now you got Pat Stuckey strutting around town saying how his kid was braver than the cops, standing up to Louie Jaffe. Saying how if Caleb and those other boys hadn't scared Louie off that morning, he would have killed more people."

"Pat Stuckey said that?" Jake said.

"It's getting out of hand," she said. "I'm afraid somebody's going to get hurt."

"I'll talk to Stuckey again," Jake said.

"Please just be careful," she said.

"I'm always careful."

When Gemma turned to him, she had tears in her eyes. She quickly brushed them away with a towel.

"Gemma."

"Jake," she said. "I mean it. Whoever did this. He's still out there. I don't think it was Louie either. But it was someone. If something happened to you like it did to Ben ... well ..."

Jake smiled and went to his sister. He put a light hand on her back. She came to him, throwing her arms around him, holding him tight.

"Hey," he said. "Take it easy. I'm careful. I'm always careful."

"Travis is all alone. He doesn't have a sister or a brother. You and me? We had each other. He's gotta go through this by himself. It's killing me to think about."

"I know," he said. "Shh. I know."

"Promise me," she said, punching him not entirely lightly in the shoulder. "I mean it."

"I'll be careful. I promise."

Sniffling, she straightened and let Jake go.

"Can you promise me something too?" he said. "Keep your ear to the ground on Travis and Ryan. I've got them in practice, but I need you to use that mom radar you have. You catch wind of any of them trying to do anything stupid ..."

"I will," she said.

"Good. Now scoop out that cobbler. It smells delicious."

Nodding, Gemma busied herself at the crockpot. He went to the front room and watched his nephews as they finished up the walk. They worked well together. Ryan was patient with his little brother. He felt a pang as Gemma's words went through him again. Ryan and Aiden had each other. He had Gemma. But Travis. She was right. In a way, he was all alone.

THIRTEEN

The next morning, Detective Ed Zender came back to work. He had a back brace and a cane, but Jake had to give him credit for showing up. Ed looked more pained than usual, trying to get comfortable in his desk chair.

"I'm really sorry about Ben, Jake," Ed said.

Jake knew he was sincere. He had his issues with Ed. The senior homicide detective, Ed had begrudged Jake's promotion to the unit. At first, rather than working together, Ed had been more worried about protecting his turf. But after a year, they'd settled into a peaceful, if not always amiable coexistence.

"Ben was a good guy," Ed said. "Always said hello or had a kind word. His wife Abby was a gem and a half. She used to take care of my mom over at Pine Grove in her final years. Nurse Abby was the only one Ma would let near her toward the end. Damn shame when she got sick. Now this. It's just a ... well ... a damn shame."

"Thanks, Ed," Jake said.

"I tried to make it over to the funeral parlor. Heard you had some excitement."

"Just some dumb kids trying to be internet cops," Jake said.

Jake saw Ed had his digital file on Ben Wayne's case open on his computer. He was reading through Jake's report on his interview with Louie Jaffe.

"Crazy Louie," Ed said. "You really think he had something to do with this?"

"My gut says no," Jake said. "I've never known that guy to bother anyone who wasn't on his property. Even then, he's never done anything to technically break the law. Skirted it plenty. But this?"

"Yeah," Ed said. "I'm supposed to believe he drove over to Nelson Palmer's property and capped Ben Wayne for no good reason?"

"That's where I am with it," Jake said. "But I've got these three kids saying Louie's Jeep was parked on the road a half mile down from the two-track leading into Palmer's woods the morning of the shooting. Louie's got a slippery alibi at best. Swears he was hunting his own property. He *did* bring a deer out to Sanderson's to be processed the next day. I just checked with him."

Ed kept scrolling through the report. "Who are your three witnesses?"

"Caleb Stuckey, Kaden Price, and Jonah Zielinski."

Ed shook his head. "Doesn't anybody name their kids normal anymore? What happened to the Steves or the Joes?"

"You're getting old, Ed," Jake said.

"Kaden Price," he said. "By any chance might that be Ansel Price's kid or grandkid? Ansel was a foreman out at the clay mill. He's been retired for a while, but he plays in a monthly card game down at the Elks Lodge. I get out there when I can. I've known Ansel forever."

"What kind of guy is he?" Jake asked.

Ed raised a brow. "Well, not to put too fine a point on it, but he's a son of a bitch. Back when I worked field ops, I used to pop in on him. My wife Rachel was friends with Ansel's sister. She was always worried Ansel was too rough with his sons. They showed up to school with black eyes. That kind of thing. Now, Ansel's changed. Found God. Quit drinking. He's always been very respectful of cops. His dad was on the job in Cleveland a million years ago."

"Hmm," Jake said, standing over Ed's shoulder.

"I think Ansel's grandkids are living with him now. His son got laid off from Emerson Tool and Dye last year. Ansel's been griping about it, but I think he secretly loves having them."

"Ed," Jake said. "You think you could give Ansel a call? Find out when Kaden's there by himself?"

"What are you thinking?"

"Well," Jake said. "Based on what you're saying, I'm thinking maybe if the kid is scared enough of Grandpa Ansel, and we show up with badges, maybe Kaden might remember even more about what happened the morning of the shooting. I questioned the three boys together over at Pat Stuckey's shop. Caleb was the ringleader for sure. I'm just thinking maybe if I got either Kaden or the other boy, Jonah, alone, they might have a different story."

Ed nodded. "I'd be happy to give Ansel a call. You sure you want me in on this?"

Ed gave Jake a sideways look, his brow arched. This was a running issue with them. Ed liked to play the martyr if he didn't think Jake included him enough.

"I just asked you, Ed," Jake said. "You've got an in. I think we need to use every angle we've got."

Ed's smile was genuine. He grabbed his desk phone and dialed a number. Five minutes of bullshitting later, and Ed had secured a visit over at Ansel Price's house.

"You're gonna owe me for this one," Ed said.

"How's that?"

"Well, Ansel said he was just about to call me. Said he's got something else on the Louie Jaffe situation he thinks we're gonna wanna hear. He kept Kaden home from school. They're both waiting to talk to us."

"Good work, Ed," Jake said. Twenty minutes after that, Ed and Jake were knocking on Ansel Price's front door.

———

Kaden Price sat in his grandfather's living room, picking at a scab on his elbow. He wouldn't look Jake in the eye. He was a different kid than the cocky loudmouth who sat at Caleb Stuckey's side two days ago.

"Don't just sit there," Ansel Price shouted. The old man stood with his hands on his hips, towering over the boy. "Tell him what you told me."

"I didn't tell you anything," Kaden said, some of his bravado returning.

"Fine," Ansel said. He reached over and picked up a smart phone in a silver case. He handed it to Jake.

"He left this on the kitchen table," Ansel said. "Took me all of two seconds to root out what these little idiots have been up to."

"You can't look at it!" Kaden shouted. "I didn't give you permission. I know my rights."

"You ain't got no rights to this phone," Ansel said. "You're twelve. And you don't pay the bill!"

Ansel pulled a piece of paper out of his pocket. It was a cell phone bill. "Says so right here," he said. "Phone's in my name. It's the 2081 number. See it? Look at all those texts. This is supposed to be for emergencies only. Not for committing crimes! This detective is going to take your ungrateful little butt to jail."

"Hold on," Jake said. "Just show me what you want me to see."

Ansel tapped on the lock screen. "Told him he couldn't have it at all unless I could get into it."

"You shared your password with your grandpa?" Jake asked.

"He makes me," Kaden said.

Ansel handed Jake the phone. "There," he said. "These three criminal geniuses laid out their whole dumb plan. Maybe if ... I don't know ... they'd actually *talk* to each other in person instead of through screens, they'd get away with more."

Ansel kept right on yelling as Jake scrolled through a group text between Caleb, Kaden, and Jonah. It started just a few hours after Ben's body was found. As Jake suspected, Caleb appeared to be the ringleader.

Caleb: You know it had to be that crazy Jaffe. I heard Trav's dad got gutted. He was gonna grind the meat up for burgers.

Jonah: That's sick.

Caleb: Time to fix him for good.

Jonah: Hell yeah! He'll probably crap his pants when they hook him up to the chair.

Caleb: They don't use chairs anymore idiot.

Kaden: How U want to play it

Caleb: Meet at your place. We call the cops from there. Can't be here. The old man is on my ass this week. Then over to Jaffe's. Bring your pea shooter.

Jonah: Maybe we should shoot his nuts off. I liked Trav's dad.

Caleb: We're gonna fix it. Don't worry.

"Kaden," Jake said, handing Ansel back the phone. "You never saw Louie Jaffe's Jeep near Nelson Palmer's property, did you?"

Kaden quit picking his scab and folded his arms over his chest. "I don't have to say a word."

"Yes, you do!" Ansel shouted. "I don't care if you're twelve. You can pack your things and go find your mother. Live with her."

"She's crazier than you are!" Kaden shouted.

"You tell the truth!" Ansel said. "That old man did nothing to you you didn't deserve. You were messing with him, weren't you? Went up there and shot out his windows, didn't you?"

"Yes," Kaden said. "You happy? Yes. That was Jonah's idea."

"What happened, Kaden?" Jake asked.

"He shot Jonah," Kaden said. "I told you that. Took a chunk out of his leg."

"Yeah? The other day he said it was his arm. You told me Jaffe came after you when you were on the road," Jake said. "But that's not true, is it? You were on Jaffe's property."

"He pulled a gun on us!" Kaden said. "Threatened to kill us all."

"You were trespassing," Ansel said. "Man has a right to defend his property. He's a veteran. Served his country in a war nobody likes to talk about. Jaffe's earned his right to peace. Not to have a bunch of hoodlums like you shooting out his windows. Jake, Jaffe's got PTSD. Did you know that? These little turds probably scared the crap out of him."

"Kaden," Jake said. "This is serious. You understand there are people in this town and online who believe you boys. They've spread rumors that Louie Jaffe is a murderer."

"He is!" Kaden said. "He's crazy. The whole town knows it. It's only a matter of time before he kills somebody."

"But not this time," Jake said, trying to keep his cool. "You didn't see his Jeep where you said you did, did you?"

"No!" Kaden said. "But if you won't arrest that kook, then it's on you when he hurts the next kid."

"We're done here for now," Jake said. He gestured toward Kaden's phone. "Can I take this?"

"It's yours," Ansel said. "He ain't getting it back. He can use a pay phone for emergencies."

"There's no such thing," Kaden muttered.

Ed just shook his head as Jake turned to leave. Jake held the door open, waiting for Ed to shuffle out. Luckily, Ansel Price had a ramp installed. Jake didn't know if Ed could have handled too many steps.

Jake helped him into the car then climbed in himself.

"Of all the stupid pranks," Ed said. "Ansel's right to be so mad. Jaffe doesn't deserve any of this."

"A wild goose chase," Jake said, pounding a fist into the steering wheel. The force of it made Ed jump. "They've done damage. Real damage. And wasted time I don't have."

"I've seen that stuff online," Ed said. "Everybody's so quick to believe the worst. They've thought of Louie as some kind of boogeyman for years. This just gave 'em all license to be proper assholes."

Jake pulled out of the Prices' driveway. It was just before noon. Ed was only planning on working half days this week.

"You want me to just drive you straight home?" Jake asked. "I can swing by and pick you up in the morning if you want."

"I'd appreciate it," Ed said. "My wife was gonna pick me up. It'll save her the trip. I've got a doctor's appointment in the morning so I'll be in later."

Ed droned on about a million other things as Jake made the fifteen-minute trip across town. Ed lived in Arch Hill, not too far from the sheriff. Jake thought about giving her a call and stopping by. She'd want to know about this latest mess with the Price boy.

He said his goodbyes to Ed as his wife helped him up the walk. Jake touched his phone icon on his dashboard app to call Sheriff Landry. Before Jake could punch in the number, his screen lit up with an incoming call. Gemma.

"Jake," she said, breathless. "I need you to meet me at Ben's house."

"What is it?" Jake said, his heart dropping. He knew his sister. Her tone. She sounded terrified.

"I just got a call from Erica," she said. "She's out of her mind. Jake, Travis is missing. He's gone."

FOURTEEN

"Just don't tell her to calm down," Gemma said. She met Jake at the end of Ben Wayne's driveway. As usual, his sister was dressed entirely inappropriately for the weather. She teetered on three-inch stiletto boots with two inches of snow on the ground.

"Tell me what happened," Jake said.

"He's gone. Travis took off somewhere."

"Where's Birdie?"

Gemma looked over her shoulder. "She's inside. For now."

Jake started to move past his sister. As she turned to follow him, she nearly slid down the driveway. Jake reached out, grabbed her arm, then helped her back up the walk.

"You're gonna break your damn neck," he said. "Put some actual snow boots on."

"I'm working today," she said. "Or was."

Gemma was one of the top real estate agents in Worthington County. Which sounded like a bigger deal than it was. But with the tourist industry starting to pick up in Blackhand Hills, Gemma had a five-year plan to set herself and her boys up for life. Of all the get-rich-quick schemes she'd tried, it turned out Gemma had a real knack for selling houses. It was the longest she'd ever stuck with a career.

They found Birdie leaning over the kitchen table, looking at a computer screen. She straightened as Jake walked in.

"Thank God," she said. "Did you bring it?"

"Bring what?"

Birdie looked from Gemma to Jake. Her face fell, and anger came into her eyes. "You didn't tell him."

"Erica," Gemma said. "I asked him to come. You haven't ..."

"I need my brother's phone," she said. "It's still with your forensics guys, I assume. We need to check and see if he has one of those tracker apps."

"Birdie," Jake said. "Start from the beginning. What happened?"

"Travis is in the wind," she said. "He told me he was staying over at a friend's last night. Dillon Harper."

Dillon was in the same grade as Travis. He wrestled 132 on the J.V. team. He lived on the family farm in Navan Township.

"We got a robocall on the landline an hour ago," Birdie said. "The school absence line. He didn't show up today. I called the Harpers. They didn't know anything about Travis spending the night. Dillon went to school like normal. They texted him and the kid played dumb. He says he hasn't talked to Travis in two days."

"When was the last time you saw him?" Jake asked.

"Yesterday," Birdie said. "We had dinner together. I wanted to watch a movie or something with him. Travis asked if he could go to Dillon's. He said he just needed to get out of the house. I thought it was a positive sign."

"On a school night," Gemma said.

"I didn't think of that," Birdie said, flapping her hands in exasperation. "I don't know what I'm doing, okay? I don't know what the protocol is with a sixteen-year-old boy who just lost his only parent. He's been so angry. Depressed. We had a normal dinner. I made spaghetti. I don't cook. It's one thing I know how to make, and Travis liked it. He had two helpings. He thanked me. It's pretty much the one time he's acknowledged me at all. Then he asked me about going over to the Harpers. He *asked* me."

"It's okay." Jake and Gemma said it together.

"You didn't do anything wrong, Birdie ... er ... Erica," Jake said.

"He was lying to me the whole time though," she said. "And now it's been fifteen hours since I've seen him. He could be anywhere."

"Relax," Jake said. "The kid probably just needed some space. He's had people around him 24/7 for the last few days. With the funeral. All the craziness online. He probably just wanted some time to blow off steam."

"He didn't go to school!" Birdie said. "He just started back yesterday. That was his idea too. I told him I thought he should just wait until after the first of the year. They're starting winter break at the end of next week. I thought it would be good for him to just take that time. Go back when the new semester started. He insisted though. He said he wanted things to start getting back to normal. We talked about it at dinner. It was the first real conversation we've had since all of this started."

"You're doing your best," Gemma said. She went to Birdie and tried to put an arm around her. Birdie took a step backward out of her reach.

"Don't. I know you mean well. Dammit. Everyone means well. But something's wrong. We have to find Travis."

"We will," Jake said. "Did he take his car?"

"He took Ben's truck," Birdie said. "They just brought it back yesterday after BCI swept it."

"Have you tried calling him?" Jake said. "I have to ask."

"Yes," Birdie said. "I've left him about a dozen voice mails. Texted him. He's not answering. That's why I'm trying to figure out if Ben had one of those tracking apps."

She grabbed the laptop off the table and turned it toward Jake. "It's Ben's," she said. "I tried the websites of a couple of the more popular apps. To see if he had accounts that would autofill on any of them. I know that's a long shot but ..."

"No," Jake said. "It's a good idea."

"I can't sit here another second," Birdie said. "I have to do something. I have to go look for him."

"What about Ryan?" Jake said to Gemma. Within the confines of wrestling season, Travis Wayne and Jake's nephew Ryan Stark were tight. One grade above Travis, Ryan had started taking him under his wing.

"He was in school today," Gemma said. "I checked. He was heading home for lunch. I told him to meet me here. He doesn't know we know Travis is AWOL."

"Good thinking," Jake said. "Give them less time to coordinate their stories. You mind if I check his room?"

Birdie led the way. She opened the door and a wave of smells hit Jake in the face. A combination of stale laundry, Axe body spray, spoiled food, and the pungent aroma of raw teenage boy.

Travis's room was littered with cups, bowls, crumpled chip bags, and empty pop cans. A bearded dragon eyed Jake with suspicion from a tank in the corner. Travis had a laundry hamper in the other corner but it was empty. Like most boys his age, Travis would rather ball his clothes all over the floor.

"Yeah," Jake said. "I can see this is gonna be pointless. Impossible to tell if he's packed anything."

"I haven't wanted to nag him," Birdie said. "That's something Ben always said. If Trav wants to live like a pig, he would just shut the door. He said he got tired of arguing about it."

Gemma smiled. "Well, he was always a better man than me. Ryan's room looks just about identical."

Jake walked in. Oddly, amid all the clutter and mess, Travis's bed was neatly made. Jake kicked a few piles of clothes out of his way. His foot made contact with something hard. Reaching down, he looked up at Birdie.

"Well, like I said. It was a good thought. But you're wasting your time trying to track Travis through any app." As he picked up Travis's cell phone, Jake felt a flicker of real fear for the first time. Wherever Travis went, he didn't want to be found. It was worth it enough to leave his phone behind.

Jake tried to open the phone, but Travis had it password protected. He could give it to the forensics detective later, but it might be hours before they got into it.

From the window, Jake saw Ryan pull up in his beat-up Ford Focus. Gemma saw too and went racing for the front door.

"Jake," Birdie said, staring at Travis's empty bed. "This is bad."

"One step at a time, Birdie," he said. "Let's see what Ryan knows."

It took all of two minutes before Jake knew his nephew was lying. He refused to meet Jake's eyes as Gemma peppered him with questions about Travis's whereabouts.

Birdie sat in the corner, glaring at Ryan. The kid broke into a cold sweat before Jake even said a word to him.

"Ryan," Jake said. "Did Travis make you swear not to talk to us?"

"What? I don't know. I mean, no."

"You saw him yesterday," Birdie said. "Ryan, you took him to school yesterday morning. You brought him home after practice. He had to have said something to you."

"It was just a normal day," Ryan said.

"Normal except for him wanting to get out of the house," Birdie said.

"Right. Right. He said that."

"You didn't offer to take him to your house?" Jake said. "I mean, Travis was staying with you before his aunt got to town."

"Oh. I don't know."

"He didn't tell you he was going to Dillon Harper's?" Jake said.

"Oh. Wait. Yeah. I think he did. Yes. He did. He said Dillon invited him over for pizza."

It was the thinnest of lies, of course. Jake knew it was possible Travis had just flat out lied to Ryan, but he doubted it.

"Ryan," Jake said. "You can drop it. He wasn't at Dillon's. He never told you he was at Dillon's. I don't know what's going on, but I know you do. What did Travis tell you?"

"I can't lose him, do you get that?" Birdie said, becoming unglued. "My parents can't lose him. They've lost their son. Whatever's going on with Travis, you're not helping him."

When Ryan Stark broke, he broke hard.

"I told him not to," Ryan said. "I swear I had no idea he was going to go through with it. I said I'd go with him. You know. To keep him from doing anything stupid. But he backed off. He said I was right. That it was a stupid idea and he should just let Uncle Jake do his job."

"What?" Gemma said. "What was so stupid?"

It was then that the horror of the situation hit Jake. He rose, walking to the back bedroom. Ben's room. It wasn't the primary bedroom. After Abby died, Ben wouldn't sleep there anymore. He chose the second bedroom at the end of the hall.

"Jake?" Birdie called out. She started to follow him.

They'd gone to Barney's together last year. Ben had wanted Jake's opinion. Jake had recommended a small safe that fit right under Ben's bed.

Jake crouched down. The door of the safe nearly hit him in the eye. It was open. The small metal gun case inside of it was empty. Ben's 9 mm wasn't there. "Ryan," Jake shouted. "You need to tell me what Travis wanted to do. Now!"

"He just wanted to talk to the old guy," Ryan cried out. "I swear. He said he just wanted to talk to him."

"Old guy," Jake said, rising. "You mean Louie Jaffe. You're telling me Travis went to confront Louie Jaffe?"

"Jake?" Gemma stood at the bedroom door, side by side with Birdie.

Jake held the empty gun case in his hands as he slowly rose.

FIFTEEN

"He's not going to do anything," Ryan said.

Jake went back out into the front room where Ryan sat. Gemma was close on his heels.

"Not going to do anything?" Gemma screamed. "Ryan, I told you. You swore you were going to keep an eye on Travis. You promised you were going to tell me if he got ideas into his head. Jake, they're all wound up. The whole wrestling team. They've been deep into those internet groups with all the conspiracy theories. I told those boys it served no purpose."

"He won't do anything," Ryan insisted. "He promised."

"Ryan," Jake said, trying to keep his temper in check. Ryan, after all, was just a kid himself. "He asked you to lie for him."

"I didn't know he hadn't come back," Ryan said. "I swear. Not until Mr. Thomas pulled me out of class asking. I didn't know. When you called, I came right over. I'm telling you now. He was fine. We had a long talk. I told him I'd go over with him after school today and we'd talk to Jaffe together."

"You what?" Gemma's tone reached a pitch that cleared Jake's sinuses. "Your keys. Now. You're taking the bus to and from school from now on."

"Mom!"

The house shook. Jake turned. Birdie had been standing at his left shoulder. She wasn't there anymore. Tires crunched over the gravel and snow.

"Dammit," Jake said, walking to the front window. "Dammit!"

If it hadn't before, hell had officially just broken loose. Jake squeezed his eyes shut and let out a hard sigh as Birdie Wayne tore out of Ben's driveway heading west. Jake knew there was only one place she'd want to go.

Birdie knew every back road Jake did. He drove as fast as he could over roads slick with ice. He rolled up on Louie Jaffe's property maybe two minutes after she did. She'd parked her rental car at the end of his quarter mile driveway. Her footprints cut through the snow and went straight up toward the house. Of course she realized Jake would go after her.

Jake zipped up his jacket. New snow was starting to fall in fat, fluffy flakes. They were calling for three more inches by this evening.

"Birdie!" Jake called out. Louie would know she was coming. If Travis Wayne had been dumb enough to confront the old man head-on, Jaffe would have seen the kid from a mile away too.

Jake stopped short as he saw Ben's truck parked at an odd angle right in front of the house.

"Dammit," Jake muttered. Travis had been exactly dumb enough.

As a shadow moved around the corner of the house, Jake acted on instinct, reaching for his weapon.

"He's not here," Birdie called out. She came into view, her own, army-issued Sig Sauer drawn; she held it two-handed, pointed at the ground.

"What the hell did you think you were going to do?" Jake yelled.

"Save that kid from making the dumbest mistake of his life," she answered. "We're too late. There's nobody in the house."

"You went in the house?" Jake said. "Birdie ... you have to ..."

"To what?" she spat. "I have to do what? Wait for you? Wait for backup? Wait for you to get a search warrant?"

"Well ... yes ..."

"I'm not the cops," she said. "And I don't need a warrant."

"Then you're trespassing at a minimum," he said. "Breaking and entering ..."

"I didn't break anything," she said. "The back door was unlocked."

"You know what? Stop talking. I don't want to know."

"Fine," she said. "Go deal with your chain of command. I'm taking a walk. They went that way."

The snow had almost filled them in, but Jake saw two distinct sets of footprints coming off the front porch and leading back into the woods.

Birdie was on the move.

"Wait!" Jake called after her.

"No!" She whipped around. "You call this in. The second Louie Jaffe sees lights and sirens heading up his way, how do you think that'll go over? Not to mention Travis. He's liable to panic. If he hasn't already."

Her voice came out in a choked garble. She had tears streaming down her face.

"I can't lose them both, Jake," she said. "I won't. So you can stand there if you want. But I'm heading into those woods."

"Yeah," Jake said. "All right. Come on. We'll go together."

Without him even telling her, Birdie took a tactical position slightly behind Jake. Between the two of them, they formed a circle of threat and 360-degree vision as they made their way toward the woods.

They followed the fading footprints where they entered a narrow trail leading downhill.

"They didn't come in here together," Jake said. "One set of prints is shallower than the other."

"He laid in wait," Birdie said. "One of them did, anyway."

"No," Jake said. "Like you said. Jaffe's going to know everyone and everything that comes in and out of here. Trav's been gone for hours. Jaffe probably lured him away from the house."

"My God," Birdie said. "He set a trap for him."

Jake hoped it wasn't true. Jaffe's words the last time they spoke cut through him.

I'll defend myself. I'll defend my property. If people leave me alone, I'll leave them alone. If anyone else tries to mess with me …

if they come up here shooting at me or my place, they ain't getting out of here alive!

"Travis," Jake muttered. "You stupid, stupid kid."

They made it about a hundred yards into the thickest part of the woods. Then, Jake smelled smoke. He was about to say something to Birdie, but a sound echoed through the woods, cutting straight through Jake's soul. A single gunshot.

"No!" Birdie shouted. Then she was off like a shot in the direction of the sound. Jake was in lock step with her.

He pulled his cell phone out and punched in dispatch.

"Darcy!" he said, breathless. "It's Cashen. I'm out at Louie Jaffe's. I've got shots fired. Shots fired! Send me backup, Code 3!"

A second gunshot pierced the air. This one different from the first. A rifle shot. Jake dropped his phone and drew his weapon.

"Jaffe!" he called out. "It's Jake Cashen. Put your weapon down. You hear me? Travis? Lay your weapons down. Both of you!"

He lost sight of Birdie.

"Jaffe!" he yelled.

He heard a scream. Jake's heart twisted at the sound of it. It was Travis.

Birdie reappeared ten yards to the left of him, her own weapon still drawn. They came to the scene together.

Louie Jaffe had Travis pinned down. He lay on his back. He held Ben's pistol, clutched to his chest, the barrel pointed straight out. Jaffe sat perched in a tree stand above them all, his rifle pointed straight at Travis's head.

"Drop your weapon!" Jake yelled. "I mean it, Jaffe."

From the corner of his eye, he saw Birdie aim at Jaffe.

"You think you can get a shot off?" Jaffe said. Jake wasn't sure which one of them the old man was talking to. From his position, he had the perfect sniper's nest.

"I think you all need to drop your weapons," Jaffe said. "You're on my property. No warrant. No cause. And this one just took a shot at me."

Jake knew the first gunshot they'd heard had come from Travis, from his father's Nine. Good God. The boy had tried to kill Jaffe.

"Travis," Jake said. "Drop your weapon. I'm not kidding around now. Birdie, you too."

"Not a chance," she said. "Not while that psycho has a rifle pointed at my nephew's head."

The three of them formed a triangle of death. Travis and Birdie both pointed at Jaffe. From his perch, Jaffe was able to take his pick between the two of them.

"He killed my dad!" Travis yelled through his tears. "He blew his brains out. You saw what he did. Why aren't you shooting him?!"

"No," Jake said. "Travis, Louie Jaffe isn't who you think he is. Louie, do you hear me? This boy is misinformed. And he's just that. A boy. He's grieving."

"Well, that's real sad," Jaffe said. "Only like I told you. He came on to my property and tried to blow my head off."

"You killed my dad!" Travis said.

"Enough!" Birdie shouted. "Not another word out of you, Travis."

"Travis," Jake said.

"No!" the boy shouted. "I know what he did. Kaden Price saw him! He threatened to kill hunters. His Jeep was there. He waited for my dad and me to go in."

"No," Jake said, trying to find the calmest tone he could. "It's a mistake. Kaden and the other boys were lying. They made the whole thing up."

"You're lying!" Travis said. "You're just trying to get me to do what you say."

"I'm not lying," Jake said. Instinct took over. Or lunacy. Later on, Jake wouldn't be able to remember which. But he holstered his weapon, raised his hands, and stepped into the line of fire.

"No," he said. "It's the truth, Travis. Kaden's grandpa got a hold of his phone. Those three boys cooked the whole thing up in a group text. What they were going to say. How they were going to try and implicate Mr. Jaffe. Then those internet idiots ran with it. It's all a horrible mistake. Louie Jaffe wasn't there the morning your dad was killed, Travis. It's just what Kaden and his friends wanted people to believe. You hear me, Jaffe? I know the truth. Now you let me take this boy out of here."

"Told you what would happen if you all came back here trying to mess with me," Jaffe said.

"What?" Jake said, putting his body between Louie Jaffe and Travis. "You gonna shoot me? You gonna shoot this kid? You do that then you're the monster everyone in town thinks you are. Or, you can let me get back to work. Let the sheriff get in front of reporters this afternoon and set the record straight about all these false rumors. I can clear your name, or you can go down for killing a cop and a kid."

"I've done nothing wrong!" Jaffe shouted. "I've got the right to defend my property and my person."

"You have," Jake said. "Anything more than that now and you're a murderer. Travis, you hand me your dad's gun now."

He made perhaps the second dumbest decision and turned his back on Louie Jaffe. He held a hand out and leaned over. When he got close enough to him, the fight went straight out of Travis Wayne. All at once, he was no longer a sixteen-year-old young man. He was a little boy. Jake took the pistol from him. He held out his hand. Slowly, Travis rose to his feet.

"Birdie?" Jake called out as he pulled Travis against him. Travis broke. He sobbed into Jake's chest.

"You have to find him," Travis said. "You have to find who killed my dad."

"I know," Jake said. "I know."

Louie Jaffe zeroed in on Birdie. She hadn't budged. Jake pulled Travis out of the circle.

"I'll get them home," Jake called out to Jaffe. "Nobody's going to bother you, Jaffe. It's over. I'll do what I said. We'll set the record straight within the hour."

"He shot at me!" Jaffe shouted.

"You want to do something about that?" Jake asked. He put a hand on Birdie's shoulder. With Travis behind them both now, she slowly lowered her gun.

"Get him out of here," he whispered to her. Birdie acted lightning quick. She holstered her weapon and grabbed Travis.

Tucking his head against her chest, she pulled him back down the path.

Jake turned to face Louie Jaffe. He was already climbing down from his tree stand, his rifle slung over his shoulder.

"I'm sorry about this," Jake said. "He's a lost kid. He's mad with grief. And he won't ever bother you again. I'll see to it."

"I'll hold you to that," Jaffe said. "And I'll defend myself and my property. It's my right."

"Of course it is."

He and Louie Jaffe stared each other down. Jaffe squared his shoulders.

"I'm sorry about the boy's father. I told you. He was always decent to me."

"He was decent to everyone," Jake said. "He was ... my friend."

Jaffe gave Jake a slow nod. "You need to talk to Trip Sanderson."

"Sanderson? The butcher?" Jake asked. Jaffe nodded.

"You ask him about all these tree huggers. They've been traipsing up and around the county getting into everyone's business."

"What tree huggers, Jaffe?"

"Arch Hill ain't gonna be what it is. Not everybody's happy about it. I'm not happy about it. But that ain't my property or my business. This is."

Jake squinted at Louie Jaffe. The man was talking in riddles. "Tree huggers," he said. "What about Arch Hill, Jaffe?"

"You know what's goin' on," he said. "The minute they start letting those assholes from Columbus and Cincinnati move in here, we're all gonna feel it. Buying up those luxury homes. They'll start passing laws even you won't wanna enforce."

"Columbus … you're talking about the new sub going in?"

"Rich assholes," Jaffe said, shaking his head. "Tourists and rich assholes. That's who's gonna start to overrun this county. You wait."

"What's Trip Sanderson got to do with any of that?"

"You ask him," Jaffe said. "Those idiots think cutting down a tree is murder. What do you suppose they think about harvesting deer?"

Jake nodded. He could only half understand what Louie Jaffe was trying to say. He supposed it was at least worth a conversation with the butcher. Trip had been the one to confirm Louie's story about shooting a deer the morning of Ben's murder. Louie had brought it in to be butchered.

"Jaffe," Jake said, trying to refocus the old man's attention. "What happened here today …"

Jaffe put up a hand. "Is nobody else's business as long as you set those people straight. You. Not that lady sheriff. You. And you keep that boy away from here. I'll leave him to his grief. You understand?"

It was Jake's turn to nod. Louie Jaffe could have pressed charges. Jake would have been duty bound to arrest Travis for any number of things all the way up to attempted murder. Instead, Louie Jaffe held his hand out for Jake to shake. Jake took it.

"He just got a little lost," Jaffe said. "No harm done. He might a been shooting at squirrels. They've been a nuisance lately."

With that, Louie Jaffe gave Jake a salute, turned on his heel, then headed back up toward his house.

Sixteen

*L*ook at him, *the killer thought. Young enough that you could still see a little of the jock punk he once was. Jake Cashen. Cashen. It was easy enough to find him online. Easy enough to confirm he was everything the killer guessed about him.*

"There have been some reports," Jake said, leaning into the lectern microphone. "Falsehoods about Louie Jaffe. While I wouldn't normally comment on an ongoing investigation, it's become necessary due to some irresponsible social media posts. Let me be perfectly clear. Louie Jaffe is not a person of interest in the death of Ben Wayne. He's been a victim of online harassment and bullying that needs to stop. As I said. Rumors and falsehoods have been perpetrated by a group of keyboard warriors who don't know what they're talking about. I've had about enough of it. Let me be clear to those individuals responsible. You are not helping. You are hindering this investigation. You are hurting innocent people and obstructing justice. We'll be handing our information over to the prosecutor's office. You can be sure of it. I will not stand for bullies of any kind."

"Detective Cashen," a reporter called out. "What do you say to those who feel they've turned over information that your office has refused to act on?"

"Information?" Jake said. "I can assure you we are following every credible lead in this case. Credible leads. Do you understand? What I'm talking about today is not credible. It's a bunch of cowards and armchair detectives who don't care about the truth. They only care about going viral. Online bullies. And as I said, they'll be dealt with."

A woman stood beside him. She had probably been a knockout in her younger days. Short. Kinky hair with silver through it. Big eyes. The town sheriff. She leaned in, taking the microphone away from Detective Cashen. Oh. He probably didn't like that, the killer thought. He was probably exactly the kind of guy who couldn't stomach working for a female boss. Maybe he didn't come out and say it directly. He probably talked about her behind her back. They always did.

"Thank you," the sheriff said. "We aren't going to be taking any questions today. As Detective Cashen said, this is an ongoing investigation. We're only making a statement at all due to the unusual circumstances and online bullying that's been happening. As Detective Cashen also said, we'll be referring that part of this case to the Worthington County Prosecutor's office. You can direct your questions on that to Tim Brouchard. That is all."

Jake looked pissed. Oh yes. Big man. Alpha male. The killer went down a quick internet rabbit hole that confirmed every suspicion.

Cashen was a jock all right. The worst kind. A wrestler. There was his picture. Captain of the Stanley High School wrestling team. State Champions. They threw a damn parade in his honor.

The killer's breath went out. There, in the grainy photograph from twenty years ago, a seventeen-year-old Jake Cashen stood beside a taller, lankier boy. His teammate. His co-captain.

Ben Wayne.

A buzzing sensation went through the killer. A detonation of nerve endings. They would erupt. Explode. Oh. This was good. It was so good. Jake Cashen had lost his best friend. Ben Wayne was supposed to be a masterpiece in and of himself. No. No. He was just the beginning.

"You don't see me," the killer said, pausing the computer screen, zeroing in on Jake Cashen's face. "You think you're bigger. Tougher. Smarter. Let me give you something else to chase."

It was time. Today was the day. The killer could never predict when it would come to a head. It was just a feeling. An intuition. A call that couldn't be ignored.

You couldn't plan too far in advance. You had to feel your way, the killer thought. There was still time. Still early enough in December there would be one out there. Waiting. Ripe for the kill.

The killer didn't remember getting into the truck. Or making the conscious decision where to go. But an hour later, the killer drove down Bacon Road. This was state land. Riskier in some ways, sure. But with the big snowfall the day before, only the most hardcore hunters would bother. Plus, there was still snow coming down. It would make for the perfect cover. No need to worry about footprints or tire tracks.

The killer found it quickly enough. A lone red pickup truck parked on the side of the road. They were asking for it, this victim. They had bumper stickers all over the back. Proud member of the NRA. The Marvell County Archery Club. He had a bleached-out rack mounted just above the back window. A trophy buck. There was even what looked like dried blood in the truck bed. So this hunter had already bagged a deer, probably. Greedy. Cocky. All of the above.

The tracks were easy enough to find. The killer used them, stepping inside each to make it that much harder to trace. The hunter was about two hundred yards in from the road in a thicket. The idiot was watching videos on his phone, his bow perched against a tree near his blind.

The wind picked up, howling just enough the killer was able to perch up making barely a sound.

The killer waited a few minutes, adrenaline making that popping sensation course through every vein. It would be easy to take a shot now. So easy.

The killer took deep, slow breaths, feeling better to lower the blood pressure. Focus. Savor it. Through the rifle scope, the killer zoned in.

He was older than the killer liked to mess with, preferring to take down stronger, faster men in their prime. This one? He wasn't ancient by any means. Probably sixty though. He had a grizzled face with plenty of gray stubble and lines carved around his mouth. He smiled at something on his phone, displaying yellow teeth, the front one chipped.

No. Not in his prime at all. On the other hand, how many deer had this one killed in his life? How many carcasses could be laid at his feet for the sport of it? The rack on his truck made the killer's blood run hot. Here he sat, watching his phone. His five-hundred-dollar phone. His forty-thousand-dollar truck. He didn't need this kill to feed himself or his family. He just wanted another rack to hang off his wall.

Anger bubbled through the killer. No. There was no room for it. Not here. Not now. Anger would lead to carelessness. This had to be perfect.

For Jake.

The man's phone rang, startling him. He quickly answered.

"Hey," he said. "I'm out in my blind. Can it wait until later? Oh. Okay. Sure. I'll swing by the Dollar Kart on my way home. How many do you need?"

The Dollar Kart. Where he could stuff his cart with lunch meat, bacon, hot dogs, and a thousand other types of raped and dead things processed for mass consumption.

He clicked off his phone, slipped it in his pocket, and grabbed his bow from its perch at the side of the tree.

There was movement through the trees. The man raised his bow. The killer took aim.

"Not today you won't," the killer whispered. Oh, this would be perfect. Even better than the killer hoped.

A large doe stepped through the trees, stuffing her face from the bait pile someone had left. Where was the sport in that even?

The man drew back his bow.

Zing! Crack!

The bullet entered right behind the man's eyes. Through his right temple. Just like Ben Wayne. An instant before he would have loosed the arrow that would have killed that doe.

So perfect. So just. The doe stood paralyzed for an instant. She made eye contact with the killer, then shot down the ravine. Lucky. Glorious. Alive.

The man twitched on the ground for a moment. It took a moment for the wild electrical impulses to work their way through his nerve endings. A death dance. The killer smiled, watching through the rifle scope. The wind changed and the killer could smell the man as he soiled himself.

Not pretty. Not dignified. But what he deserved. He died with his bow still in his hand. The killer committed it to memory. It would be useful later. It would make the perfect souvenir.

The killer waited, drinking in the sight of the kill from the rifle scope. Snow fell down harder. Perfect. So perfect. As if God blessed the kill.

Finally, the killer walked out of the woods and back to the truck, the snow filling in every footprint.

SEVENTEEN

"I think you're in the clear," Ed Zender said. He was seated at his desk, feet up, hands linked behind his head.

Jake was in no mood to fish for information from him. That was Ed's usual M.O. Say something just vague enough he could hold his listener captive while he drew out the rest of his story.

Jake tossed his keys on his own desk. His head pounded. He'd just spent the better part of the morning fielding wild-goose-chase tips coming into the Crimestopper Hotline after giving the press conference he'd never wanted to give. Before that, he'd spoken to Trip Sanderson, the butcher. Trip had confirmed Louie's tip. A small group of animal rights protesters had caused a minor ruckus at the shop on opening day. Though it hadn't been enough for Trip to even call the sheriffs. Trip didn't recognize any of them and hadn't gotten license plates. It was likely one more dead end.

"I just got off the phone with Louie Jaffe," Ed said. "I took the liberty of reaching out to him again."

The pounding in Jake's head grew more intense.

"I didn't ask you to do that, Ed," Jake said. "Louie just wants to be left alone. In fact, I promised him we'd do exactly that."

Ed sat up and waved a dismissive hand. "You should have come to me in the first place before you went running off to his property again. Louie respects me."

Jake swallowed the retort he had in mind. He could only imagine what Jaffe really thought of Ed.

"Anyway," Jake said. "What do you mean, I'm off the hook?"

"He's not going to pursue anything against Ben's kid. You know he could have. On about five different charges."

Jake took a breath. It was in him to unload on Ed.

"He was pretty hot still when I called," Ed said. "Boy, you shoulda heard him. Brouchard could probably make a case for attempted murder against that poor Wayne boy. What the hell was he thinking running up there with a loaded pistol?"

"He wasn't thinking," Jake said. "That's the whole point. That kid didn't just lose his dad. He *found* his dad with a bullet in his head, Ed. Think about what that would have done to you at sixteen years old."

"Yeah. Yeah," Ed said. "I guess maybe you'd know more about that than I would. Well, anyway. Like I said. I talked Jaffe down. He promised he's not gonna pursue the matter against Travis any further."

"Ed," Jake said, losing his patience for good. "I know that. I've been handling it for the last twenty-four hours. Louie Jaffe isn't the problem. The problem is a bunch of idiot wannabes with internet muscles spouting off online."

"You think your little presser is going to put that to rest?"

"Nope," Jake said. "I'm pretty certain it won't. But I gave Jaffe my word."

"Well," Ed said. "I get why you did it. I'm just not sure it was the best idea. Don't you think it's better if the real killer thinks we're focusing on Jaffe?"

"What else are you working on, Ed?" Jake said, trying desperately to change the subject.

"Not much. Ben Wayne's case is the hottest thing we've got going."

Jake gripped a pencil so hard he cracked it in two.

"Sorry," Ed said. "I guess I forget sometimes how close the two of you were."

"Thanks," Jake said. "I appreciate the thought. If you don't mind, I'm gonna try to get through these phone records. I got the full report on Ben's home computer and cell phone from BCI late last night."

"Oh sure, sure," Ed said.

Jake turned his back to Ed, hoping that would be the end of it. Jake slid a flash drive in his laptop. Mark Ramirez's digital forensics report pulled up. Jake looked at the incoming and outgoing calls and texts off of Ben's phone for the few days prior to the shooting.

It was mundane mostly. At the same time, beautiful. Ben had called his father the morning prior to the hunt. They spoke for almost an hour. Jake knew it would have been physically difficult for Rudy Wayne to talk that long. It meant Ben had been patient with his father. It meant Ben had likely done most of the talking.

There was a missed call to Jake's own cell. He closed his eyes, remembering where he was the last time Ben had tried to get in touch with him. Work, probably. A few days before, they'd run into each other in town and Ben invited Jake over for dinner. He'd gotten a new smoker he wanted to try out. They'd talked about Ryan and Travis. Jake knew he wasn't going to be able to go out on opening day. So Ben had offered to invite Ryan out with them on Palmer's property. God. If Ryan hadn't been sick that morning …

Jake had asked Ben to call him later in the week so he'd have a better handle on his schedule and they could figure out dinner. He never took the call. He'd meant to call Ben back. He just hadn't gotten around to it.

"Anything?" Ed asked. Jake hadn't heard Ed sneak behind him.

"No," Jake said. "Not a damn thing. There was nobody new in Ben's life. Nobody old that would have wanted to hurt him."

Jake scooted his chair back. He grabbed his computer bag off the desk, ready to slide his laptop back into it. He could look at the rest of this stuff at home.

As he picked up the bag, he noticed a new pile of mail underneath it. He grabbed it. Junk mostly. But at the very bottom was a legal-sized yellow envelope. Thin. It was addressed to Det. Jake Cashen, Sheriff's Department, printed on a white label strip with black ink.

Jake took the letter opener off his desk. It was one his nephew Aiden got for him last Christmas. The handle had a cartoon police officer on it, smiling with his hands on his hips.

Jake sliced open the end of the envelope and peered inside.

A single piece of paper fell out. At first, Jake thought it was blank. He turned it over. It took a moment ... an instant. Then all the blood drained from his head.

"Ed," Jake said. He let go of the paper, letting it flutter to the desk. "When did this get here?"

Ed shrugged. "Same time as always, I guess. This morning."

Heart pounding, Jake slowly rose. It was a detailed pencil sketch. A human hand, relaxed, the thumb and opposite fingers curled into a C. It rested in leaves. There was a ring on the middle finger. The details of it made Jake feel as if he'd swallowed a mouthful of ash.

"What's the matter?" Ed said.

"Get Darcy," he said. "I need to know when this was delivered."

Ed reached for the paper.

"Stop!" Jake said. "Don't touch it!"

Ed leaned over Jake's shoulder. "What am I looking at?"

Jake picked up the letter opener and pointed the sharp end at the ring. "It's Ben's hand," he said.

"What? How the hell can you tell that?"

"His ring!" Jake said. "He's wearing his State Champ ring. I've got the same one at home. Ben never took his off. He was wearing it when he died."

"Lots of people have that ring," Ed said. "At least fourteen were on your team, weren't they?"

Jake fired up his laptop again. Within seconds, he had the crime scene photos pulled up. "Look at his hand," Jake said.

Ben had fallen to the ground on his side. His left hand rested in the leaves, curved into a C shape. Exactly as the drawing depicted. There were small drops of blood across his wrist, part of the splatter pattern from the fatal shot. Jake looked closer. Though the drawing had no color, done only in pencil, he saw the fine detail of the same splatter pattern across the wrist.

"Well, I'll be damned," Ed said.

Jake reached in his drawer and pulled out a pair of latex gloves.

"Lemme get a picture of that before you tag it," Ed said. He grabbed his cell phone off his desk.

"Don't use that," Jake said. "Not unless you want some future defense lawyer getting permission to paw through your entire phone."

"Good point," Ed said. Jake grabbed a digital camera he kept in the desk and snapped pictures of the drawing, and the envelope where it had fallen. Then he put on his latex gloves.

Ed handed him an evidence bag. Jake slipped the drawing and envelope inside it. Only then did he turn the envelope so he could read the postmark.

"Columbus," he said. "Great."

"No help there," Ed said. "Maybe those labels on the front might mean something."

Jake dialed Mark Ramirez's phone number. He answered on the second ring.

"Hey, Mark," Jake said. "You in the office? I've got something I need BCI to take a look at."

"I'm glad you called, Jake," Mark said. "You were on my list to call today. I've got something I think you'll want to take a look at too."

"I'll head your way," Jake said. "I can be there by four."

"Are you sure you can get your overtime approved?"

"I don't care," Jake said. "Just stay there. I'm on my way."

EIGHTEEN

"Thanks for getting down here so fast," Mark Ramirez said. Jake held the evidence bag containing the drawing he received under his arm. Ramirez's office was in the very basement of the building. Cold as a meat locker, it had no windows and thus no natural light. Jake knew everyone else in the building called it the dungeon. At the same time, Jake understood exactly why Mark Ramirez liked it so much.

It was quiet. Secluded. Far away from the normal office traffic in the rest of the building. Nobody came down here unless they meant to. It allowed Agent Ramirez to work in peace without having to field stupid questions from dozens of people every day.

"I've got something for you," Jake said, putting the evidence bag on the table where Ramirez sat. He had three thin files stacked beside him and a small projector screen set up on one end of the room.

Ramirez leaned over, grabbing his glasses out of his front pocket. He slipped them on and peered at the drawing encased in plastic now.

"What am I looking at?"

Jake had printed a copy of the crime scene photo that best showed Ben's left hand as it lay on the ground. He set it beside the photograph.

"Somebody mailed that drawing to me," Jake said. "Look at the positioning. It's an exact match to the way Ben was found. Whoever drew it even has the leaves positioned the same way. See there's a large maple leaf just above his pinky? The corner of it is torn off in a jagged edge."

"I see it," Mark said. "Blood spatter's the same too. Where the hell'd you get this again?"

Jake showed him the second bag where he'd placed the mailing envelope.

"It came through regular, departmental mail," Jake said. "Columbus postmark, two days ago."

"No help there," Ramirez said. "I'll get my lab on this right away."

"I'm the only one who touched it," Jake said. "The drawing, I mean. You'll find my prints along the very top where I slipped it out of the envelope. I used a letter opener. I dropped it the second I realized what I was holding."

"Gotcha," Ramirez said.

"Someone's making this personal now," Jake said. "Somebody who knows I'm on the case is trying to mess with me."

Ramirez sat back, scratching his chin. "Well, you're looking at somebody who's familiar enough with the crime scene."

"It's someone who was there," Jake said. "That's my gut feeling."

"It could be someone who's also seen this picture, Jake?" Ramirez said, handing the crime scene photo back to him. "I know you've thought of that."

"I have," Jake said. "But the angle's just different enough from the photo to the drawing. I don't think it's a copy of the photos we have. Take a look." Jake handed Mark his phone. He'd pulled up every crime scene photo he had that showed Ben's left hand as it lay on the ground.

Mark peered closer at the drawing, then scrolled through the pictures. After a few minutes, he handed Jake his phone.

"You're right that none of them are exact. That still doesn't mean ..."

"It wasn't one of our people," Jake said.

"You think it was one of mine?" Ramirez asked, though there was no defensiveness in his tone. That's another thing Jake liked about Mark Ramirez. The man kept his emotions out of everything he was doing. He had one objective. Process and protect the evidence. He was a scientist in that way.

"I don't think it's anyone connected to the case on the law enforcement side," Jake said. "This is a message from the killer."

"No note."

"It was addressed to me," Jake said. "The sender could have drawn anything from the scene. Ben's face. His head wound. His whole body. That's not what they drew. They drew Ben's hand and made sure I could see his ring. That ring."

Jake pulled an identical ring out of his pocket and set it in front of Ramirez.

"You took this out of evidence?" Mark said, eyes wide.

"No," Jake said. "That's my ring. I have the same one. Ben and I were co-captains of our State Champ wrestling team. I think the killer looked me up. I gave that press conference a couple of days ago and the killer saw it. I'm the face of this now. It wouldn't have been hard to figure out some details from my past. Back in the day when we earned those rings, it was big news to the local papers. We gave maybe a half a dozen interviews together."

"He's taunting you. Or she's taunting you," Ramirez said.

"It's not a coincidence I get that crap sent to me right after I give a press conference on the case."

"That makes a certain amount of sick sense," Mark said. "But I processed that scene. There's no evidence the killer walked near Ben's body. They weren't close enough to study his hand, as far as I know."

"They wouldn't have to be," Jake said. "The killer had a high-powered rifle likely with a scope. He could have seen plenty. And we know it was a good twenty minutes from the time Travis Wayne heard the shot before he found his dad."

"He could have taken pictures of his own," Ramirez said. "If he had a long-distance scope, he could have had a long-distance camera lens. This could have been his way of taking a souvenir without physically touching the body."

"It's worth considering," Jake said. "And I'd sure appreciate it if you'd put a rush on processing that drawing. I don't have high hopes you'll find anything."

"Don't be so sure," Mark said. "Whoever did this has some real artistic talent. I find it hard to believe they could have done this while wearing gloves. But you never know. Give me a couple of days max and I'll get back with you."

"Thanks, Mark," Jake said. "What else did you have for me?"

For an instant, Ramirez looked puzzled. Then his eyes brightened. "Oh! I swear, sometimes I think I'd forget my head if it wasn't attached."

Ramirez slid the files down the table. "You asked me to keep an eye out for other unsolved killings that might bear some similarities to your guy. These could be something. They're probably nothing. But I figured you could have a look and compare."

Jake took the files. Mark reached over and tapped on the first one.

"Two of these happened in pretty close proximity to each other. Coldbrook County. Two years ago. First guy, sixty-five-year-old retired school principal. African American. Woody Jessup. He was out catfishing on the Giant Oaks River last time anybody saw or knew where he was. Missing for almost a week. Divers found him trapped under a beaver dam. Shot once through the temple, just like your guy. Accidental but never solved."

Jake flipped the file open. Woody Jessup's badly bloated and decomposed body stared up at him. Though the rest of the details of the case were nothing like Ben's, Jake knew it was worth taking a closer look at. He flipped the file closed.

"This is good," Jake said. "No. Ramirez, this is excellent. I'll take a look at all of these."

Ramirez shrugged. "I gotta be honest. I think you're looking for a needle in a haystack with those. They're all over the place. All kinds of victims. But all killed with high-powered rifles. All unsolved or ruled accidents. I'm not sure I know what to hope for in what you find."

"Thank you," Jake said. "And I know what you mean."

"Good luck," Ramirez said. "I'll warn you. Those cases out of Coldbrook County. You might run into asses and elbows if you start poking around in there. I don't care much for their homicide detective. Guy named Ray Mosley. He's a real son of a bitch if you've never had the pleasure. I have. He's a decent detective, but one of the most insecure, defensive guys you'll ever meet. Never understands when someone's actually trying to help him, if you know the type."

"Unfortunately, I do. I work with one of those. Thanks for the heads-up," Jake said.

"Ah," Ramirez said. "How is Ed Zender these days?"

"Same old Ed," Jake said.

"Can't imagine he's gonna much like it if this case starts getting national attention and he's not lead. Just a word of warning. Watch your back if that happens. I think Zender for the most part means well. He just ... well ..."

"Does a poor impression of it," Jake said.

"Yeah," Ramirez said.

Jake slipped the files into his bag.

"We'll keep each other in the loop," Jake promised.

"Like I said. I'm kind of hoping you can't make anything out of those other cases," Ramirez said. "If you can. Well. We've got bigger problems then, don't we?"

"I get it," Jake said. As he rose and shook Ramirez's hand, he read the same fear in Mark's eyes. If there was a connection between any of these cases and Ben's, then there was a good chance they were dealing with a serial killer. With the drawing sent to Jake, whoever it was had just upped the ante.

NINETEEN

He couldn't go home. After eight p.m., the office was empty and quiet. Jake walked in, locked the door, and dumped Ramirez's files out on the round break table they kept in the corner of the room. He wiped away the granules of sugar and dried coffee rings. He went to the coffeepot. Typical, Zender or Gary Majewski hadn't bothered to dump out this morning's grounds or the dregs from the pot. Jake rinsed everything out and started a fresh pot. As it began to drip through, he opened the file on the top of the stack.

Victim was female, African American. She was killed last year in Fairfield County. She'd been stopped on the side of the road, fixing a flat tire. They'd recovered a bullet out of the driver's side door. She'd been shot twice. Once in the chest. Once in the head. Her purse was missing.

The next file was a double homicide in Cuyahoga County. Two white males were shot from a high-powered rifle while sitting in their vehicle. Drug paraphernalia was found on the seat between them.

Another victim was killed just two weeks ago while sitting in his living room watching a hockey game. The rifle shot came through a bay window at the front of the house. White male. Fifty-eight years old. No suspects.

Four other files outlined victims killed in the same county three years ago. No commonality. Two were white. One was African American. One Hispanic. Drive-bys in rough parts of town. Though no suspects were ever charged, in each of those, the shootings took place in front of multiple witnesses.

As the hours ticked by, Jake's vision started to blur. There had to be something. Something!

He picked up the Woody Jessup file and reread the details. Sixty-five-year-old African American male last seen catfishing in a small boat on the Giant Oaks River. He was reported missing when he didn't return home for dinner. It took a week before Jessup's bloated body was found trapped beneath the beaver dam about a mile downriver from where his boat was found. He'd been shot once through the head.

Another file. A twenty-five-year-old white male was killed in Fayette County a year ago last September. He'd been jogging along a rural road. No one saw anything. He'd been found in a ditch by a passerby, shot once through the right temple.

Two other victims were killed outside a gas station in Clinton County. A married couple. Grainy security footage showed them arguing in front of Pump #3. Then they disappeared from view. A few hours later, the pair were found dead in a nearby woods. Both shot through the head. The woman showed signs of sexual assault.

Then there was Cory Boardman. Jake's pulse skipped as he read the file. Boardman was also killed in Coldbrook County like Woody Jessup, the fisherman. A bow hunter, he was thirty-five,

Caucasian, and he'd been struck through the right temple by a rifle shot. His friend found him. They were hunting a friend's land, a hundred-acre tract of pristine woods. A small portion of the Giant Oaks River ran through it. Boardman died two weeks after Woody Jessup.

Jake put Jessup and Boardman's files side by side. One was hunting. The other fishing. One was black. One was white. One on the riverbank. One near the woods. There were a dozen other tiny details that made them different from each other and even more different than Ben's killing. And yet ...

Jake's brain buzzed. He couldn't sit still. He started pacing in front of the table. He'd finished almost the entire pot of crappy coffee.

Jake pulled out the crime scene photos from Boardman's file. He'd fallen face down in the leaves.

Jessup. Boardman. A fisherman. A hunter. Ben Wayne. A hunter. All three, high-powered rifles took them out from a distance. Like a sniper hit.

He picked up the file from Fayette County. He almost dismissed it. It didn't fit with the others. The victim was a jogger. Jake read through some of the witness statements. His sister gave a detailed interview as she was the last person to have spoken to him. "Trevor wouldn't hurt anyone. Not a person. Not an animal. He was vegan, for God's sake."

A throwaway comment. But enough to eliminate this victim from the others. And yet ...

Jake pulled up a map on his laptop, pinpointing where the jogger's body was found. Two things stuck out to him. The victim had been jogging along a rural road. It bordered one of the largest tracts of state hunting land in the county. What if ...

Jake sat down hard. He was right. He knew it. He checked the
date the jogger was murdered against the DNR website. A
jogger. Not a hunter. But he'd been killed on opening day for
bow season that year just a few hundred yards from where
dozens of other hunters were.

A knock on the door startled Jake out of his own head. He'd lost
all track of time.

"Hey, there," Sheriff Landry said, poking her head in. "I heard a
rumor you were trying to blow my OT budget for the month."

She came further into the room. She was carrying two large
paper bags. She held them up. "Did you eat?"

The moment she said it, Jake's stomach growled loudly by way
of an answer. She laughed. "I'll take that as a no."

Landry joined him where he was standing and peered down at
the table. It was a mess of files and notes. On the portable
whiteboard beside it, Jake had started writing up a timeline and
drawn a crude map.

"This something you're ready to share with the class?" she asked.
She busied herself pulling heavenly-smelling food out of the
paper bags.

"Hope you like Pad Thai," she said. "These are leftovers from
the command officer's luncheon."

She handed Jake one of the white takeout boxes and a pair of
chopsticks. Jake tore into it, not caring if it was crap on a shingle.
His traitorous stomach growled again. The food was delicious.

"Thanks," he said, his mouth full.

"About this mess?" she asked, taking a seat at the table. "I'm
worried about you, Jake. What's going on here?"

"I don't know yet," he said. "At least, I'm not sure."

"You need a second brain on it?" she asked.

"Maybe," he said. "I asked Mark Ramirez from BCI to give me what he could find on similar shootings to Ben's. Unsolved cases where the manner of kill was a high-powered rifle shot. They're a hell of a lot rarer than you'd think."

"This many?" Landry asked, touching the large stack of files.

"Over a dozen in the last five years," he said. "This is just Ohio. Most of them look like they're probably gang or drug related. But these three."

Jake showed Meg the file she had on Woody Jessup, Cory Boardman, and the jogger. Landry worked her chopsticks with skilled precision as she leaned over the files, taking in the basic facts like he had.

"Hunters or fishermen," she said, pointing to Boardman and Jessup. "These two. What's the commonality with this guy?" She pointed a chopstick at the Fayette County file.

Jake showed her the map showing the proximity of the road to state hunting land in Fayette County. "And he's shot on opening day for bow season."

Landry sat back. He watched as her eyes darted over the map image. "You think he was a mistake? Unplanned?"

"Maybe," Jake said. "Maybe our guy went out there, hoping to bag a hunter. Maybe something happened. The woods would have been crawling with every local yahoo at that time of the morning. He'd want somebody isolated. That might have been hard to find."

"So he gives up but this poor sap happens to be jogging on by, all alone."

"Yeah," Jake said. "Maybe."

"Well," Landry said, tilting her head to the side. "I mean, this guy's not completely dissimilar to the others. He's an athlete. Like Ben was. Top of his physical peak maybe."

"Right," Jake said, jazzed that Landry was picking up on the same red flags he was.

She sat back hard, put her to-go container on the table and rubbed her forehead. "My God, Jake. You honestly think we're dealing with a serial killer?"

Jake pulled up the picture of the drawing he'd received. "Ramirez is processing this for me too. He's out there. He knows I'm looking for him ... or her."

"They'll kill again," she said. "I want you to be wrong. Lord. I really want you to be wrong."

"But you know I'm not," Jake said.

"Jake," she said. "If these crimes are connected, you know we need to get in touch with the FBI."

"No," Jake said, his tone sharper than he meant. "Not yet."

"Ben was your friend," she said. "If you're getting too close to this ..."

"I'm not," he said. "I just need a little more time."

"You're not the only one paying attention to this investigation, Jake. It's not just you on the line. If you need help ..."

"I don't need help from the Bureau. Not yet."

She sighed. "I know you didn't end things on good terms with them. I trust you. You know that. But you also have to let me protect you. Maybe ..."

"No," he said. "I've got a handle on this. That's a promise."

She pursed her lips, but didn't push him any further. "I hope you're wrong. I hate it when you're right," she said. "Intensely hate it."

Jake knew what she meant. The last major murder in town had shaken up the entire department. He'd have given anything for it to have turned out differently than it did. He wished he'd been wrong about that one too.

"You didn't just come down here to bring me food, did you? What's going on?" he asked.

"I got a call from Tim Brouchard about an hour ago," she said. "He got a tip called into his office. There's an environmental group causing some trouble in Marvell County. Appears to be the same group who caused some trouble at Trip Sanderson's too. Apparently they've been harassing hunters. Throwing red paint on their trucks. Walking into state land with blow horns and crashing cymbals."

"Why am I just now hearing about it?" Jake said. "Why isn't Brouchard calling me?" Louie Jaffe's warning popped back into his mind. He'd warned him about "tree huggers."

"Sanderson never called the cops," she said. "Sounds like whatever happened out at his shop was mild. This group is getting bolder now. Somebody sent Brouchard a video."

Landry pulled up her phone. She turned it toward him as she pushed play on her video app.

The video was choppy. Whoever started recording got mostly the tops of their own shoes at first. Then the video stabilized and panned upward.

Two irate women yelled at the person holding the camera, calling them just about every vile name in the book.

"You're a murderer!" one of the women said. She appeared to be in charge. She held a picket sign that said, "Stop the Murder of Innocent Animals!"

The woman beside her wore a dress that appeared to be made out of raw hamburger. She had what Jake hoped was fake blood smeared in her hair.

"You're a killer!" the woman shrieked. "You should be gutted and strung up yourself!"

She spit in the face of the person holding the video. Things went sideways after that. Jake saw a lot of pushing and shoving, but the phone dropped to the ground.

"This was this morning," she said. "This group stormed into a deer processing station just over the county line. Those two women in the video are being held for assault."

"I want to talk to them," Jake said.

"I figured you'd say that," Landry said. "I told Brouchard you'd head out there first thing in the morning. In light of these other cases Ramirez gave you, I'd say work as much OT as you need."

More than anything else, Jake wanted to be wrong. His gut told him he wasn't.

TWENTY

Marvell County had a smaller tax base than Worthington County. As such, Detective Dave Yun was pretty much a one-man band when it came to major and minor crimes. He was overworked, underpaid, underappreciated, but Jake had always found him to be one of the most easy-going guys he'd ever met.

The Sheriff's Office was housed across the street from the courthouse in the county seat of Oakton, Ohio. Yun had a cubicle, rather than an office. He popped his head over the partition as Jake walked into the bullpen.

"Oh well," Yun said. "I was just about to head out for coffee. You can walk with me."

"Out?" Jake said. "It's snowing. How far out do they make you go? You telling me Sheriff Mumford won't even spring for beans?"

Yun smiled. Sheriff Melvin Mumford was a bit of an Ohio legend. The longest-serving sheriff in the state, they'd have to drag him out in a box before he retired.

Yun wore a rumpled brown suit with a red tie. His stick straight black hair stuck up in the back. He grabbed a donut off the table on the way out and offered one to Jake.

"I'm good," Jake said.

"We're just down the hall," Yun said. He led Jake to a tiny break room. On the far wall was a one-way mirror. Jake could see straight into the one and only interview room in the Marvell County Sheriff's Office. Currently, a woman sat at the table. She was reed thin with steely gray hair she wore long down her back in a thick braid.

"Is that her?" Jake asked as he poured himself a cup of coffee.

Yun had a file tucked under his arm. He tossed it on the table and offered Jake a seat.

"The name she gave my responding officers was Jasmine Phoenix. But a different name popped up when we ran her fingerprints."

"Shocking," Jake said as he sat down and opened the file. The same woman, maybe a few years younger, stared back at him from a mugshot.

"Esther Doreen Cahill," Jake read. She had a string of arrests ranging from trespassing and petty theft to assault. Most of them had been either dropped or pled out.

"They call themselves the Animal Rights Underground. Or the ARU," Yun said.

"Catchy," Jake said.

"They're from Oberlin originally," Yun said. "But they've been expanding. Heard their group even got as far as the Upper Peninsula in Michigan. Staged a series of protests when they took wolves off the endangered lists. From what I understand, her group got some media attention going after some Ohio farmers too. Made some sort of human fence to try and keep some hunters from culling some coyotes who went after livestock."

"I vaguely remember," Jake said.

"They're into all kinds of stuff now," Yun said. "They send people out to disrupt hunters on state land on opening day."

"That's what I heard," Jake said. "Air horns and bullhorns. I think a small group of them caused some trouble for one of our butchers on opening day."

"Yeah," Yun said. "I'd say that's probably the least radical thing they do. Over in Pike County last year, a couple of them ran around tossing buckets of human urine all over the place on state hunting land. Even that wasn't so bad.""

Jake raised a brow. "You're a weird dude, my friend."

Yun smiled. "Well, I mean, at least piss buckets are pretty harmless. Non-confrontational. Lately they've gotten more aggressive. They're actually confronting hunters at deer checkpoints, coming up and harassing these guys before they even get out of their trucks. Throwing fake blood in their faces. I arrested one of them over at the bait shop. Guy was trying to prevent them from selling hunting and fishing licenses."

Jake set the file down and looked through the glass. Esther/Jasmine was busy picking at her nails, seeming entirely unfazed as she sat and waited for who knew how long.

"Have you questioned her yet?" Jake asked.

Yun nodded. "For a lot of good that did. I've got surveillance footage from the butcher over on Wellman Road. One of her associates marched in there with her bullhorn and started harassing his customers. While she was doing that, Esther here snuck around the counter and started spraying bleach all over the meat the butcher was trying to process."

"The deer's already dead?" Jake said. "What good will that do?"

Yun shrugged. "Beats me. You think she really might have something to do with what happened to your buddy Ben Wayne? By the way, I'm real sorry about all that. I didn't know the guy or anything, but what I've read. Geez. Was his kid really the one who found him?"

"Yes," Jake said. "A lot of the details we're trying to keep out of the media."

"Of course," Yun said.

"But I'm dealing with a sniper-type killing. Ben was taken out by a high-powered rifle. He probably didn't know what hit him."

"I guess there's a blessing in that," Dave Yun said. "Little else. Man, I'd hate to think this lady has resorted to that kind of thing. Look, I'm not a hunter. I'm a vegetarian, actually. I don't begrudge anybody else what they eat though. But I just don't see the logic. If you're trying to protect animals, why in the world would you go around killing humans? Seems kinda extreme."

"Did you pull any weapons off her or her associates?" Jake asked.

Yun shook his head. "Just a bottle of bleach spray. She had some wire cutters on her. They were cutting through barbed wire to get on private property. But no guns that we could find. Be my guest though. You're welcome to interview her. She's not very talkative though."

"I appreciate it," Jake said.

"Take all the time you need," Yun said. "I'm gonna finish up my paperwork at my desk. When you're done, come find me."

"Will do," Jake said. Yun got up and left. Jake waited a few minutes, observing Esther Cahill/Jasmine Phoenix through the glass.

She seemed calm enough, still just absently picking at her nails. She tapped her fingers on the table a few times, impatient, but she wasn't ranting or railing like he'd seen her in the video.

Jake got up and went around to the adjoining door. He opened it. Esther looked up, puzzled as Jake stood there.

"Good morning," he said.

"I don't suppose you're my court-appointed lawyer," she said. Jake put a hand on his hip, spreading his jacket so she could see his gun and badge.

"No, ma'am," he said. "My name is Detective Jake Cashen. Have you asked for a court-appointed lawyer?"

She laughed. "Hardly. I know my rights."

"Great," he said. "I suppose you're getting sick of sitting here. Is there anything I can get you to make you more comfortable?"

"Jake Cashen," she said. "I feel like I've heard that name before."

"I'm from Worthington County," he said. "Blackhand Hills. Do you have much occasion to get out there?"

"Blackhand Hills," she said. "There's the next great state tragedy."

"How so?"

"People can't leave well enough alone. They want to carve into those hills. Put up zip lines and luxury resorts."

Jake shook his head. "You don't have to tell me. My grandpa owns a two-hundred-acre tract of land in Poznan Township in the southeast part of the county. Pristine woods. The river runs through it. You wouldn't believe the kind of money they're offering him to put rental units on it. He won't budge though. He's as stubborn as they come. The land's been in our family for over a hundred years."

"Your family?" she said. "And who'd they steal it from?"

"Fair point," Jake said. "You mind if I sit?"

"I don't care what you do," she said. "So what's a Worthington County detective doing all the way over in Marvell County?"

"I'm working a case," he said. "So ... Ms. Phoenix. Or Ms. Cahill. Which do you prefer?"

"Sounds like you've got all that figured out," she said. "Doesn't that file you're holding tell you everything you need to know about me?"

"Doesn't tell me anything," Jake said, setting the file between them. He slid it closer to Esther. "How long have you been here in Oakton?"

She went back to picking her nails. "You planning on charging me with something?"

"I'm hoping we can have a conversation," Jake said. "That's all. But that's entirely up to you. Someone I know, someone who meant a lot to me, got hurt. Now, I don't know if it was on purpose. I don't know if it was an accident. I'm just trying to get to the truth."

"The truth." She leaned forward. "I doubt that very much. Was your friend the one butchering innocent animals?"

"Ms. Cahill, my friend was spending time with his son. Do you have kids?"

She leaned back. "Do you?"

"No," he said. "No kids. No wife. It's just me."

"And your granddad," she said. "The one with all that valuable land you're just waiting to inherit, right?"

Jake smiled. "Sure. Only my granddad's too stubborn to die anytime soon. And he'd probably blow the head off of anyone who tried to sell that land out from under him. The two of you would probably get along great."

Esther Cahill smiled. It almost seemed genuine. Then the door opened and her smile faded, replaced with the hard stare she gave him the moment he walked in the room.

"Jake," Dave Yun said, almost whispering it. "I'm sorry. Can you step out here for a moment?"

"Are we done here?" Esther Cahill said. "If you're not going to charge me."

"Oh, we'll probably charge you," Yun said, his voice taking a hard edge that gave Jake the first sign there was something else wrong.

"Just sit tight," Jake said to Esther. "I'll find out what's going on."

He closed the door behind him. Yun ran a hand over his face and strode to the other end of the hall. Jake followed. When Yun turned to him, his color didn't look good.

"We just took a 911 call," Yun said. "A couple of kids were out snowmobiling off Dunkirk Road. West part of the county. They found a dead body next to the road. Shot through the head, Jake. They think he's been out there a couple of hours."

"Shot through the head," Jake repeated.

"Jake," Yun said. "The guy was wearing hunter's orange."

Jake felt the blood drain from his face. "Dammit."

"Yeah," Yun said. "I'm heading out there right now. I thought you might want to tag along. I'll have one of the deputies sit with Jasmine or whatever she's calling herself."

"Thanks," Jake said. "Let's go."

Twenty-One

There was already a crowd starting to gather by the side of Dunkirk Road in the westernmost part of Marvell County. Thankfully, two deputies had already set up roadblocks coming and going. But Jake knew every hunter in the township probably already knew what was going on. The police scanner brigade would likely already be on the way next.

Jake parked directly behind Yun and joined him as he stood in the open field next to a heavily wooded area on the side of the road. Yun stood with his hands on his hips, his tie flapping in the breeze. It was freezing out, but Yun hadn't worn more than his suit jacket. Ahead, parked along the side of the road, Jake spotted two trucks. One a rusted-out gray. The other, a newer F-150 in cobalt blue.

"What've you got?" Yun asked the young deputy standing a few yards away. He identified himself as Deputy Fred Midge. Beside him in the field, a white male lay on his back, spread-eagle. Even from here, Jake could see he'd been shot through the temple. Hungry crows circled overhead. The snow-covered ground was splattered red with the victim's blood and worse.

A second deputy stood further in, closer to the woods, his hands on the shoulders of another man in hunter's orange. The poor guy was doubled over, hands on his knees, puking his guts out.

Deputy Midge answered Yun's questions. "Well, we responded to a 911 call. The caller was Breck Taylor over there. Sean Taylor's boy."

"Sean runs the bait shop over on Mill Pond Road," Yun said to Jake over his shoulder. "The one I was telling you about where that whack job was messing with guys trying to buy hunting licenses."

"Anyway," Midge continued. "Breck was just finishing up his morning hunt. He's parked about a quarter of a mile up that way. He saw Kenny Mihalek's truck parked there and pulled in behind it. He said he could see Kenny lying out there and thought he had had a heart attack or something. He ran up trying to see if he needed help."

Kenny Mihalek was far beyond help.

"We got everything blocked off," Midge said. "We were just waiting for you to get here. M.E.'s on the way."

"Thanks," Yun said. He gestured to Jake and the two of them walked over to where Breck Taylor had just finished losing his breakfast. Taylor was young. Very young. Maybe twenty, twenty-one. He stood upright, tears streaming down his face.

"Hey, Breck," Yun said. "You doing okay? You think you could walk me through what happened?"

"I just talked to him," Breck said. "Kenny was parked out here when I got here this morning. I got a late start. I've got a one o'clock class over at Marvell County Community College. I opened for my dad this morning at the bait shop. He's set up about ten miles north of here on his buddy's private land. I can't get a hold of him."

"What time did you get out here this morning, son?" Yun asked.

"Seven," he said. "Kenny came into the shop this morning. Told me he was coming out here. We shot the breeze a little about where he liked to set up. He gave me some suggestions where I might have luck too. I didn't see anything. I got out here too late. And I had to get ready for class so I packed up and came out of the woods just over there. That trail through the clearing. I saw Kenny's truck. Then I saw him lying on the ground and I knew something was wrong. I called out to him but he didn't answer."

"Got it," Yun said.

"So I called out. Hey, Kenny! I knew something was wrong. I knew it. So I came running. At first, I thought maybe it was his heart. But then ..."

Breck doubled over again and dry heaved.

"Did you see anyone else out here this morning?" Yun asked.

Breck straightened and shook his head. "No, sir. Heard plenty. There were a few guys hunting a little further down in the valley. But they were nowhere near me or Kenny. There's two of 'em over there."

Breck pointed. A pair of men stood behind the police tape, texting on their phones. One of them started recording a video.

"Hey," Jake said. "You want to show a little respect?"

"Take that thing away from him!" Yun shouted to Deputy Midge. "Clear those idiots out of here. Get names and numbers on everybody. Move that roadblock back a good half a mile in each direction. I don't want anyone close enough to piss me off."

"Kenny's got grandkids," Breck said. "They're little. Oh man. I think the oldest is only eight or nine. My kid sister babysits for them."

"I know," Yun said, patting Breck on the back. "I know, son. You didn't hear anything? Didn't see anybody you didn't know?"

"Well, sure," he said. "Like I told you. I don't know those guys that were set up down in the valley. And when Kenny and me were talking, it was about those kooks who went over to Bowdrie's Butcher Shop yesterday causing a nuisance." Jake knew Nate Bowdrie. He'd wrestled his son a million years ago.

"What do you know about that?" Yun asked. As he did, Jake turned and walked over to Kenny Mihalek's truck. The keys were still in the ignition. This was Marvell County, where you could leave your truck sitting like that and not worry about anyone driving off with it.

He looked inside the truck. There was a wallet sitting on the console between the front seats. Mihalek had a cooler wedged under the back seat. Jake walked to the back, careful to stay on the paved road. It was covered in slush and salt. The trucks had likely come through early this morning. That surprised him. Dunkirk wasn't what he'd call a well-traveled road. Marvell County itself didn't have a lot of business or industry. It was all farmland. Two subdivisions had gone in in recent years and the downtown area consisted of a single traffic light. As far as Jake knew, there were only two restaurants in town and they didn't even have so much as a McDonald's. County residents did their shopping in Worthington County to the east or Fairfield County to the north.

It had stopped snowing early this morning. Maybe four a.m. There was an inch of solid cover. Jake could make out footprints leading from the woods all the way to Kenny's truck. Kenny's, no doubt. Just eyeballing the treads in Kenny's Thorogood boots, Jake could see the pattern in the snow matched.

"Where did you come from?" Jake whispered. He walked back to the body, joining Midge and Yun beside it. Mihalek ended up on his back. He was shot through the left temple. The large exit wound blew out the right side of his head.

Jake looked up. The killer could have been perched somewhere across the road.

"You came from somewhere, you son of a bitch," Jake muttered. The salt trucks and plows obscured tracks or prints that might have shown up on the opposite side of the road. Kenny's truck was partly plowed in. With his four-wheel drive and sturdy snow tires, he wouldn't have had much trouble pulling out though. But Kenny's truck had to have been there when the county trucks came through.

Jake walked back to Dave Yun and Breck Taylor.

"Did you talk to any of them? See them?" Yun said.

"No," Breck said. "My dad talked to Nate Bowdrie though. Before those nut jobs came into the bait shop. My dad and Nate, they're pretty tight. He was asking Nate what kind of car those dumbasses drove. He wanted to know what to look for in case they came in harassing our customers. Which of course they did last night. We're starting to sell some ice fishing stuff. People are always coming in to grab a case of beer or the donuts we still bake fresh. But we still sell hunting licenses so my dad knew we might get targeted. And sure enough."

"Breck said he heard some of those people from Jasmine Phoenix's group were harassing those hunters in the valley this morning. He doesn't know if Kenny ran into them or not," Yun explained.

"You don't think they'd actually hurt anyone?" Breck said. "That don't make sense. They want to save deer, but they're okay killing people?"

"We don't know that," Yun said. "Not a good idea making those kinds of assumptions. Okay, Breck? I'm gonna need you to zip it on that, son. We're gonna have enough trouble with rumors going around as it is. I don't need some kid going off half-cocked like they did in Worthington."

Yun turned to Jake, his face turning a shade of purple. "Oh, hey. I'm sorry about that. That was your cousin who went after that old man on his property the other day?"

"Christ. You heard about that all the way out here?" Jake said. "And no. Friend of the family. Don't worry about it. You're absolutely right. You mind coming over here and taking a look at something with me?"

Jake gave Breck Taylor a polite smile. He and Yun walked further down the road out of earshot.

"You might want to call the road commission and figure out when their trucks came through," Jake said. "Mihalek's truck is packed in from the plow. If your man was parked further down the road waiting, you might be able to figure out where. Or maybe the road commission crew saw something."

"I'll check into it," Yun said. "Thanks, Jake. Man, I really want this to have just been some kind of accident. But that head wound."

"Your M.E.'s going to tell you it was a high-powered rifle."

"Yeah," Yun said. "I just ... man. We've got a psycho out there somewhere, don't we?"

"Dave," Jake said. "You're gonna have your hands full out here."

"I already called in BCI," Yun said. "Mark Ramirez is on his way."

"Good," Jake said. "He did my crime scene for Ben Wayne. He's exactly who you want in the loop on this. I have to warn you though. These internet crusaders are going to be crawling all over the place now. I wouldn't be surprised if that nitwit you just called out for recording from his phone isn't posting on their social media page already."

"Dammit," Yun said. "That's the last thing I need."

"You mind if I go back and finish my conversation with Jasmine Phoenix? If she had nothing to do with Kenny Mihalek, then she doesn't know about this yet. If she did have something to do with it ... well ..."

Yun's shoulders dropped. "You'd be doing me a hell of a favor, Jake. Yes. By all means. Have at her. I trust you a hundred percent on that. That'd be a big relief to know you've got her statement locked down while I deal with whack-a-mole out here until Ramirez shows up."

"Not a problem," Jake said. "Glad to do it." Behind them, Breck Taylor started dry heaving again. Jake and Yun exchanged a look. Jake squared his shoulders as he walked back to his car and readied himself to interrogate Jasmine Phoenix.

TWENTY-TWO

J asmine Phoenix sat eating a kale salad as Jake walked back into the interview room. She seemed completely nonplussed by his presence, crunching away as he took a seat at the table across from her.

One of Yun's deputies had handed him the thinnest of files on her just as he came back into the building. By day, the woman was a substitute teacher in the Oberlin City School District. She and another woman had formed the Animal Rights Underground as a non-profit five years ago. They had a website and a social media page. From what Jake could tell the ARU started out as an animal rescue organization. It had now morphed into the guerilla activism that brought her here today.

"Can I get you anything else?" Jake said. "That wasn't much of a salad."

Jasmine put her plastic fork down and carefully dotted the corners of her mouth with a napkin she then neatly folded next to her plate.

"I asked them not to bring me anything plastic," she said, looking at her garbage with disdain. Jake reached across and tossed all of it into the waste bin in the corner.

"Do you know how long that will take to break down?" she asked.

"I'm sure you're about to tell me," Jake answered.

"A thousand years," Jasmine said. "This planet is drowning in plastic bags, water bottles, K-Cups."

"Wet wipes too, I hear," Jake said. "You know I read an article that said the River Thames is changing course on account of an island that's formed entirely of those flushable toilet wipes people buy. I can't even imagine it. Saw a picture of some woman standing on the thing. How can they market those things as flushable when they do that kind of damage?"

"You think toilet wipes are our biggest problem?"

"Then there's that algae bloom in the Great Lakes. You know, a few years ago, we had people from Michigan coming all the way down here to get bottled water because they couldn't drink what was coming out of their own tap. That always seemed nutty to me. Your water source is polluted so you buy up cases of plastic bottles that you're just gonna throw in the garbage. Does your group do anything about that?"

"Like what?" she asked.

"Well, you know. Adopt-a-Road or whatever. We do that up in Worthington County. The Sheriff's Department. We pick up trash on a stretch of County Road Twelve three or four times a year. It's disgusting the things people throw out of their car windows. It's a small thing, I suppose. But I figure if everybody on the planet would commit to doing just one thing like that every now and again, I think it could make a difference, don't you?"

"What's your point, Detective?" Jasmine said.

"I think I made it," Jake answered. "See, what you people do, I just don't get. You're certainly getting attention. I suppose if that's your goal, then fine. But do you know very much about the people who live around here?"

"I know none of them have a care in the world for what's going on around them. With their big trucks and their small minds ..."

Jake sat back in his chair, taking a more casual posture. He crossed one ankle over the opposite knee.

"Well, most of the people in *this* town don't work in it. They drive to New Lexington and Columbus. While I suppose it'd be fine in the middle of the summer, you ever try driving a Prius through ten inches of snow on a backcountry Ohio road in February, ma'am?"

Jasmine Phoenix narrowed her eyes at Jake. If she could have shot lasers out of them, he knew his chest would have a gaping hole in it right about now.

"You probably have an excuse for everything, don't you?" she said.

"I wouldn't say excuse, no," he said. "But I know most of the folks who live around here are hardworking, good people who are just trying to put food on the table. That includes Nate Bowdrie. He owns the butcher shop you barged into. Did you know his youngest daughter, Michelle, is the first one in his whole family who's gone to college? Bowdrie's trying to send her without taking out a dime's worth of loans. So when you start disrupting his ability to do *his* job, he might start taking it personally."

"Then Nate Bowdrie is a death merchant," Jasmine said.

"He processes ground beef," Jake said. "T-Bone steaks. Makes jerky. He's got a mortgage and a small business loan on top of the cost of tuition to send his youngest kid to school so she can get a business degree and help out at the store."

"I know what you think of me," she said. "I know what you think in general. You're a good ole boy, just like the rest of them, Detective Cashen. Do you hunt?"

"Yes, ma'am," he said. "Like I told you, my grandpa has two hundred acres in Worthington County. Foot of the Blackhand Hills. It's beautiful there. We eat what we harvest. Gramps used to butcher it himself until his eyes started to go. We donate at least half of our venison to St. Isadore's Church every winter. They run a soup kitchen. Best venison stew you've ever tasted."

"How sweet," Jasmine said, her voice dripping with venom. "How saintly."

"I don't know about that," Jake said. "I only know things aren't ever black and white, Ms. Phoenix. That goes for you too. I'm sure you believe in what you're doing. Just as I'm sure these hunters you've got a beef with are just as worried about the environment and conservation as you are."

"Save me your spiel about how those killers are actually saving lives. You going to start spouting off about highway deaths? Deer vs. driver car accident fatalities?"

"It is a problem," Jake said.

"It's a problem because, once again, you have people encroaching on spaces where they don't belong."

"You gonna start tearing up highways next?" Jake asked.

"If I have to, yes," she said. "Animal rights are human rights. When are people like you going to start getting that through your thick skulls?"

"Well, that's not how the law works."

"It will be," she said. "I work with some very powerful people, Detective Cashen. People who will take our case all the way to the Supreme Court."

"What case would that be? Nobody's arrested you. Yet."

"We're seeking a declaratory judgment that animals should be afforded the same rights as human beings."

Jake raised a brow. "Hmm. Well, that would be something. Heck. That might even be something I could get behind. If I'm following your logic ... with my thick skull, that is. If you caught somebody trying to hurt an animal. Or ... hunt an animal, you'd be able to protect that animal like you'd protect a human under the same circumstances."

"Exactly," Jasmine said. "They can't speak for themselves. We have to do it for them. It's our moral obligation."

"Self-defense. Defense of another person. Yeah. That would be something. I suppose you'd need to test that out though, wouldn't you? I mean ... you said declaratory judgment. That's when you get some judge to say you're right without a real case in front of them, right?"

"Maybe your skull isn't so thick after all, Detective Cashen."

Jake smiled. "Careful, all those compliments might go to my head. But what I'm thinking ... maybe you'd have a better shot at testing your theory if you actually tried to kill somebody just for sitting in a deer blind. That'd be a hell of an argument to make in a murder trial. I think that'd get national news. International news even. You'd have fundraisers lining up."

"It's coming," she said.

Jake nodded. "Why'd you pick Marvell County though? There're a million other places with bigger populations, bigger news markets. You've been out here for what, two days?"

"We go county to county," she said. "There's no such thing as too small as long as the DNR is sanctioning murder in this state."

"Sure, sure," Jake said. "You got here the night before last?"

"Yes," she said.

"Where'd you stay last night?" he asked. "I know Detective Yun got word you and your people were staying at the Sunset Motel over on Prater Street. Nice place."

"It's a hovel," she said. "But those fundraising dollars you speak of aren't exactly rolling in just yet."

"So where'd you go last night after you left Bowdrie's?"

"You already know we went to that bait shop. I talked to the owner there. Then we went back to the motel," she said, annoyed.

"Just you and your people? I saw on that video of you yesterday morning, it was you and some other lady. The one who actually threw the paint on those hunters at the DNR checkpoint. Was it just the two of you or do you have more people with you down here?"

"Just us," she said.

"Gotcha."

It would be easy enough to check. Hopefully, the Sunset Motel had surveillance cameras. Jake made a note to have Yun pull them to see Jasmine's movements throughout the night and this morning.

"Says here you're a substitute teacher," Jake said, opening the thin file he had. "How'd you get involved in the ... what is it ... ARU?"

"That's none of your business," she said.

"Probably just rescuing cats, huh?" Jake said. "Well, that's pretty noble. What kind of things do you teach?"

No answer.

"You went to school for something," Jake said. "English? Math? History? I bet that's it. You've got that look about you."

"What look?"

"Or government. You should be a government teacher. You sure seem to know a lot about how the court system works."

"You don't have to be a government teacher to know that. You just have to read and pay attention, Detective."

"Ah," Jake said. "I heard you made your way up to my neck of the woods too. Paid a visit to Trip Sanderson's butcher shop. Messed around on state land."

Jasmine Phoenix grew stonily silent. She stared at Jake, her mouth tightly shut.

"You had a guy with you," he said. "At least that's what one of my deputies said he heard. Kid was running around peeing on trees, using an air horn to try to scare off the deer and other hunters."

"We do what we have to do," she said. "Like I told you."

"Right. Only peeing on trees isn't gonna do anything. You know that? Every other mammal out in those woods is pissing on something. Deer don't much care. You might want to switch tactics. Hair. That'd do it. Tell your boy to maybe try tearing out clumps of hair and spreading it around. Do you remember where you were exactly?"

If possible, her lips closed even tighter.

"You heard we had a shooting out there," Jake said. "A friend of mine got killed on opening day. It's been in the news."

"Yes," she said. "I recognize you from your press conference."

"Well, Ben Wayne, that's the man who was killed. If you think your boy … or whoever was out there that day might have seen something, I'd sure like to talk to them."

"I didn't say we were out there that day," she said. "You did."

"Did I? I don't think so. I said one of my deputies heard you were out there. You saying you weren't?"

"Your friend was a hunter?"

"He was."

"Did he kill any deer that day?"

"No, ma'am," Jake said. "Somebody put a bullet in his head before he got the chance. Lucky day for the deer, I suppose. His boy got one though. Just before it happened."

"Then he's a murderer too," Jasmine Phoenix spat her words. All traces of her composure were gone. "Both of them. Father and son. Generational killers."

"You saying my friend deserved what he got?"

"Don't put words in my mouth," she said. "I'm not stupid. And I'm not crazy."

"I certainly hope not," Jake said. "But you were out there. And you're telling me if you saw someone about to shoot a deer, you think you'd be justified in killing them first. To save the deer. On account that buck's got just as many rights as the hunter. Right?"

"Yes," she said. "It would be justified. That's an innocent animal."

Jake sat back.

"It's the only way you people will ever understand anything. Guns. Death. That's what you understand. You take and you take. So somebody needs to start taking from you!"

Jake leaned forward. Before he could answer her, the door burst open.

"You're to cease all questioning of my client immediately!"

A middle-aged, balding man charged through. He was sweating. He had coffee stains on his tie.

"Who are you?" Jasmine asked.

"Have you asked for a lawyer?" the man said.

"She hasn't," Jake said, rising.

"I want a lawyer," Jasmine said. "I'm done talking to you. You said I could go. I'm leaving."

Jake held up his hands. Jasmine grabbed her purse. Her new lawyer held his arm out for her to take. She did. He tossed a card on the table in front of Jake. It read Seth Bielman, Attorney at Law, Columbus, Ohio.

Jake grabbed it and clipped it to the thin file he had. Thin. Yes. But maybe just enough to get a search warrant.

Twenty-Three

For a moment, an instant, Jake's head spun. The walls closed in and the surrounding voices seemed to come through tin cans.

Kenny Mihalek lay on his back, Christ-like with his arms outstretched, his private parts covered with a thin sheet. Bloodless now, his chest cavity gaped open from the Y-incision.

"Thanks for looping me in," Jake said, though it didn't sound like his own voice to him.

Ben, he thought. This could be Ben. It *was* Ben. Mihalek had a similar build with lanky arms and legs. Blond hair with strands of silver starting just above his blown-out temples.

"Shot entered here," Dr. Foley said. He shined a red laser pointer at the wound on Mihalek's right temple. "Hell of a shot."

"Can you gauge the distance?" Detective Yun said. Jake stepped closer. Mihalek's eyes were fixed open. His jaw hung slack, as if his scream were frozen in place. Maybe it was.

"It's hard to say," Dr. Foley said. The man was one of the youngest M.E.'s in the state. Two years younger than Jake; by appearance, it could have been twenty. Foley still had the rosy cheeks of youth that made Jake wonder if he could even grow a full beard.

"Not close range," Foley said. "I can tell you that much. The shot was too clean. I mean, it cut its path of damage, but there were no powder burns or anything on the skin itself. I can take a rough guess, not for testimony, mind you, but I'd say your shooter was no more than a hundred yards away."

"We're still canvassing," Yun said. "Trying to figure out if anyone else might have seen something."

"That's state land," Foley said. "There had to be tons of people around."

"What do you know about the angle of the shot?" Jake asked.

"Your shooter was elevated," Foley said. He picked up a notepad from a side table. Within seconds, he drew a remarkably detailed picture of a male figure sitting in a deer blind. He traced a straight line from the figure's head angled upward.

"I'd say it's a pretty safe bet your shooter was sitting in a tree or a tree stand," Foley said.

"A sniper's nest," Jake said.

"That's exactly it," Foley said. He put down his pen and pad and walked to the head of the exam table. He picked up a metal specimen bowl.

"Got your bullet frag right here," Foley said.

Jake's pulse skipped. That's the one piece of evidence they'd yet to find at Ben's crime scene.

"We found more of it lodged in the tree trunk right next to where Kenny lay," Yun said. "We put a rush on it, but barely needed to."

"I've seen this before," Foley said. "Your guys confirmed it, but this is a 7.62 by 54mmR. It's pretty unique. They made these for the Russian military."

Jake's gaze fixed on the small silver, flattened bullet fragment clutched between the tweezer prongs. "Who the hell uses a 7.62?" he whispered.

"It's fascinating," Dr. Foley said. His eyes lit up as he let the fragment drop back into the tray with a metallic ping. "The Mosin-Nagant rifle is chambered for these. Definitely not something that'd be legal for deer hunting in Ohio."

"Not an accident," Jake said. Though he'd known it in his bones since the moment he got the call about Ben, the proof sat in that cold metal tray.

"No hunter did this," Jake said. "He wasn't out there trying to shoot deer."

"No, sir," Foley said. "I'd say you had a hunter out there, all right. But not the normal kind."

"Thanks for this," Jake said. He directed it at both Foley and Yun.

"I appreciate it, Dr. Foley. How soon before you can get me your full report?"

"Oh, give me two hours. I'll get it transcribed."

"Can I get a copy of that?" Jake asked.

"Of course," Yun said. The two detectives left Dr. Foley to finish up his grisly work. Yun ushered Jake out to the hospital parking lot.

"You really think your guy is connected to this?" Yun asked.

"I think I want to run Foley's report by my own M.E. We shouldn't get ahead of ourselves."

"You're right though," Yun said. "I wanted to hold out hope that we just had a tragic accident out there. That's bad enough. But the idea somebody was out there hunting hunters. It's gonna get out."

"About that," Jake said. "As soon as somebody figures out you called me, we might have a problem."

"More than usual?" Yun smiled.

"There's an online group following the Wayne murder case," Jake said. "They have their own ... theories."

"Great," Yun said. "Appreciate the heads-up. Nobody's gonna hear from me that you have any interest in the Mihalek case. But we're smaller than you over in Worthington County. My people won't say anything, but I have no doubt somebody's seen you."

"I guess we can't control that. I can wrangle my end. We're officially done commenting on an ongoing investigation."

"Press will get the same non-answer from my office," Yun said. "That's a promise."

Jake shook Yun's hand. Both men knew they couldn't really control the speculation. But it was nice to know Yun was on the same page.

"Let's just keep sharing," Yun said. "I'll make sure you get Foley's full report as soon as I do."

Jake thanked Dave Yun once again, then headed for his car. It would be a long drive back to the office. And he had one more stop on the way.

Twenty-Four

Barney Jr.'s voice took on a breathless, giddy tone as he leaned over the gun case toward Jake.

"That's the one," he said. "Come on. I need to show you something."

Barney opened the flap in the counter, allowing Jake to come through it and join him in the back room. Barney had a rifle perched against the wall next to his desk. He picked it up and tossed it to Jake. Jake caught it deftly in one hand.

It was the Russian-built, 7.62 Mosin-Nagant.

"Ever held one of those before?" Barney asked. "It's a thing of beauty. A Russian masterpiece. They're artists, those Russians. Just the feel of it. The power of it."

"You're pretty sure it's what I'm looking for?" Jake asked.

"The Mosin-Nagant was mass produced by the Russians," Barney said. "Mostly around the WW2 era. They are a gun guy's gun. Just like the AK-47, they were built cheap but sturdy. Reliable. Russians know how to make a good, tough rifle."

"Yeah," Jake said. "It's ugly as hell. What else can you tell me about it?" Barney lit up. Jake started to regret the question.

Barney smiled. "I was hoping you'd ask. This one's got a sordid history. In the Battle of Stalingrad, Vasily Zaitsev got famous with this. He was responsible for two hundred and twenty-five confirmed Nazi kills. Pride of the Soviet military. The soldiers would taunt the Nazis with just his name. Couple of movies and a bunch of books about him if you want to check him out. This was his weapon of choice."

The thing didn't look like much to Jake. It seemed too long and heavy.

"There's a famous Finnish sniper who preferred this one too," Barney said. "Simo Hayha, nicknamed the White Death. Had at least five hundred and five confirmed enemy kills. He didn't even use a scope. Iron sights only. Another Soviet, Lyudmilla Pavlichenko, was called the "Lady of Death." She had three hundred and nine confirmed kills. She used ..."

"I get it," Jake said. "Barney, how easy is it to get one of these? How many are out there?"

"Oh they're still sold all over the world from surpluses. Any gun show in the U.S. is gonna have 'em. No serial numbers, no real records."

Jake handed the rifle back to Barney. "Not what I wanted to hear. Barney, you're sure you haven't sold any of those types or rounds to anyone recently?"

"Nope. I'm not selling much of anything right now," Barney said. "That's what's really pissing me off about those Dark Side of Blackhand Hills people. I'm losing business."

"I don't understand that," Jake said.

"They plant people," Barney said, lowering his voice to a whisper even though they were behind the closed door of his office. Barney turned his computer monitor around. It displayed a four-way split shot of real-time camera footage from his store surveillance software. From here, Barney had a clear view of both the front and back entrances, the area just above the cash register, and a wide shot of the entire sales floor. Currently, he had three customers browsing at different points.

"Any one of them," Barney said. "I'm getting all kinds of lookie-loos lately. People coming in to browse but not buy. Then some jackhole will post who they saw me talking to or whether Jaffe's been in. You watch. I hope you're monitoring that website because trust me. By this evening, there will be a whole thread about you coming in here to talk to me."

"They can't think you had anything to do with what happened to Ben," Jake said.

"They're bored. They're nutless. I don't know. Maybe you've got some people out there who don't like my business so they're using this whole thing to rattle my cage. It's working to drive my loyal customers right out of the store. They don't want to risk coming in and having their comings and goings plastered all over the internet."

"I'm sorry about that, Barney," Jake said. "I don't even know if there's anything to do about it. If we put out another statement, it'll just draw more attention to you, even if we're disavowing any connection."

"I know," Barney said. "What idiot said all press is good press?"

"Well," Jake said. "I appreciate your help and your insight. I don't know what, if anything, will come from it ..."

"None of that matters to me," Barney said, his voice breaking. For all his bluster, Curtis Barnaby was truly soft-hearted.

"He was nice to me," Barney said. "Both you and Ben. Always nice to me. I got bullied a lot when I was in elementary. Cuz of my size. The way I looked."

"I know, Barney," Jake said.

"You and Ben ... I remember one recess you went after Buddy Gerald and what was that other meathead's name. Brzezinski? Baranski? He ended up moving to Columbus or somewhere by junior high. Anyway, when you saw them trying to knock me down ... when I was just trying to walk away and eat my lunch ... you and Ben got in there and made them back down. Ben muscled Buddy pretty good. Made him cry. I'll always remember that, Jake."

Jake smiled. He himself didn't remember the incident. He knew Barney had often been the target of the meanest kids in school growing up.

"Glad we did something right," Jake said.

"Oh, you did all of it right. Those kids were afraid of you after that. All the way through high school. You and Ben and Lance Harvey were the reason there weren't more fights like that in high school. They knew you guys wouldn't put up with it. You were our heroes."

"I'm no hero," Jake said.

"Well," Barney said. "I sure did appreciate it. I don't care what they say about me. If I can do anything to help you find whoever went after Ben like that ... God. Jake. I wish I could kill them myself. Ben didn't have a mean bone in him. Not one. Nobody who knew him would have wanted to hurt him, Jake. He was a saint."

"I suppose Ben would argue that," Jake said. "But yeah. There weren't too many guys better than him."

"You gotta find out who did this," Barney said. "You have to."

"I'm doing my best," Jake said.

Barney launched himself at Jake then, enveloping him in a bone-crushing bear hug as he sobbed against Jake's shoulder. Jake went rigid, holding Barney up. He stood there until it became uncomfortable. Finally, Barney straightened and blew his nose on his sleeve.

"You gotta catch that son of a bitch," he said.

Jake leveled a hard look at Barney. There was only one thing he could say. One thing he could feel. "I will Barney," he said. "God help me, I will."

TWENTY-FIVE

Woody Jessup. Cory Boardman. Ben Wayne. Kenny Mihalek.

Jake wrote each name on an index card and stuck thumbtacks through them. He pushed them into the map he'd hung on the office corkboard.

All four had been killed with a single shot through the head with a high-powered rifle. Three of them were killed while deer hunting. One killed while fishing. That just left the Fayette County jogger, killed just a few hundred yards from prime state land on opening day. The wild card. In his gut, Jake believed that victim wasn't the killer's intended target. He was an afterthought. Wrong place. Wrong time. A target of opportunity. He wasn't ready to fill out an index card for him just yet.

He had his laptop open on the desk. He'd found the social media page for Animal Rights Underground. Jasmine Phoenix was listed as the page's administrator and only moderator. He scrolled through each of her posts, noting the dates, times, and any check-ins.

She was in Marvell County when Kenny Mihalek was killed. Yun was busy executing a search warrant for her hotel room and car. But so far, they'd found no physical evidence connecting Phoenix or any of her minions to the crime scene. So far. Yun promised to forward her phone forensics report as soon as Ramirez from BCI finished it.

Jake scrolled farther and farther back. The group's posts had grown more radical over the past eighteen months. Many of them had sensitive content warnings on them as she posted images depicting animal cruelty.

Phoenix had led a protest at a medical research facility in Cleveland. She'd been arrested at that one but charges were dropped the next morning. After that, her group seemed to shift their focus to hunters specifically.

Jake found a picture of Jasmine wearing a shirt made of what looked like raw slabs of bacon. She held a bullhorn; her face contorted with rage as she confronted a hunter at a deer checkpoint.

"He's not hunting pigs, lady," Jake muttered.

In another photo, Jasmine and two associates chained themselves to a tree outside another butcher shop in Coldbrook County. Jake checked the timestamp. It was one week after Cory Boardman turned up dead. Not a smoking gun by any means, but she'd been there.

Jake pulled out the business card her lawyer had given him. Seth Bielman. The guy was an environmental lawyer, not a criminal defense attorney. A quick google search revealed the loose legalities of Jasmine Phoenix's theories on animal versus human rights came from Bielman. Bielman had a blog where he argued the same things.

"He thinks she's how he's gonna make his name," Jake said.

Jasmine Phoenix's personal profile mirrored what she posted on the ARU page. Jake dug deeper, finding a separate profile for Esther Cahill. She seemed like a different woman altogether. She wore coke bottle glasses with stringy gray hair parted down the middle.

There was nothing much here. Just memes about horses and cats. She frequented a craft store in Oberlin.

Esther's work history had seven different entries. She listed every school where she substitute taught. Jake pulled them up one by one. Each was an elementary school in or around Oberlin. He landed on Meadowdale, a Montessori school in Elyria. Scrolling through some of the class photos posted, a zing of heat went through him as he landed on one in particular.

This was a second-grade class, assembled in the school library. Each child proudly held up their renditions of Monet's famous *Water Lilies* painting. Some of them were quite good, by Jake's critique. The caption on the photo is what stopped Jake's heart.

"While Mrs. Willis enjoyed her maternity leave, her second-grade class, led by Ms. Cahill, tried their hand at Impressionist paintings."

Art class. Esther Cahill worked as a substitute art teacher.

In the corner of the corkboard, Jake had pinned a copy of the drawing he'd been sent of Ben Wayne's dead hand.

"You doing okay?" Meg Landry's voice pulled Jake out of his head. He checked his watch. He was late for their morning coffee meeting.

"Sorry, boss," he said as he stood in front of the corkboard.

An art teacher. An art teacher!

"What do you have, Jake?" she said.

"I don't know," he said. "A lot of guesses and theories. But … there's something."

"You spent the day over in Marvell County. Do you think their victim is connected to Ben Wayne?"

Jake started to pace. "My gut? Yes."

Meg Landry's face fell. She sank slowly into the nearest chair. It happened to be at Jake's desk. "What do you need?"

"Take a look at this?"

Jake showed Landry Esther Cahill's picture at the Meadowdale library. Landry's brow furrowed as she read the caption. Her eyes then immediately went to the picture of the drawing on the corkboard.

"Just because she filled in for an art teacher doesn't mean she was an artist, Jake."

"I know," he said. "Except … I think she was. Again, gut feeling. But she was that, I don't know, artsy type."

"Yeah. I don't think that's gonna hold up in court, Detective," Landry deadpanned.

"This woman is trying to test a legal principle. She wants a court to rule that animals should be considered human beings. So that they would benefit from the same protections."

Landry tilted her head. "As in killing one would carry murder penalties?"

"Right."

"I gotta admit, in some cases, I don't know that I disagree."

"I get that," Jake said. "She was talking about declaratory judgments. But more than that, she was talking about launching a test case."

"What do you mean?"

"I mean," Jake said, jabbing his finger on the index card bearing Kenny Mihalek's name. "She finds Mihalek. Shoots him before he can kill a deer. She argues defense of another person. The other person being the deer."

"Does she have an alibi for the morning of Ben's shooting?"

"I didn't get that far," Jake said. "Her lawyer barged in."

Landry went pale.

"Relax," he said. "It was a clean interview. She wasn't under arrest. I asked her if she wanted a lawyer and she said no. It was only after this clown showed up that she clammed up."

"Well, then. Again, I'm asking you what you need."

He turned to her. "She seemed to know who I was," Jake said. "She called me Detective Cashen from the get-go. I didn't tell her my name first. Granted, she'd been sitting in that interview room for a while. Somebody else might have told her. Only none of the deputies near her knew I was planning to sit down with her until after I did."

"You think she saw your press conference on Louie Jaffe. Then she sent you that drawing?"

"It's possible," he said.

"You said your gut's telling you all these killings are connected. Is your gut also telling you Jasmine Phoenix, Esther Cahill, whatever her name is today ... is she involved?"

"I need time," he said. "And I need you to be okay with me devoting most of it to this case. I want to head back over to Coldbrook County. I want to talk to whoever cleared Cory Boardman and Woody Jessup's cases."

"Is Ed back full time?" she asked.

"He's back Ed time," Jake answered.

"We're stretched pretty thin as it is," she said. "Jake, I know you still don't want to hear this. But we should call in the FBI."

"I don't have enough. I just have a hunch."

"I'd say you have more than that. Jake ..."

"I know what I'm asking," he said. "And I know this is no more than likely a wild goose chase. It's just ..."

"Your gut," she answered.

"Am I crazy?"

Landry got up. She walked over to the corkboard and took a closer look. Jake had the files on each shooting spread out on the table. She picked up Woody Jessup's picture.

"If you're right about this and we don't follow proper protocol, it's not just your feet to the fire. Do I need to remind you enough people still consider me an outsider in this county? I don't have a lot of friends among the County Commissioners. And you have even less. Despite your family name."

Jake laughed. "My family name's never been an asset."

"You know what I mean. Nothing would make your Uncle Rob happier than to see you taken down a peg by the FBI. But it's my name at the head of this department, not yours."

"A couple of days," he said. "That's what I'm asking for."

"You might not be a welcome visitor, Jake," she said. "I know the detective down in Coldbrook County. Met him last year at a conference. He was ... not friendly. Your basic good ole boy, as I recall."

Jake smiled. "My specialty."

"Yeah," she said. "I'd say you're more his type than I am. When do you want to go?"

"Now," he said. "Like I said, give me a couple of days. If I don't follow this ..."

"I get it, I get it," she said. "You asked me if I think you're crazy." She was still holding Woody Jessup's photo. She picked up Cory Boardman's.

"Four," she said. "Four men over eighteen months. Three of them in the last four months. Jake ..."

"I know," he said. "If my gut's right, it means this psycho is picking up steam."

"Go," she said. "And Jake? Hurry."

TWENTY-SIX

"You're outta your goddamn mind!"

For the briefest of moments, when Jake laid out his questions on the deaths of Cory Boardman and Woody Jessup, he thought a light bulb had gone off in the head of Detective Ray Mosley. Instead, he lit a fuse.

Sweat dripped down the side of Mosley's head beneath his broad-brimmed campaign hat. He stood with his hands on his hips, the buttons of his brown shirt straining over his belly. Mosley wore black, orthopedic shoes. He had a round, doughy face with beady brown eyes and a nose that was no bigger than a cherry, and just about as red. Mosley's breath heaved through his tiny nostrils as he glared at Jake.

"Those were hunting accidents, plain and simple," Mosley said. "I don't need you traipsing through here stirring up cases that have long since cleared."

"I'm not asking you to do any more work, Ray," Jake said. "I'm just asking you to share notes with me."

"Eyes on your own paper, hotshot," Mosley said, shaking his head. "I knew those men. I went to school with Woody Jessup. We played football together. His sister was a bridesmaid at my wedding."

"I'm sorry for your loss," Jake said. "Ben Wayne was a close friend of mine too."

"These were accidents, kid. You've been watching too many episodes of *CSI*."

"Accidents," Jake said. "Both of these men ... all *four* of them if we include Ben Wayne, and now Kenny Mihalek, were either actively hunting or killed in close proximity to where hunters were ..."

"Exactly," Mosley said. "Ya know ... when hunters hunt, they use live rounds, Jake. It was an accident. A horrible accident. In Boardman's case, his buddy damn near killed himself a month later. Did you know that? Poor kid was racked with guilt. We could never tell where the shot came from, but odds are it was from someone in their party. That eats at a guy. But it's over. Almost two years ago now. People have moved on. Gotten over it as much as they can. Quit trying to dig up old graves."

"Hunting accidents," Jake said. "Boardman was killed during bow season. And how many guys do you know that go squirrel or rabbit hunting with high-powered rifles?"

"That's not my problem. I told you. Jessup and Boardman have been cleared. Closed."

"You're worried about your stats?" Jake said.

"I'm done talking," Mosley said. "You wanna go sniffing around Marvell County, have at it. I'm not gonna have you mucking things up down here. Case closed. Now if you don't mind, I still work for a living. I need to get back to it."

"I still have questions, Mosley," Jake said, rising. "I'm asking for a copy of your complete files. You gonna make me get a court order?"

"I just might," Mosley said, getting in Jake's face. Jake curled his fists but dug them into his sides. He went rigid, staring Ray Mosley down. Take a swing, he thought. One shot. Do me the favor.

But Mosley saw something in Jake's eyes. He jutted his chin, but backed down.

"You can show yourself out," Mosley said.

"Thanks for your help, Ray," Jake said through gritted teeth. Mosley brushed past him, making a point of jamming his shoulder into Jake's. As he did, the scent of whiskey made his eyes water. Christ. It was eleven a.m. The guy was plastered.

Jake let out a breath then headed out. He passed by the front desk.

"Detective, wait." Jake stopped. The desk clerk looked pained. She was pleasant. Apologetic. Helpful. The exact opposite of Ray Mosley.

"He's really a good guy," she said. She'd introduced herself as Lucy when Jake walked in. "Ray's just had a tough couple of years. His wife left him. And she was his second. She's married to the fire chief now. It was the town scandal. She took him for everything. And she'll get half his pension too. Mosley wants to retire but won't now. The sheriff doesn't have the heart to force it ..."

"It's fine," Jake said. "It's ... whatever."

"It's been a couple of years, but what happened to Cory Boardman ... it had an impact around here. Everybody knew him. His death is still a sore spot for a lot of people."

"What about Woody Jessup? Nobody cared?"

Lucy bit her lip. "Woody wasn't the nicest of fellas," she said. "He kind of made a point of *not* having too many friends. Cory though? He was just a sweet kid."

"Any chance you can get me that file Mosley won't cough up?"

Lucy shook her head almost violently. "I can't do that. They'd fire me. But if you really want to know about Cory, you should just ask around. Start by having a cup of coffee over at Klineman's Diner just down the street. It's almost lunch time. Cory worked construction. They all eat there on their lunch breaks. Look for Sam Stahl. He's my nephew. He was hunting with Cory the day he died."

"Sam Stahl?" Jake asked.

"Right. He and Cory both work ... er ... worked ... for the same construction crew. They're putting in these new luxury townhouses on Stone Creek Road. It's a big to-do. They cleared some hundred-year-old oaks. That had everybody in an uproar. You ask me, Cy Rifkin, that's the man who sold the land to the developers ... well, he had every right to do what he did. His kids weren't interested in keeping up that property. Why shouldn't Cy get what he could out of it while he was still alive to enjoy it? He and his wife took the money and bought a condo in Florida. Living the dream."

"Bless you," Jake said, flashing her a smile that made her blush.

"You wait right here."

Lucy picked up her desk phone. She made a quick call. A minute later, she handed Jake a piece of paper with an address and phone number on it.

"That's Sam's personal cell. Like I told you, he's about to take lunch. Klineman's Diner is on Halsey Street four blocks over."

"I could kiss you," Jake said. Lucy's blush deepened.

"If you were twenty years older, kid."

"I'd still be out of your league," Jake said. He thanked Lucy again and went out of the building, heading in the direction Lucy had pointed.

TWENTY-SEVEN

The diner was just as Lucy described, full to the brim with the local lunch crowd. There were no empty tables, just a few stools at the counter. He scanned the dining room, looking for a man fitting Sam Stahl's description according to his aunt. Red hair. Glasses. A big smile with a broken front tooth that he wouldn't fix because Dean Construction didn't offer a dental plan.

Jake spotted Stahl sitting in a back booth with two other men. As he approached, Sam saw him. He leaned over and whispered something to his companions. They promptly got up and moved two tables over. Lucy had been as good as her word. She'd texted Sam to give him a heads-up that Jake was on his way.

"Mr. Stahl?" Jake asked, extending a hand to shake Sam's. Sam rose halfway out of his seat and returned the handshake. Jake would have preferred to talk to him somewhere more private, but the place was loud with conversation and rattling silverware and piped-in southern rock.

Jake slid a business card across the table and took a seat in the opposite booth. Sam fingered the card and gave Jake a weak smile.

"Thanks for meeting with me," Jake said. His entrance had caused a few stares from the surrounding diner patrons, but by the time he sat, everyone had gone back to their meals.

Sam Stahl sat sipping an iced tea, his half-eaten BLT on a plate in front of him. The kid sweetly offered Jake the other half as soon as he sat down.

"I'm okay," Jake said. "But thanks."

"You can order," Sam said. "Trina keeps the kitchen open until 12:30 during the week. If you don't like BLTs, her patty melts are darn near perfect."

"I'll keep that in mind for next time," Jake said. "Thanks for agreeing to meet with me."

Sam smiled as a gum-smacking Trina came to clear the table.

"I don't mind," Sam said. "Though I don't know what else I can tell you I didn't already tell Detective Mosley."

"Your Aunt Lucy said you were pretty torn up after what happened to Cory," Jake said. "I'm sorry for your loss. My friend, Ben Wayne, died under similar circumstances last month."

"Were you with him?"

"No," Jake said. "His sixteen-year-old son was. He's the one who found him."

Sam's eyes instantly reddened. "It's an awful thing. Something I'll never get out of my head. I can still see Cory like that. I can't … I can't remember him any other way now."

"I'm sure that's not what he'd want," Jake said.

"His mom asked me about it a lot. She got kind of obsessed for a while. Needing to know every detail of Cory's last moments. I don't tell her everything. She asks if he suffered. You know. Was it instant? Do I know if he felt anything? I told her he didn't know what hit him. I told her one minute he was walking to his truck. The next, just ... lights out."

"You shouldn't torture yourself. Odds are that's exactly how it happened, Sam."

He nodded, then got a far-off look.

"Would you mind going over with me what happened the morning Cory was killed? You were with a group of friends?"

Sam's attention snapped back to Jake.

"New friends," he said. "I just moved to here five years ago. My fiancé, Sydney, is from here. I met her in college. Cory is actually her cousin. Was. Anyway, he invited me to tag along with his usual crew."

"Who was part of the usual crew?" Jake asked.

"That'd be Andy Rifkin, Henry Potter. Cory and me."

Jake wrote down the names. "So it was four of you that went out that morning?"

"Just three," Sam said. "Me. Cory, Henry. Rif ... um ... Andy Rifkin was supposed to come but he was sick that day."

"Can you start from the beginning? Who planned the hunt?"

"That'd be Andy Rifkin. Or ... Rif. That's his nickname," Sam said. "I met him through Cory. They all went to high school together. With Sydney too. My fiancé. Anyway, Cory told me

Andy had permission to hunt this hundred-acre tract off Goose Creek Road."

"Who owned the land?" Jake asked.

"It used to be part of Rif's family farm. His dad sold it, but they still had permission to hunt. That's what Rif said. Anyway, there was some question about where we were supposed to be. Rif was supposed to come out there and walk it with us. Some wires got crossed. Cory had an app on his phone that showed the boundaries and where we were setting up didn't look like it was part of the property Rif initially told us. I was kinda pissed about that. Rif set this whole thing up. Then he's not there. Cory called him. Rif sent him a text with a picture of the map with the boundary lines drawn. Actually ..."

Sam pulled out his cell phone. After about thirty seconds of scrolling, he produced a text chain between the men from his hunting party. He handed the phone to Jake.

"Do you mind sending me a screenshot of this map?" Jake asked. He wrote down his cell number. Sam texted him the map photo.

"Anyway," Sam continued. "It seemed fishy to me. This was a totally different area than what Rif initially told us. Cory was asking him over and over if he had it right. We didn't want to be hunting somewhere we weren't supposed to be."

"Of course," Jake said.

"You hunt?" Sam asked.

"When I can," Jake said.

"Around here?"

"No," Jake said. "My grandfather has some land in Worthington County. About two hundred acres in Blackhand Hills."

"Man," Sam said. "I bet that's something. I hear it's gorgeous there."

"We like it." Jake smiled. "So what happened after you got your location sorted out that morning?"

"Everything seemed fine then, after all that. We split up. Got settled in our ground blinds. Then Henry sends a text that some other hunters confronted him. Hot as hell. Telling him we didn't have permission. It got pretty heated. So he sent a text to all of us saying he was gonna bail and suggested we all do the same. I'd about had enough. I hadn't seen any deer sign anywhere. It wasn't this prime land Rif promised. It was just a waste of everyone's time. So we all packed it in and said we were going to meet up at the pizza place on South Road. Just a total bust. I took days off work. For nothing. I started walking back to where I parked my truck. That's when I heard the gunshot. I knew it came from the direction where Cory was set up. I started running. When I got to him, he was laid out on his back on the side of the road. Like he was heading to his truck but didn't make it. Shot went through his temple."

"Did you see anyone else?"

"No, sir," Sam said. "Not a soul. It was Henry who had the run-in with the other property owner. But he wasn't armed. It was just an old guy in a four-wheeler."

"Where did you park your vehicles?" Jake asked.

"On Goose Creek Road," Sam said. He showed him the map on his phone again. Sam pointed to a small stretch of road, south of where he'd been set up.

"I called for help," Sam said. "Texted the guys. Called 911. I knew Cory was dead, but wanted to be sure, you know? So I went back to my truck and tried to flag someone down. Nobody would stop."

"Did you see many other cars?" Jake asked.

"Three," Sam said. "Not one of them would stop. There was this old lady in a Cadillac. Her I could understand. I had to have looked crazy. Another couple driving an RV. They didn't even look at me. Then a guy driving this blue Explorer. I thought he was a cop at first. Thought I saw the lights on top. But it was just a roof rack. He slowed down but gave me the finger when I tried to run toward him. Henry pulled up right after that, thank God. But it was too late."

"No one in your party had a rifle?" Jake asked.

"No," Sam said. "I swear to God. No. That's what's always made me so mad about this whole thing. We were bow hunting. Nobody had a rifle. Talk to Henry. He swore up and down that the guy who confronted him wasn't carrying one. That poor guy."

"Do you know the name of the farmer who ran your friend Henry off?" Jake asked.

"Um. Lud something. Henry will know. But I heard he got pretty torn up over the whole thing. Everybody assumed he ran us off with a rifle. But he didn't. We were in the wrong. Rif was in the wrong. He's a jerk."

"You blame Andy Rifkin for what happened?" Jake asked.

"I blame him for sending us out there," Sam said. "He organized the whole thing. He was a real dick about it too. Went around town saying what happened to Cory was our fault. Called us a bunch of idiots. He and Cory were tight. I know it hit him hard. He probably felt guilty. But he'll tell everyone who will listen that Cory would still be alive if he'd have been out there babysitting us that day."

"That's rough," Jake said.

"Sydney and I broke up over it for a while. She called off the wedding. Her aunt, Cory's mom ... she blames me too. One half of Sydney's family won't talk to the other now. Because Rif couldn't keep his mouth shut about it. We're better now. We're probably going to elope."

"I'm really sorry all of that happened to you," Jake said.

"Sure. I don't know what good any of this will do. I'm running a risk even talking to you about it. But I want to know what really happened to Cory too. Mosley says it was an accident. I just don't get it. Nobody had a rifle, that I know of. And how he was shot. That wasn't ... it wasn't a lucky shot. You know? It didn't look like an accident."

"You told him that? Mosley?" Jake said.

"Yeah. But it didn't go anywhere."

"Well, I appreciate your insight. I don't know if this is going to go anywhere either. If it does ... I'll let you know."

"Yeah," Sam said. "I just hope this doesn't stir up Sydney's family."

"It won't if I have anything to do about it," Jake said. "That's a promise. It might have a connection to my case, it might not. But you've been really helpful, Sam. I wouldn't mind talking to your friend Henry too. And do you know where I might find Andy Rifkin?"

"Henry works with me at Deans. He's out sick today but I'll write down his number for you. As for Rif, you can find him at Coldbrook Auto. He sells used cars."

"Thanks, Sam," Jake said. "Again, this has been extremely helpful."

Jake reached across the table and shook Sam's hand.

He had more questions than answers. More than anything, he wanted to have a look at Ray Mosley's full report. A court order would take weeks. But his next stop was the Coldbrook County Medical Examiner's Office.

TWENTY-EIGHT

J ake should have known there'd be trouble the moment he pulled into the parking lot of Coldbrook County Hospital. He saw patrol cars pulling out of the lot. One of them driven by Detective Ray Mosley, the other by the sheriff himself. Mosley made eye contact as Jake turned in, but quickly avoided his gaze, pretending not to see him.

The volunteer standing at the lobby desk plastered on a fake smile as Jake approached. His gut told him Mosley had already warned her about him. It was a small county hospital. The woman was probably related to either Mosley or the sheriff or at least only one degree of separation removed.

"Coroner's office is on the fourth floor," she said.

"That's refreshing," Jake said, trying to keep his tone light. "Nine times out of ten they're in the basement."

"You can take those elevators," she said, dismissing Jake. He steeled himself for whatever brick wall he'd run into in the form of Dr. Noah Culpepper, M.E.

Culpepper's receptionist made him wait twenty minutes, even though Jake had called ahead. He ignored six calls from the office in the meantime. Two from Landry, three from Zender, and one from Darcy. His sojourn to Coldbrook had borne little fruit, and a lot of headaches.

"Sorry to keep you waiting." Dr. Culpepper stepped out looking straight out of central casting. He wore a white lab coat, had fewer strands of hair than he had fingers, and his complexion had a grayish pallor that came from rarely seeing sunlight.

"Thanks for seeing me," Jake said, shaking the older man's hand.

"Probably could have saved you the trip," Culpepper said, though his expression was pleasant enough. "You want some coffee? Or we've still got some donuts floating around here somewhere. My girl brings them in from one of the local bakeries. Homemade fresh every morning. I recommend the cinnamon cake ones."

"I'm good," Jake said. "Thanks."

Culpepper ushered Jake into his office and promptly lit a cigarette.

"They still let you do that in here?"

"Beauty of working up on the fourth floor is that nobody ever comes up here to check on me. The traffic I do get generally comes in body bags so who's going to report me?"

"Fair point," Jake said. "Listen. I won't take up too much of your time. I was hoping you'd be able to answer some questions about two autopsies you performed."

"Cory Boardman and old Woody Jessup," Culpepper said, taking a drag. "I figured that's what this was about. I understand you've been rattling some cages around town."

"I don't know how much rattling I've been doing. I talked to Detective Mosley."

Culpepper's face broke into a wide smile. "Yeah? I think I can guess how that went."

"Mosley was ... well, we have different opinions about what might have happened to Jessup and Boardman. I'd really like your insights."

"To what," Culpepper said. "Break the tie?"

"It's not a competition," Jake said. "And I'm not looking to win any prizes. Look, I'm working a homicide down in Worthington County. The victim was a friend of mine. Ben Wayne. He was shot through the head by a high-powered rifle while he sat in a deer blind just a few hundred yards away from his only kid. I have reason to think that my case wasn't an isolated incident. I'm looking at a few others, including Jessup and Boardman, that to my mind, are starting to fit a very disturbing profile. If I'm right, well ..."

Culpepper rolled his eyes. "You think you're hunting a serial killer, hotshot?"

"I think I'm trying to solve a murder, doctor."

"Mosley ruled both of those cases as accidental."

"I'm aware. I'd like to know what you think. You did the post-mortems on both men. What can you tell me?"

Culpepper let out a sigh. "Look. I'd love to help you out. But if you're asking me to second guess or get in the middle of whatever beef Mosley has with you ..."

"No beef," Jake said. "But I gotta admit, I can't figure out why everyone in this town is making this so hard. I'm not here to cause trouble for anybody. I'm trying to get answers. Answers that I'm sure Jessup and Boardman's families would also like to have."

"That may be. Cory's mom ... Shirley Boardman is my cousin, actually. It's been real rough on her, what happened. She and her husband separated right after Cory's funeral. The stress of it all opened up some fault lines in their marriage. I'm not sure digging this all up again is what she needs."

"I'm sorry about that. I really am. But if her son was murdered, and there's a chance his killer is still out there and ready to kill again ..."

"That's a pretty big if," Culpepper said. "Look, this was Mosley's case. I'm sorry. But what you need, you'll have to get through him. I'm not in the business of stepping on anyone's toes. If you want my files, I'll gladly give them to you, if Mosley is agreeable to it."

"He won't cooperate," Jake said.

"Try again," Culpepper said. "Try harder. Mosley has his issues, but he's a good cop."

Jake bit the inside of his mouth to keep from blurting out what was on his mind. By his estimation, Mosley had come to hasty conclusions. Jake rose and extended his hand to Culpepper once more. The man had made his position clear. It was time to cut and run. Come at this from another angle. Only Jake had no idea which one and every instinct he had told him he was running out of time.

Twenty-Nine

"Jake!" Spiros Papatonis's booming voice filled the restaurant. He stood at the griddle, twirling a spatula as Jake walked in.

"Sit, sit," Spiros said. The man could fry eggs faster than anyone Jake had ever seen. Before Jake could even properly say hello, Spiros had his simple breakfast of eggs, toast, and wedge of melon plated and sliding down the counter, defying physics and stopping exactly in front of Jake.

Not to be outdone, Spiros's wife Tessa shuffled over to him, pouring a piping hot cup of coffee with a dollop of heavy cream.

"You look skinny," she said, standing with her hands on her hips.

"The wrestling team's giving me a workout," Jake said, patting his growling stomach.

"They look good," Spiros called out. "You think Ryan's got a chance to win States this year?"

"If he can get his head out of his rear end long enough," Jake said.

Tessa laughed. "He's seventeen. They're born that way. Eat!"

Jake dipped his fork in his eggs and did as he was told. Spiros came out from behind the cook line and joined his wife in front of Jake.

"I've been worried about you," Spiros said. "Look at those dark circles under your eyes. You haven't been sleeping."

"You're worse than she is," Jake said. In the last year, Spiros and Tessa had more or less adopted Jake. He'd delivered them long-sought answers on their daughter's cold case murder. Her smiling picture stared down at him from a frame on the wall. She'd been beautiful, Nina Papatonis. Vibrant. Their reason for living once upon a time. Somehow, Spiros and Tessa had found a way to go on.

Booming laughter reached Jake's ears from the back of the restaurant.

"You forgot what day it is?" Spiros asked.

"What?" Jake said.

"Tuesday," Tessa answered. "You never come in on Tuesdays anymore. They've noticed."

They were on to him. There was no point in making excuses. It was true, Jake had avoided coming into Papa's Diner on Tuesday mornings for the last year. Today, he'd gotten his days mixed up.

"They ask about you," Tessa said, dropping her voice to a whisper.

Jake stabbed a fork through his eggs and filled his mouth, avoiding answering her.

Tessa waved an irritated hand at him. "They worry about you," she said. "And they mean well. Maybe you should go easy on them."

They were the Wise Men. Or so they liked to call themselves. Tessa usually called them the Wise Asses. The infamous group of retired local cops. They had breakfast at Papa's every Tuesday morning.

"I saw them at Ben's funeral," Jake said. "We talked."

"You did more than talk," Spiros said. "Those old farts did you a favor. We all saw it. You lost your temper, and you were about to do something you couldn't walk back. Go back there. Talk to them. Thank them."

Tessa's face went dark. She reached out and put a hand on Jake's arm. Her eyes misted with tears.

"I worry about you too," she said. "Ben was a good friend. He loved you."

"I know," Jake said.

"That boy," Tessa said. "Travis. That poor sweet boy ..."

"Don't rile yourself up," Spiros said, putting an arm around his wife. "Jake doesn't need you crying in his coffee. The boy will be okay. He's tough."

Jake nodded. "Thank you for caring."

"You keep an eye on him," Tessa said. "You tell him to come see me. I'll make him an apple cobbler."

"He's cutting weight," Jake said. "You're a bad influence."

Tessa shook her finger at him. "Then you send him when wrestling season is over. Come with him. I'll fatten you both up."

"I don't doubt it," Jake said, laughing.

The voices in the back got even louder. Virgil Adamski told an off-color joke that made Tessa blush. Behind her, Spiros doubled over in laughter.

Jake had just finished his plate when Bill Nutter walked into the main restaurant, carrying an empty pot of coffee. He stopped short, his face falling for an instant, then splitting into a grin when he saw Jake.

"Hey, Bill," Jake said, waving his own cup of coffee at him. Tessa reached for a fresh pot. She poured some into Jake's cup, then traded it for the empty pot Bill held.

"Good to see you," Bill said. "Come on back and join us. Tessa just made fresh baklava."

"You cleaned me out," Tessa said, but beamed.

Jake's instinct was to make an excuse. He had to get back to the office. While true, something had nagged at him ever since he got back from Coldbrook County. Whether he liked it or not, he needed a fresh set of ears. Bill Nutter, Virgil Adamski, and Chuck Thompson had almost a century of institutional knowledge among them. And Jake was running into dead ends. Also, he'd never properly thanked these three for stepping in at Ben's funeral.

"Come on," Nutter said. Maybe he saw something in Jake's expression. But the older man put an arm around Jake and practically pulled him off his stool.

"Look who I found," Nutter said. As he led Jake to the back room, Adamski and Thompson let out a whooping holler, welcoming Jake to their ranks.

An empty chair in the corner sent a pang through Jake. Retired Detective Frank Borowski used to sit there every Tuesday morning too. Now he was gone.

A plate of baklava sat in the middle of the table. Chuck reached over and put a fresh piece on a smaller plate, handing it to Jake. Flaky and delicious, the thing melted on his tongue.

"We've missed seeing you," Bill said. "Chuck and I were just talking. We've been hearing rumors that Ed Zender's finally thinking about hanging up his shield."

"News to me," Jake said, debating whether he should have another piece of baklava. Tessa appeared out of nowhere, slapping another piece on his plate as if she could read his mind. She slid it in front of him then disappeared back into the kitchen.

"Well, he should," Virgil said. "He's been sitting on his ass for the last, what, six weeks. Came in here the other day carrying one of those hemorrhoid donuts."

Jake laughed. "I don't think that's his problem. He had back surgery."

"He brought it in so everybody would ask him what's wrong," Chuck said. "Even Tessa was rolling her eyes at him."

A fresh round of mostly good-natured ribbing at Ed's expense worked its way through the men. Then, they grew quiet. Jake saw Virgil eye Bill. Bill cleared his throat and turned to Jake.

"So," he said. "You wanna talk about it?"

"How do you know I have anything I want to talk about?" Jake asked.

The men exchanged looks. They seemed to have their own unspoken language. The language of old men who had seen the worst of people. Who understood the horrors of the job, but had come through to the other side.

"Jake," Virgil said. "Rudy Wayne was my neighbor."

"I know."

"We heard a rumor that you spent some time in Coldbrook County this week," Chuck said. "Something going on down there related to Ben's case?"

There was no point in trying to cover. They knew Jake well enough to know he wouldn't have gone to Coldbrook for personal reasons. Not while Ben's killer was still out there.

"Jake," Bill said. "These knuckleheads online are now saying this group out of Oberlin might be behind all of this. You know how we feel about those keyboard warriors, but ..."

"Rumors," Jake said. "That's all that is. Are they saying anything about me being in Coldbrook?"

"No," Chuck said quickly. "Nothing on that. I just heard it from Ed."

"Ed shouldn't be flapping his jaw," Jake muttered.

"You're here," Chuck said. "You've been avoiding Tuesday mornings for the last year. But you're here. If there's anything you want to run up the flagpole, we're here for ya, Jake."

"I appreciate that. And yes, I was down in Coldbrook County trying to track down a lead. But it was a dead end. So far."

"Dead end or brick wall?" Bill asked. "Ray Mosley is one of the biggest assholes I've ever crossed paths with." It earned him an odd, angry look from Virgil.

"Ray?" Virgil said. "We went to the trooper academy together. You mean to tell me he's still on the job? I would have thought he'd retired years ago. He's gotta be close to thirty-five years on."

"Well, we didn't exactly make friends," Jake said. "He's got a couple of closed cases I wanted to take a look at. He ruled them accidents, but both victims took rifle shots to the head. Look, this can't go further than this table, but there were certain similarities with Ben's case and another one in Marvell County last week. I just ..."

"Shit," Chuck said. "You think you're dealing with a serial killer?"

"Shh!" Both Virgil and Bill spoke over Chuck.

"Lock it down, big mouth," Bill said. "Christ, Jake. Are you sure?"

"It's what my gut is telling me." Jake was reluctant to share any more.

"Let me guess," Virgil said. "You don't want to hand this off to the Bureau. Can't say as I blame you. I wouldn't want to either and I don't have a history with them like you do."

"You think that tree hugger group could be behind this?" Chuck asked. "That's what they're saying on the internet now. They've moved off harassing poor Louie Jaffe."

"I'm just looking for Mosley to share notes with me. He ruled both of his cases as accidental. First guy, Woody Jessup, was shot in the head while fishing for catfish on the Giant Oaks River. Second guy, Cory Boardman, was shot coming out of the woods on opening day for bow season last year."

"Accidental?" Bill said. "Rifle shots to the head? Mosley lost his damn mind?"

"Yeah," Virgil said. "That's Mosley for you. Let me guess, he didn't like the idea of reopening cases he's already closed and cleared. He's always been nuts about his stats."

"His stats?" Bill said. "Who gives a rat's ass?"

"That's just the way Ray is," Virgil said. "He's a good guy. And he used to be a damn good detective. But it's been more than ten years since I had anything to do with him professionally. He could be slipping or getting lazy."

"He probably doesn't feel like doing extra work," Chuck said. "That's what it sounds like, anyway."

"Well," Jake said. "He pretty much threw me out of his office. He locked down his M.E. from talking to me too. I made a little headway with one of his clerks. She gave me the name of one of the guys Cory Boardman went hunting with that morning. I talked to him. The kid's not buying the accidental shooting story either but caught hell for saying anything about it. It caused some family drama. He's engaged to Boardman's cousin or something."

"Great," Chuck said.

"Listen," Virgil said. "Ray and I do run into each other every once in a while. My brother's got a hunting cabin down in Coldbrook. Every time I visit, I'll grab a beer with Ray. It's been a few years. But I can reach out."

"You think that'll help?" Jake said.

"It might," Virgil said. "Frank knew him too."

The men grew quiet, reverent at the mention of Frank Borowski. It was a subject Jake swore he would never bring up to them again. That wound was still far too fresh.

"I'd owe you," Jake said. Virgil met his gaze. The older man knew exactly how much Jake's words cost him. Not long ago, Jake swore he would never let himself make the choices these men had made. Or Frank.

"No," Virgil said. "This one's on the house, Jake. Give me a day or two. But I'll make sure Ray Mosley gives you everything you need."

THIRTY

S mug. So smug. Jake Cashen sat at that table trying to look relaxed. Trying to make it seem like this was just a casual conversation. Trying to find common ground. *I'm just like you. I'm not a threat.*

A liar. A predator.

The killer had studied everything about Cashen. Sitting up close. Seeing every pore in Jake's face. He had a scar on his chin. Faint. But the cut had been deep once. His hands were rough. So he worked with them. Not some desk jockey. He had said something about his grandfather's property in Blackhand Hills. Two hundred acres of prime hunting land.

Jake probably had a freezer full of venison. Easy pickings. He probably treated the animals like pets until he blew a hole in their hearts.

You wouldn't understand me, the killer thought. *I let you think you do. You act sympathetic. You want me to think you're on my side. You were just here to get more information. Learn the facts.*

The worst kind of predator is one who tries to make you think he's only the lamb.

The killer printed out everything available online about Jake Cashen. A treasure trove.

Mommy and Daddy died when he was just seven. A murder-suicide. The local papers were short on details. But they were pretty people, Jake Sr. and Sonya Cashen. She'd been a local beauty queen in her younger days.

Rich kids, the killer thought. The mother was an Arden. She came from a wealthy family. They owned the company town back in the day. So Jake's big tragedy was losing them. So what? He'd probably gotten sympathy from everyone in town. A golden child. They felt sorry for him.

The killer tacked up the picture of a young Jake Cashen along with his friend, Ben Wayne. Co-captains. They were still in their wrestling singlets in that one. Buff. Built. Ready to take on the world.

Adrenaline coursed through the killer's veins at the image of Ben Wayne as he lay on the ground, his life leaching out of him.

"You can't touch me," the killer thought. "You'll never be as smart as I am. You'll never be as powerful."

Top cop. The killer smoothed the folded pages of the article, mentioning Jake Cashen's part in a major RICO case. Little Jake, backwoods orphan, made it all the way to the FBI. He'd gone up against the worst of the worst. Drug dealers. Mafia kingpins. An untouchable.

The killer's heart skipped. Untouchable. The killer had been just a few feet away from Jake.

Untouchable. We'll see, the killer thought. We will see.

Kenny Mihalek. That was his name. Just a working-class guy. That's what his friends said when the news reporters got a hold of them. No enemies. Would never hurt a fly.

Why do they always say that? Never hurt a fly. Except Mihalek had gone out there that morning ready to slaughter innocent animals. He would never raise a weapon again.

"There's your justice, Jake Cashen," the killer said.

Mihalek had died well, at least. He bucked once as the bullet entered his brain. It was fun to watch them fall. Some fell right where they stood. Others took a step or two; those were the best ones. That moment when the body knows it's about to die, but the brain cannot comprehend. They try to outrun it.

You are gone, the killer thought. There is nothing left of you. You don't exist. You were a killer. There is one less of you now. Good riddance. Bonus if I can take you out before you have the chance to breed.

Kenny Mihalek had no children. Score 1. Ben Wayne had a son. I should have waited, the killer thought. I had wanted to. I could hear him, calling out, running toward the sound of the shot.

Too late. But oh, if I could have killed both of you that day. Two generations. Wiped out. No more of your toxic male genes to spread.

The killer picked up a pencil. This would be quick, today. The larger masterpiece was still unfinished. It would be beautiful. Mihalek's death was the most magnificent yet. One step backward. His head had turned toward the killer at the last second. He knew something was out there. He knew he wasn't safe.

Bam!

The shot tunneled right behind Mihalek's eyes. Just like Ben Wayne. Instantly blind. Was there pain? The killer hoped there had been pain, if just for a moment.

"I want you to know," the killer said. "It's better if you know."

The killer traced the lines of Mihalek's face in pencil. His eyes had frozen open. Most of them did.

He died with his hat in his hand. When he fell to the ground in a graceful arc, Mihalek had been clutching it. His entire body had twitched as the killer watched through the rifle scope. But the dead man's hand curled around that knit cap and held it in a true death grip.

John Deere. The killer sketched the logo on the cap. So strange that Mihalek had held it that way. Almost a grisly product placement.

The killer brushed loose pencil shavings away from the drawing, leaning forward to blow those that remained.

It wasn't the killer's best work, the sketch. But it would serve its purpose. The killer folded it neatly, then slipped it inside the large yellow mailer. The label maker sat on the table. One push of a button and Jake Cashen's address at the Worthington County Sheriff's Department was spit out in one, unbroken piece.

The killer carefully cut the address into strips and taped them to the outside of the envelope. A "forever" stamp today. A simple liberty bell. The killer peeled it from the roll. There would be no DNA to test. No saliva. No sweat. No stray hairs.

"For your collection," the killer whispered, before sliding the envelope into a bag for later mailing. Not today. Tomorrow perhaps.

The killer walked to the closet where each of the larger drawings were kept with care. So many of them now. Each labeled.

Mihalek's was the newest. But the killer kept a new, empty sleeve. Until today, there had been no name on it. But an hour ago, the killer wrote one, using big, looping cursive, just like the others.

He would not be the last. But he might be the greatest. The killer smoothed a gloved hand over the last, empty frame with its shiny new label on the bottom.

For you, Jake Cashen. Then the killer closed and locked the closet door.

THIRTY-ONE

First thing the next morning, an email from Dave Yun reset the entire trajectory of Jake's day. In the subject line in all caps, Yun had written:

PHOENIX/CAHILL PHONE DUMP. HAVE A LOOK AND CALL ME.

Jake transferred the .zip file and waited for it to open. Yun had the last month of activity on Esther Cahill/Jasmine Phoenix's phone. He checked it against the timeline of Ben's shooting and Kenny Mihalek's. In Ben's case, the cell tower data put Phoenix in Oberlin, not Worthington County. That alone didn't mean anything. She could have left her phone at home. She could have had an associate head out to the Palmer farm without her. Still, he looked for a pattern to her movements.

She was in Marvell County when Mihalek died. He already knew that. It would take more time to triangulate exactly where she might be in relation to the various towers and Mihalek's movements. But she was in the area.

"But not Worthington County," Jake whispered.

"What's that?" Ed said. He came over and stood over Jake's shoulder.

"I'm reading the phone dump from that woman Dave Yun picked up in Marvell County."

"That animal rights nut?"

"Yeah."

Jake scrolled up through the report. On the morning Ben died, Jasmine's phone hit a tower two counties over. He looked it up on the map. She'd been driving. The hits put her on I-75 and heading south.

Jake scrolled further back.

"Well, look at that," Ed said. He pointed a greasy finger on a line of text dated two weeks prior to Ben's killing.

"She was in Worthington County," Ed said.

Jake sat back. "She hit the tower a quarter of a mile down the road."

Jake read the small line of text. Jasmine placed two outgoing calls less than a minute in length. Ten minutes later, she had an incoming call from the same number lasting four minutes.

"That's a county number, Jake," Ed said, picking up what Jake did. But there was something else. This was a number he knew. His blood heated with fresh anger. He hit print then shot straight up out of his chair and shoved it under the desk so hard it bounced back.

"What is it?" Ed said.

"I'll be back," Jake said, grabbing his coat off the rack. He tore the page from the printer tray on his way out and stuffed it into his pocket.

THIRTY-TWO

"I need to see him," Jake said, trying to keep his voice low, and failing.

"You need an appointment, Detective," his receptionist said. "Commissioner Arden has a full schedule today."

"Clear it," Jake said. "Uncle Rob's going to be talking to me for a little while."

"Detective!" she shouted as Jake blew past her desk. If Rob Arden's door had been locked, Jake figured he'd kick the damn thing in.

His Uncle Rob was on the phone, white-faced as Jake stormed in.

"Hang up," Jake said.

Arden's jaw dropped. His cheeks turned bright red.

"Now see here," he started, rising out of his chair. He hung up the phone.

"Sit down," Jake said.

"I'm sorry, Commissioner Arden," Arden's frightened receptionist poked her head through the door.

"Close the door," Arden said. "This will just be a moment."

"Don't count on it," Jake said. He took the printout from Jasmine Phoenix's phone dump and slapped it on the table in front of his uncle.

"You called them out here," Jake said. "That animal rights protest group. You arranged for them to come out here and mess with hunters on county property, didn't you?"

"I don't know what you're talking about," Rob said.

"This!" Jake said, jabbing a finger onto the relevant lines of the report. "She called you. Jasmine Phoenix, Esther Cahill, whatever her name is. There are multiple incoming and outgoing calls between the two of you. She came to the county. You met with her. There's only one reason for that. You wanted them out here. Why?"

"They're constituents," he said.

"Like hell. That group's out of Oberlin, not here. You paid her to come out here and hassle hunters in your own backyard. You wanna tell me why or should I guess?"

"They're a political interest group," Arden said. "I make a point of listening to all sides of an issue."

"That's crap," Jake said. "When I run a list of donations to the ARU, I'm going to find you made a sizable one, aren't I?"

Arden slowly sat back down in his seat. It was enough of a confirmation.

"I heard her group was up by Echo Lake," Jake said. "You've had pushback from a couple of the hunt clubs about the new development going in over there. So what, you figured you'd hire these protestors to scare them off?"

"Don't you lecture me," Arden said. "You just stay on your side of the tracks."

Jake laughed. "Do you know Jasmine Phoenix is a person of interest in a shooting up in Marvell County? And I haven't cleared her from her involvement in Ben Wayne's death. You wanna rethink your position?"

Rob Arden's lips started to turn blue. "You can't ... I'm not ... there wasn't ..."

"You're gonna want to be real careful what you say to me next," Jake said; planting his hand flat on Arden's desk, he leaned forward, getting in his uncle's face.

His face. There was little about it that reminded Jake of Rob's only sister, his mother Sonya. She had dark hair, luminous green eyes, and an upturned nose. The deepest set of dimples that Gemma had inherited. Rob had been a few years older than Sonya. From the moment she died, Rob and the rest of the Ardens had disavowed any relationship with Jake and Gemma, her only children.

"You think I paid that woman to come out here and kill Ben Wayne? Don't you dare put that out there! I'll ruin you. I'll make it so you won't even be able to work as a meter reader."

"Don't overestimate your influence, *Uncle* Rob," Jake said, emphasizing the word he knew Rob Arden hated most of all.

"You want to look at my phone too?" Arden said. He pulled it out of his pocket and threw it on the desk. "I've got nothing to hide."

"I need to know what you and Jasmine Phoenix talked about. Every detail. If you lie, I'll know. I'll put you in handcuffs right here and march you straight down the hall in front of everybody in line out there paying their tax bills."

"You wouldn't."

Jake took his cuffs out and slammed them on the desk next to Rob's phone. Finally, all the bluster left Rob Arden's tone. He folded his trembling hands.

"Fine," he said. "You're right. I called her. I'd heard her group was staging protests nearby. I was only trying to make sure they could do so safely. If they were going to come here anyway, that is."

"Sure," Jake said. "You told her where to set up camp, didn't you?"

Rob took a breath. "I merely suggested where she might be the safest."

"You're lying."

"I didn't think it was good for anyone if she came into town."

"You're lying!" Jake said. "You specifically wanted her on Echo Lake, didn't you? Everyone knows you're backing that new development going in. How'd you sell that?"

"Fine," he said. "But they were coming here anyway. That Phoenix woman confirmed that."

"Was that before or after you paid her off?"

"It wasn't a pay-off," Rob said. "It was a donation. I donate to all kinds of environmental groups."

"You have a vested interest in Arch Hill Estates going in. You're on record with that. You've had pushback from the hunters and landowners on the other side of the lake. So you figured you'd use that group to scare them off, didn't you?"

"I don't have to answer that," Rob said.

"No," Jake said. "You just did."

"I didn't do anything illegal!"

"That will make a great slogan for your reelection campaign," Jake said.

"You can't share any of this," Rob said. "It's a private matter."

"You trying to obstruct my investigation?" Jake said.

"You stop putting words in my mouth," Arden said. He rose slowly, anger filling his eyes.

"How much?" Jake asked.

"What?"

"How much was your donation to the cause? Don't lie. I'll be able to find out on my own anyway."

Arden sighed. "Twenty thousand."

"Twenty grand," Jake said. "So that's the going rate for Jasmine Phoenix's morals? Good to know. She's okay with a subdivision going in and displacing wildlife, as long as it comes with a payday."

"It was a private donation!" Arden shouted.

"By a public official who supported the variance to allow that development to go in. Yeah. Tell that one to the voters, Uncle Rob. I'm done here. For now."

"You're on thin ice yourself," Rob said. "Don't think I don't know what you did when you left the FBI. I know who you are, Jake. You're your father's son."

Jake whirled on his uncle. He put a hand on Arden's shoulder. Arden's eyes went wide with real terror.

Jake took a breath, then slowly uncurled his fingers from Arden's shoulder. Jake smoothed Arden's jacket. Patted his uncle on the chest, then left him there, seething.

Adrenaline still fueled Jake as he stormed down the hall. He whipped around when he heard his name shouted from an open doorway.

"Jake!"

It was Tim Brouchard.

"Not now," Jake said, not at all in the mood for twenty questions on the status of his investigation.

"The whole building knows you went in there and chewed Arden a new one. You better let me know what's going on."

Shaking his head, Jake stepped into Brouchard's office.

"It's nothing. Yet," Jake said.

"Nothing?"

"Fine," Jake said. "If this goes any further, you're gonna hear about it anyway. My uncle had meetings with a prominent member of that protest group that's been going around harassing hunters and butcher shops."

"What? Why?"

"He used her to push back against the hunter groups that have tried to block the development."

"She's fine with houses going in there but not hunters?"

"I think she's fine with whatever fattens her wallet."

Brouchard stood with one hand over his mouth, the other on his hip. "Is he really that stupid? If the public finds out he was trying to threaten a group opposed to that land deal ..."

"That's his problem," Jake said.

"It could be a criminal one," Tim said. "Listen, Jake, you know I've been opposed to that development too."

"You planning on running against my Uncle Rob in the next election?"

"Would you support me if I did?" Tim asked.

Jake laughed. "Tim, I don't give a rat's ass whether he wins or loses. And I don't care a whole lot whether you do either."

"Jake, this is shady. If Rob Arden has been exerting undue influence on ..."

"Tim," Jake said. "I don't care."

"If he's committed a crime, it's your job to care," Tim said.

"No," Jake said. "Right now my job is to solve Ben Wayne's murder. Unless he's guilty of that, my Uncle Rob's dealings are so far down on my current list of priorities. I'll let you worry about that."

"But ..."

Jake didn't wait for Brouchard to finish. He showed himself out and stormed out of the county building, leaving what he knew were dozens of jaws flapping in his wake.

I f Jake hoped he'd be left in peace to work the case, they were dashed as soon as he walked back into the office. Birdie Wayne was sitting in the hallway waiting for him.

Jake's step faltered. He had a split second to slip down the other hall and avoid what he knew was an interrogation of his own.

"Jake," Birdie said. Too late.

"Hey, Birdie," Jake said, finding a real smile for her. "Everything okay?"

"No," she said, her tone hard. So it was going to be that kind of talk, Jake thought.

"Come on," he said. "We can talk in here." Jake showed Birdie to an empty interview room.

"Thank you," she said. "I'll get right to it. I need to know what's going on. I need to know how close you are to finding who killed my brother."

Jake paused, then pulled a chair out for her. She waved him off, preferring to stand. "Birdie," he said. "You know I can't get into the details of an ongoing investigation."

"Don't give me that," she said. "This is me. You know what I do for a living."

"For the army," Jake reminded her.

"Jake, I want to know why you're spending all your time everywhere but Worthington County."

"What? Who told you that?"

"It's all over the internet," she said. "I know there was a shooting in Marvell County. Another hunter. Are they connected? Did the guy kill again after he got to Ben?"

"I don't know," Jake said.

"Don't tell me ..."

"That's the truth, Birdie," Jake said. "I don't know. I'm working on finding out. I need you to trust me."

"Jake ..."

He went to her, putting a light hand on her shoulder. Birdie stiffened.

"I'm going to find who did this," he said. "That's a promise."

"Only you can't promise me that," she said. "Not really. I'm scared. Travis is not okay."

"He will be," Jake said. "I'm watching out for him. You know that."

"He's not fine!" Birdie insisted. "He doesn't sleep. He still spends all his time on the internet following that Dark Siders group."

"You have to put a stop to that," Jake said. "I kept Louie Jaffe from pressing charges by the skin of my teeth. He still could."

"I know," she said, her voice breaking. "Jake, I just feel so ... powerless. I want to do something. I want to help."

"You can't," he said, his voice barely above a whisper. "And I know that's tearing at you. But you need to trust me that I am. I am going to find who did this."

"But what if you don't?" she said. "Jake, I don't know if Travis will survive it. This is changing him."

"Of course it is," Jake said. "He needs time."

"He needs to know the person who killed his father isn't still out there. He's terrified. That's the other thing that's going on. Trav won't admit it, but he's got it in his head that this guy is going to come after him next."

"There's no reason to think that," Jake said. "Travis is safe."

"Is he?"

"Yes," Jake said.

"I don't know," she said. "I've been thinking maybe we should just leave. He could come with me to Washington. I've got an apartment on base. It's not huge but I have two bedrooms. Or I've talked about ignoring my parents and moving near them in Florida. That might be good for Travis too."

"Maybe," Jake said. "Is that what he wants?"

"He doesn't know what he wants," she said. "Neither do I."

"Well," Jake said. "You've had a lot to deal with. Maybe you shouldn't be making big decisions like that for a little while. Give it time. Christmas is coming up, you're on leave until after that?"

She nodded. "I can't even think about Christmas."

"I know," he said.

"I hate this."

"I know."

"What am I supposed to do?" she asked. "Tell me."

Jake didn't know what to say. He didn't know what to do either where Birdie was concerned. He tried to think what Ben would want. He settled on putting an arm around Birdie and pulling her close.

"I'm sorry," he whispered. "I'm here for Travis too, okay? You don't have to do any of this by yourself. Gemma's here. She wants to help. She lives for it. Take her up on it."

Birdie pulled away. She wiped her eyes and nodded.

"I'm sorry. I know you're doing the best you can. I'm just tired of feeling so helpless. I don't like sitting on the sidelines."

"You're not," he said. "You're the one stable thing in Travis's life right now. That matters. Hell, that's everything."

"I'm making this crap up as I go," she said.

Jake laughed. "Birdie, we all are. Now go on home. When there's something to tell, you're my first call. I swear, okay?"

"Okay."

As she left, Jake hoped he made her feel better. For himself, he only felt worse.

He didn't have a chance to wallow in it, however. As soon as his shift ended for the day, he took one last phone call from Virgil Adamski.

"Tell me something good, Virgil," Jake said. Virgil had agreed to try and run interference with him with Detective Mosley from Coldbrook County.

"Well," Virgil said. "I don't think it's something I want to discuss over the phone. You think you can come out to my lake house? I've got something you're going to want to see in person."

Jake checked the time. Gemma expected him for dinner. Though he knew part of that was so she could grill him just like Birdie had. "I'll be there in an hour." Jake hung up and texted Gemma not to wait for him. He ignored her response, knowing it wouldn't be good.

THIRTY-THREE

Virgil Adamski owned one of the best tracts of land in Worthington County. Twenty acres of wooded paradise that led downhill, stopping at the southern shore of Echo Lake, a man-made, private lake put in over a hundred years ago. His great-grandfather had bought this lot for five hundred dollars, a small fortune for the time. Now, the land alone was worth a hundred times that. Only Virgil had no plans to sell. He kept a double-wide on the property and escaped to it when the grandkids started driving him nuts. The original log cabin was still there too. Virgil had been meaning to fix it up for years. He'd gotten it to the point that the roof no longer leaked and the wood burner kept it warm enough for guests to sleep in, though anyone rarely ever came. His current guest was still sleeping it off on a futon.

But it was to the main house, the double-wide, that afternoon that he asked Jake to come.

Jake hadn't been down here since he was a kid. Coach Frank brought him, Ben, and Lance Harvey the summer before their senior year in high school. It was supposed to be a bonding experience. The three boys camped out in the woods. Only Lance had snuck a case of beer. When Coach Frank found out, he made them cut, split, and stack ten cords of oak and maple. All three of them ended up puking their guts out by nine a.m.

The place hadn't changed one bit. It looked like Virgil had put a new roof on, but the double-wide needed new siding. Last week's snow had melted, leaving a slushy mess leading all the way up to the house.

Virgil met him on the front porch, waving a hand high over his head. In the other, he held a cup of coffee. Virgil wore a faded Worthington County Sheriffs' Charity Catfish Tournament T-shirt. He'd been in charge of planning the thing for twenty years. The department didn't have it anymore, as none of the younger guys had stepped up to run it. It was another thing on Jake's long list of things to deal with.

"Thanks for coming out on such short notice," Virgil said. He held the rickety storm door open.

"I'm glad you called," Jake said. Virgil had told him very little else, only that he had something Jake would want to see.

"Any reason we couldn't have done this somewhere more civilized?" Jake was teasing Virgil. The property was glorious. Thick hickory trees. A perfect sandy-bottomed shoreline once the ice finally melted. But Virgil's bucolic hideaway wouldn't be the same by this time next year. The long-awaited Arch Hill Estates would be going in on the north shore of the lake come spring. After decades of wrangling with the township and county planning commission, the developers had finally won. Thanks in large part to dear old Uncle Rob.

"Figure I better enjoy it out here while I can. Next summer, the lake will be teeming with assholes on jet skis."

"I thought they were planning on outlawing that," Jake said. "No wake."

Virgil shrugged. "Who the hell's going to enforce it? Unless maybe you've got some pull with the county commissioners. Talk to your Uncle Rob for me."

Virgil raised a brow. He knew full well that Jake barely spoke to his uncle. If Rob Arden had any say in the matter, he would disavow sharing DNA with any Cashens. And Jake had just freshly poisoned their already bad blood over Arden's ties to Jasmine Phoenix.

"I'll get right on that," Jake said.

"Have a seat," Virgil said. His kitchen table was of the folding variety, but sturdy and solid. They'd call it mid-century modern now; the thing was American-made in the late forties, white with steel trim, made with Depression-era ingenuity and skill. Something Jake's generation would throw away and order new online.

"Too early for a drink?" Virgil offered.

"I'm good, Adamski," Jake said. "You've got me out here. So either you've got something to tell me you don't want to risk anyone else hearing, or you're planning on burying my body after we're done where nobody will ever find it."

Virgil laughed. He and Jake sat at the table. Jake's eyes went to the stuffed black tote bag sitting propped against the wall.

"I've talked to Ray Mosley," Virgil said, cutting to it finally. "I spent the last day and a half with him, if I'm being honest."

"Oh?" Jake said. "I hope you're gonna tell me you got somewhere with him."

"Yeah," Virgil said. "You could say that. Look. There's some stuff you need to know about Mosley."

"What stuff?" Jake asked.

Virgil's expression turned stern. He straightened his shoulders. This wasn't one of the Wise Men anymore. Whatever was on Virgil's mind, he'd pushed all bullshitting aside.

"He's in trouble, okay?" Virgil said.

Jake went still. It took everything in him not to start grilling Virgil. But he knew the older man would get to his point in his own way.

"This is hard for me," Virgil said. "There's a part of this that feels disloyal. Ray's a good guy. You gotta know that. Like I told you before, in his day, he was a hell of a detective too."

"In his day," Jake said. "Virg, Mosley is the only detective in Coldbrook County. He's all they got."

"I should have reached out to him sooner. I blame myself for that. You say you're gonna once you retire. That's the part that's hard about leaving. People ask me all the time if I miss it. The job. Not for a single, solitary second. I miss the people, though. The camaraderie. That's why we started meeting up at Tessa and Spiros's every week. It's important. This job will do things to you. And I know you're the last person I need to tell that to."

"Virgil," Jake said. "What about Mosley?"

"He's always been obsessed with his stats."

"You told me that before," Jake said.

"Yeah. Well ... he's a control freak. Always has been. Single-minded to a fault. It cost him. He's been divorced a couple of times. The last one's the reason he's still on the job. She cleaned him out. It got rough. She had a kid who died. Drugs. A lot of blame went around. Anyway, I should have reached out to him sooner. Mosley's a mess, Jake."

"I could smell booze on him when I talked to him, Virgil," Jake said.

"Yeah. It's really bad. Sounds like some of the other guys down there have been trying to save him from himself. It's not working. I'm afraid he's going to drink himself to death."

"Did you talk to him about the Boardman and Jessup cases?" Jake said.

Virgil heaved the tote bag on the table. "I did," he said. "We had a really long talk about it. I explained to him you're a good guy. Made him understand how close you were to Ben Wayne. Told him you're not looking to step on his toes or stir shit up."

"Did it work?" Jake asked.

"He gave me these," Virgil said, sliding the bag to the middle of the table. "Mosley's notes and files on both Jessup and Boardman."

"He let you leave with them?" Jake said, incredulous. "Those are his originals?"

"He trusts me," Virgil said. "And by extension, he trusts you. I stuck my neck out to get these. I hope you ..."

"Have you looked at them?" Jake asked, pulling the bag closer to him. He pulled out the top file. It was Woody Jessup's.

"No," Virgil said. "I wanted to wait until you got here. You can take all the time you need. I'm gonna head out and salt that walk again. You can call me if you need anything."

He got up. He shut the door behind him and left Jake alone in the trailer. Jake pulled both dog-eared files out of the tote bag and began to spread them in two separate piles on the table.

They were a mess. No discernable order to the information in the files. Mosley had loose notes instead of formal witness statements. Scraps of papers. Times and dates written on coffee-stained napkins with no context as to what they meant.

He'd never called BCI out to either scene. In Jessup's case, it didn't appear that Mosley did any real canvassing. He had a statement from a local bait shop owner who might have been the last person to see Woody Jessup alive. But it had been hours before his family said he'd gone out to the river.

With Jessup spending days submerged, there was no real way to pinpoint his time of death.

Jake pulled the autopsy report. That, at least, was organized. As he read the M.E.'s notes, Jake's heart turned to ice.

He set the report down and picked up Cory Boardman's file. This one was in even worse shape than Jessup's. Jake found the notes from only one witness interview in the entire thing. Sam Stahl. His story had matched what he'd told Jake, so there was that. Mosley had made a note to interview Andrew Rifkin. Jake thumbed through the pages. He could find no record that Mosley had ever even followed up with Rifkin. It made no sense.

At first, Jake couldn't even find the M.E.'s report. It was like it didn't exist. Then finally, he found it clipped behind a notebook page with scribbled writing Jake couldn't make out.

Jake studied the report. His vision blurred in and out as his anger rose. It was there. Right there. He flipped to the report on Jessup.

"Motherfu—"

He buried his face in his hands. "You son of a bitch," Jake whispered. "You lazy, drunk son of a ..."

The door to the trailer opened. For an instant, Jake thought he was seeing things. Ray Mosley himself came through the door. His eyes were nearly swollen shut, they were so puffy. His skin was ash gray. He stood in the doorway.

"You killed him," Jake said, though the words didn't feel like his own. He felt as if he'd floated outside his own body and hovered above.

"Cashen," Mosley started. Jake rose to his feet, his fists curling at his sides.

"You killed him!" Jake shouted, full voice. He slammed a hand down on the table, sending papers flying.

"Accidents," Jake said. "Jessup and Boardman. Accidents? Your M.E. found bullets in both bodies, Mosley. 7.62s. Sniper rounds. Both of them. The same exact type of bullets. Does that sound like an accident to you? You had it. It was right here in front of you!"

"Hold on," Mosley said. He started backing up out of the trailer. Jake advanced on him.

"It's been almost two years since they found Jessup!" Jake yelled. "Boardman died just a couple of months later. You should have known Jessup's death was no accident the second you got this report back from your M.E. Did you even read it?"

Mosley shook his head. His lips were moving, but no sound came out.

"It never occurred to you to call in BCI when Boardman's autopsy came back? 7.62s, Mosley. Christ. Two shooting deaths. Both with the same M.O., the same type of bullet ..."

"You're wrong ..."

"You know I'm not. You know it! Stats. You're worried about your stats. You had a serial killer running loose in your county. And you buried it. You got lazy. Now at least two other men are dead, Mosley. More. My friend ... Ben Wayne was like a brother to me. And he's dead ... because of you!"

Jake launched himself at Mosley, all reason leaching from his brain. If he'd turned the case over to BCI. If he'd shared information with other departments instead of burying these cases as accidents ...

It would have cost him nothing. Nothing!

God. Ben. Ben!

"Jake! Jake!"

Virgil's words reached him, though he sounded as if he were underwater. Blood roared in Jake's ears. It was cold outside but he didn't feel it.

Virgil had his hands on Jake's arm, pulling him backward. Jake had Mosley up against the side of the trailer. Tears streamed down the older man's face.

"Jake!" Virgil said again. He got his arms around Jake. Jake let go. He let Virgil pull him backward in a bear hug.

"He knew," Jake said. "You son of a bitch. You knew. Everyone was covering for you. Your M.E. was covering for you! That's why he wouldn't talk to me. He knew you've been checked out for God knows how long. He didn't want to be the one to blow the whistle on you."

"You don't know what you're talking about!" Mosley shouted, his bravado coming back.

"Ray, zip it!" Virgil said. "Get your ass back to the cabin and stay there."

Mosley's shoulders dropped, but he did as he was told. Virgil pushed Jake backward. The two men went back into the trailer.

Jake picked up the M.E. reports on both victims.

"They were both shot with sniper rounds, Virgil," Jake said. "Both shot through the head. He ruled them accidental. He's had a serial killer running loose out there for almost two years. Both of these shootings fit the profile of Ben Wayne and now Kenny Mihalek's killings over in Marvell. The same type of bullet. They come from a unique rifle. My God. There could be more. There *will* be more."

Virgil sat down hard. He put his reading glasses on and looked at the documents Jake shoved under his nose. Virgil's color drained. He put a hand over his mouth.

"I don't know what to say," Virgil said.

"They've been protecting him," Jake said. "Your buddy Mosley. How many more murders can we lay at his feet? Huh?"

Virgil nodded. "He's a drunk, Jake ..."

"I don't care anymore," Jake said. "I can't afford to. And goddammit ... neither could Ben."

With that, Jake stuffed Mosley's files back into the bag. He didn't ask permission. He took everything with him as he stormed out of the trailer, leaving Virgil to look after Mosley.

THIRTY-FOUR

When Jake left Virgil Adamski's trailer that night, he had intended to go straight home. Only the route back took him past Meg Landry's house on County Road Ten. Even then, he meant to drive on by. But there were lights on in her first-floor study and Jake knew she'd be the only one in there. He pulled into the drive.

Even with the late hour, Phil Landry was out in the driveway running the snow blower. A fresh two inches had fallen since dinnertime. Phil would know Meg left early, by six every morning so she was always at the office well ahead of Jake and the rest of her command officers. Or some nights, if something bad enough happened, Meg might need to leave in the middle of the night. Her husband would make sure Worthington County would have their sheriff if they needed her.

Jake parked in the street and walked up to meet Phil. Phil cut the engine to the snow blower. He wiped a gloved hand across his brow and smiled at Jake. He didn't seem surprised to see him. He didn't seem annoyed either. Phil Landry knew who he married.

"You okay, Jake?" Phil asked. Phil and Meg couldn't be less alike. Meg was a people person, comfortable in crowds, a tough negotiator, and a good boss. Phil was an engineer with the power company, spending most of his time staring at a computer screen and avoiding social functions. He was quiet. Shy. And completely devoted to Meg. He'd followed her wherever her career led, working from home when their daughter Paige was a baby.

"I've been better, Phil," Jake said. "I'm sorry to come out here so late ..."

"She's in the office," Phil said, not even blinking. "She couldn't sleep either. She won't tell me what's going on but I know it's bothering her about as much as it is you by the look on your face. You're peas in a pod. Go on in through the garage door and take your boots off."

Jake smiled. "Thanks, Phil."

He entered through the Landrys' mud room off the garage. Jake slipped out of his boots so he wouldn't track fresh slush all over Meg's white oak floors. The house was a unicorn. A two-story Tudor built in the 1910s, it sat up on a hill overlooking one of Worthington County's newest subdivisions. In the two years since the Landrys moved in, they had been painstakingly trying to restore it to its original glory. They were doing a great job of it, but it meant the house was in a perpetual state of disarray as each project got done. The latest was the downstairs bathroom. Meg insisted on keeping all the original peach-and-black-checkered tile.

Meg came out of her study and stood at the entrance to the kitchen in front of him. She didn't look surprised to see him any more than Phil had. Jake knew the same thing was on her mind as well.

"I wondered when you'd come up for air," she said.

"I'm sorry," he said. "I feel like an ass barging in on you this late."

"No, you don't," she said. "Plus, you don't make a habit of it. Come on in. You want a cup of coffee? I was thinking of brewing a pot."

"It's almost eleven at night," Jake said.

"So bourbon then," she said. "How do you like it?"

"Neat is fine," Jake said.

Meg nodded as he followed her into her study off the dining room. She pulled the leaded glass French doors shut, closing the room from the rest of the house while Jake took a seat at her desk. Meg came back with two shot glasses filled with Evan Williams Bottled-in-Bond. She'd poured hers over ice. "Thanks," Jake said.

"So where have you been all day?" she asked. "You've been AWOL."

"I have not," he said.

"You haven't answered your phone since just after noon, Jake," she said, calling him out. He'd left it on the front seat of his car when he went in to talk to Virgil.

"I wasn't AWOL," he said. "I told Beverly I was headed out to Virgil Adamski's."

"Right," she said. "I understand he was going to try to smooth things over with you and Ray Mosley. How'd that go?"

Jake took a sip of his bourbon. The booze heated him from the inside out and a sip wasn't nearly enough. He downed it and set the rocks glass on Meg's desk blotter. Raising a brow, she poured him a second shot.

"He's a drunk," Jake said. "Mosley has been coasting on his reputation for God knows how long. He cleared those two cases as accidental shootings that he shouldn't have. Both men killed with 7.62 rounds. Shot through the temples. One hunting. One while fishing. They fit the profile of Ben's shooting. And Kenny Mihalek's in Marvell County last week. Plus that jogger in Fayette County. It's a pattern, boss. I'm sure now."

Meg sat down slowly in the chair behind her desk. She downed her own bourbon and poured herself another.

"They've been covering for Mosley down there for years."

"Christ," she whispered. "You're sure? I mean, there could be ..."

"I'm sure," Jake said. "I'm gonna reach out to Dave Yun over in Marvell first thing in the morning."

"Jake," Meg said. "Yun's been trying to get a hold of you since this afternoon. I talked to him when you wouldn't pick up. Beverly clued me in."

"God," Jake said. "Please don't tell me he's got another victim."

"No," she said. "Not that. But he feels pretty confident that he can clear the Animal Rights Underground from any involvement in at least Mihalek's murder."

"Jasmine Phoenix," Jake said.

"Yep," Landry said. "Yun got a hold of surveillance tape from a parking structure two blocks from the Marvell County Government Center. Phoenix and the two people she brought with her can be seen entering and leaving. The timeline coincides with when Mihalek would have been out in the woods. They ate breakfast at a diner down there. Yun's got the receipts and talked to the waitress who served them. They couldn't be in two places at once. So whatever happened in Marvell, your Jasmine Phoenix wasn't involved."

Jake rubbed his temple. "She wouldn't have had to be the trigger person. The ARU is a growing organization. Yun might be able to rule out Jasmine's direct involvement, but she made her end game pretty clear. She wants a test case."

"Fine," Landry said. "But that's one case. One killing. You're talking about a serial killer. Why on earth would Phoenix authorize multiple killings to prove her point when one will do?"

It was a good point. One Jake didn't immediately have an answer for.

"Were you going to tell me about your run-in with your uncle on this one?" she asked.

Jake ran his finger over the rim of his glass. "I figured I didn't need to. Brouchard knew about it. It came to nothing."

"Nothing?"

"Well, nothing that has any bearing on Ben's case. My uncle is slime. That's not new information."

"Right," she said. "So why did you feel compelled to confront him about it this time?"

"The ARU are hired guns," he said. "It came to my attention Uncle Rob made a sizable donation to their cause. It was in his interests for them to cause trouble with some local hunters down the road."

"Let me guess," she said. "The same locals who've been against that new gated subdivision going in on the other side of my township here."

Jake raised his glass in mock toast.

"Terrific," she said. "Jake, this is the kind of thing I need to know about. When were you planning on telling me?"

"I'm telling you now. And it's nothing."

"It's not nothing," she said. "Those protesters got dangerously close to breaking the law. Now you're telling me a prominent member of the County Commission had a hand in it. That right there is a can of worms waiting to hit the fan."

Jake laughed at her mixed metaphor. "Fair point. But they're not my worms at the moment. I care about Ben's case. Nothing else."

"Fine," Landry said. "Your Uncle Rob is a fight for another day. So what about Mosley?"

Jake set his glass down. He waved Landry off when she offered to pour him a third drink. "Not unless you want me sleeping on your couch," he said.

"Phil can drive you home," she said. "And that couch in the corner has a pull-out."

"It's okay," he said. "Though I appreciate the thought."

"Your gut, Jake," Landry said. "What did Mosley miss other than the ballistics?"

"I talked to a friend of one of the victims. The kid who was killed, Cory Boardman, was part of a hunting party. The whole thing was arranged by their friend, Andrew Rifkin. Rifkin had them hunting in an area where they didn't have permission. Rifkin didn't tell them that. Then at the last minute, Rifkin claims he's sick and sends the rest of them off without him. Then Cory Boardman gets shot in the head."

"The victim, this Cory Boardman, he was trespassing?" Landry asked.

"Apparently," Jake answered. "The buddy I talked to, Sam Stahl, said they got some grief for it. Got run off the property."

"You think the landowner took it to another level and shot Boardman?"

"No," Jake said.

"Then what?"

"This Rifkin," Jake said. "The guy was responsible for putting his friends in harm's way. Sam Stahl was pretty specific about that. He's got a text chain with him where Rifkin sends them screenshots of a map."

"X marks the spot?" Landry said.

"Exactly."

"Does Rifkin have an alibi?" Landry asked.

"I have no idea. That's the thing. Mosley never bothered to interview him."

"What?"

"Rifkin's been shooting his mouth off all over town, blaming Boardman for his own death. Saying how if Stahl and the others had just done what they were told, nothing bad would have happened. This whole thing has torn Stahl up pretty bad. He blames himself enough already for what happened. Rifkin's been rubbing salt in his wounds. And that's all fine and good, but Mosley doesn't even have a conversation with him before clearing the case?"

"Did Mosley have an explanation for that?"

"He was pretty strung out last I saw him over at Virgil's."

Landry sat back in her chair. Her eyes narrowed and she skewered Jake with a look. "Jake," she said. "What did you do to him?"

"Nothing," he said. "I just ... voiced my frustrations."

"Terrific," she said.

"I think he'll be staying out at Virgil's for a while. I think Virgil might be trying to sponsor him."

"Good for Virgil," Landry said. "So what about you?"

"He's it, boss," Jake said. "Mosley is the only detective they have down in Coldbrook. He's in no condition to reopen either of these cases."

"What do you want to do?"

"I need some time," Jake said. "A few days."

"To go rooting around even more in Coldbrook County? Jake ..."

"I want to talk to Rifkin myself," Jake said. "That's all. Then ... we can take it from there."

"I need you here, Jake. You're a Worthington County Sheriff's Deputy. You're not with the FBI anymore. Your jurisdiction is clear."

"Meg," Jake said. It got her attention. He could count on one hand the times he'd ever used her first name.

She let out a sigh. "You're stubborn. Anyone ever told you that?"

"Once or twice," he said.

"How much longer?"

"A couple more days," he said.

"You should let me call in the Bureau," she said. "You had a hunch before. Now you're sure. This isn't ..."

"I can't lose control of this," he said. "I can't have Special Agent Lilly or whatever pencil neck they send waltzing down here trying to take over. You know he's got a beef with me. He'll get in my way. I'm too close. I can feel it."

"Jake," she said. "Don't you see? That's entirely the point. You're too close. Let someone help you."

"No!" He nearly shouted it. "No, boss. Just ... a couple more days. That's all I'm asking for. If none of my leads pan out, then we'll call in whoever you like."

"At a certain point," she said, "your past history with the Bureau is going to cause a real problem for me."

"It won't," he said. "Not this time. I swear it."

"If this goes sideways ..."

"It won't!" he insisted.

She folded her hands, resting them on her desk. "Two days," she said. "And you're taking personal time. Don't put me in the position of having to justify your overtime to the County Commissioners. Your Uncle Rob is just looking for an opportunity to screw both of us over. He says I play favorites where you're concerned. Whether it was justified or not, you've rattled his cage. He's spoiling for a fight. Pretty soon, you're going to give him one he can win."

Jake smiled. "Two more days. That's all I need. I swear."

"Don't make me regret it, Jake," she said. "And do us both a favor, stop making me promises we both know you have no idea whether you can keep. You have forty-eight hours. Then I'm calling in the FBI with or without your blessing."

As Jake rose, he knew she was serious. Meg Landry never made idle threats. In forty-eight hours, he would lose control of this case unless he solved it first.

THIRTY-FIVE

Andrew "Rif" Rifkin stood just a little close to the well-endowed woman as she leaned through the window of a candy-red Mustang on the showroom floor of Coldbrook Auto. Rifkin eyed her, making a lewd gesture that he thought only one of the other male salesmen could see. Jake sat behind the wheel of his own car, watching through the window. He'd been there an hour. Rifkin had yet to make a sale.

He said something. Invaded the woman's personal space just that much more. She went rod straight, pulling at her tight skirt. She giggled, then teetered on her high heels as she put some distance between them. Rifkin's smile faded, just for an instant. He made some joke. The woman feigned her own laughter, her hand fluttering to her throat. A moment later, her companion came to her side. Rifkin shook the man's hand, but the moment was over. The pair left him there, leaning against the Mustang, his sale hopelessly dead.

The floor manager came over to Rifkin and whispered something to him. Rifkin's smile widened but it seemed like a mask. Jake hoped he was telling Rifkin to back off. Check himself. What he probably needed was a pop in the mouth.

Rifkin nodded, then made his way to the side door. He came outside, propping himself against the wall in a small alley between the sales floor and the service department. He took out a pack of cigarettes and lit one. It was then Jake decided to make his move.

He shut his car door loud enough to catch Rifkin's attention. The man looked up, his cigarette dangling from his lip. As Jake approached, wearing his own fake smile, Rifkin quickly put out his cigarette, grinding it on the ground beneath his heel.

"Can I help you?" Rifkin asked, clearly thinking he had fresh meat in front of him and perhaps a way to salvage his disaster of a day.

"Maybe," Jake said, extending a hand. Rifkin shook his with an aggressive grip. When they broke, Jake pulled out his badge. Rifkin eyed it, but kept his smarmy smile in place.

He was tall. Six two, six three, maybe. He used it, closing the space between them, forcing Jake to look up to maintain eye contact. An old urge went through Jake. Easy target for a double-leg takedown. Get a big guy like him on the ground on his back, he'd be a defenseless, flailing turtle.

"My name is Jake Cashen," he said. "I'm a detective over in Worthington County. Is there someplace we can talk?"

Rifkin looked nervously over his shoulder. "I have to get back," he said.

"This will only take a few minutes," Jake said. "It's about Cory Boardman."

Rifkin reacted. For an instant, his face fell. Then just as quickly, he smiled. Big.

"You're a ways away from Worthington County," Rifkin said. "I heard you were talking up Sam Stahl the other day. You doing some kind of a side job? Like a private investigator?"

"More or less," Jake said. "So, is there somewhere we can talk?"

"You look like you should be in a Corvette," Rifkin said. "The brand-new one's something special. Zero to sixty in three point eight seconds."

"Oh yeah?" Jake said. "Maybe you're right."

"Follow me," Rifkin said. He led Jake back into the showroom. He walked to a locked cabinet behind the main desk and pulled out a set of keys. "I've got something you'll like."

"Bill, I'm taking the Charger out," he said. Bill, the floor manager, gave Rifkin a wave. Jake waited, then followed Rifkin out.

A shiny new red Dodge Charger sat parked right out front. Rifkin wasn't wrong. The thing was a beast and a beauty. It was also fifteen levels of not Jake's style. He climbed in the passenger seat and waited for Rifkin to get behind the wheel.

He was quiet at first, taking his time to put the car in gear and back out. Then once he pulled out of the parking lot, Rifkin hit the gas, making the tires squeal as he peeled out onto Main Street.

They drove for a few minutes, taking the back roads until Rifkin hit the on-ramp to State Route 666.

"There's a truck stop at the next exit," Jake said. "Pull in there. I'll buy you a cup of coffee."

"Suit yourself," Rifkin said. He floored the gas again, weaving and passing cars. He was showing off. Going too fast for the road conditions. ODOT had just started salting since the snow quit falling.

Rifkin zoomed off the exit and pulled into a parking spot. Smiling, he took the keys out of the ignition and placed them in the cupholder in the center console. Jake picked them up and pocketed them.

"You wanna go in?" Jake asked.

"Nah," Rifkin said. "Say whatever it is you gotta say right here."

"Cory Boardman," he said. "He was a friend of yours?"

"Not really," Rifkin answered. "I mean, yeah. We hunted together. Went to high school together. I wouldn't say we were close though. Not tight."

"There's a big difference between liking someone enough to hunt with and being real friends," Jake said. "They don't always coincide."

"Right," Rifkin said. "That's it exactly."

"Did you two hunt together every year?"

Rifkin looked off into the distance. A semi was pulling into the station. Rifkin waved a hand.

"For the last five or six years, I think," Rifkin said. "So does Cory's mom know you're sniffing around? How much is the insurance company paying you?"

"Insurance company?"

"She's something else," Rifkin said. "Always has been. That old battle-ax is trying to run Cory's life even after he's dead."

"She thinks she's owed money?" Jake asked.

"She's had her hand out ever since that poor kid died. She never liked Cory's girlfriend, Ashley. Never. Look. I've had my doubts too. Ashley got around. But you take one look at that kid and there's no doubt who his dad was."

"He's Cory's," Jake said, trying to follow without looking like he was trying to follow.

"Well he's sure as hell not mine!" Rifkin laughed at his own joke.

"Well," Jake said. "You said Ashley got around."

"Not with me, she didn't," Rifkin said. "Is that what that slut's saying?"

"Andrew," Jake said. "Do you mind if I call you Andrew?"

"Yeah," Rifkin said. "Nobody calls me Andrew. It's Rif."

"Got it. Rif. Anyway, I'm really just trying to get a sense of what happened the day Cory died."

"Are they trying to say he offed himself?" Rif asked. "The insurance company? I've heard they don't have to pay out if you off yourself."

"I have no idea what the insurance company is trying to say," Jake said. "And it's none of my business. I'm just trying to ..."

"Idiots," Rif said. "There. I said it. I'll save you the trouble. It's a shame what happened to Cory. Ashley's got her issues, but she's trying her best. She's getting no help from Cory's family. And here she is, taking care of his kid. She deserves that money. So you put that in your report."

"You think Cory was an idiot?" Jake said.

"They all were."

"I understand you were supposed to be on that trip the morning Cory was killed. I'll be honest. I'm getting conflicting stories about what really happened that morning."

"I'll bet you are," Rif said. "I told you. They're all idiots. I've kept my mouth shut for a really long time."

Jake practically swallowed his own tongue. Though Andrew Rifkin was talking in circles, the man hadn't stopped talking since the second Jake walked up to him.

"It has to have been hard," Jake said. "I mean, if you were supposed to be out there with those ... um ... idiots, as you said ..."

"Damn straight," Rif said. "They begged me. *Begged* me. Not one of them was a real hunter. I do better without them. That's the truth. I was doing them a favor by taking them out to my old man's property. We don't even own it anymore. I got special permission. My own damn fault because I felt sorry for Cory. He was freaking out about Ashley being pregnant. Like his confidence was all shot to hell. I don't know. So, he came to me. Fishing up and down for an invite to hunt that land. I felt sorry for him, you know? I should have followed my own gut and told him to piss off. Take his chances on state land. But I'm a nice guy."

"For sure," Jake said. "This property. It used to be owned by your family?"

"My great-grandpa bought it," Rif said. "Used to be six hundred acres in my family. My dad started selling it off bit by bit except for the couple of acres I still live on."

"How'd you feel about that?" Jake asked. "Your dad selling it off, I mean."

Rif shrugged. "He didn't ask me how I felt. My grandparents wanted to keep that in the family. But he got an offer he couldn't refuse type of thing. Made millions on that deal. And he's damn near spent it all. Says he's planning to spend his last dime with his last breath."

"That's rough," Jake said. "But you still had permission to hunt the land from the new owners?"

"Yes," Rifkin hissed. "Not anymore though. That's the real bitch of all this."

Jake raised a brow. Cory Boardman ended up with a bullet in his brain. But Andrew Rifkin couldn't hunt deer where he wanted to. That was the bitch of this?

"They didn't listen to you, did they?" Jake said. "Man, I can't tell you how many trips I've had like that. I'm lucky. My grandpa's got two hundred acres in the Blackhand Hills. I don't have to get permission."

"He gonna leave it to you?" Rif asked.

"Probably," Jake said.

"Man. It's gorgeous down there. I went on a trip with a buddy of mine a few years ago. Shot a ten-point."

"I'm lucky," Jake said. "But we've had our share of trespassers over the years. Bold as hell. My grandpa has had a few run-ins that came to blows."

"See?" Rif said. "That's the thing. That's why the new owners trusted me on my family's old property. I don't put up with any of that. I only bring people in I trust."

"You trusted Cory and the others. Who else was out there?"

Rif rattled off the names Jake now knew by heart. "Henry Potter and Cory were my friends since we were kids. Sam was a friend of Cory's. I didn't know him as well."

"That's what Sam said," Jake said.

"That guy," Rif said. "Like I said, he was a friend of Cory's. I was on the fence about letting him in. But Cory vouched for him. That's the only thing I regret about what went down. That little shit's been going around town saying that crap was my fault."

"How so?" Jake said. "I mean, you weren't even there."

"Exactly. I told them. I *told* them. Gave them a map. Showed them exactly where they were supposed to be. If they'd have just done what I told them, their dumb selves wouldn't have gotten into trouble."

"They were trespassing?" Jake asked.

"Of course they were. Set up somewhere they weren't supposed to be. Cory gave me all kinds of crap that morning too. Ranting and raving that I should be out there with them. That's the last thing he said to me. You believe that? I bend over backwards getting him permission to hunt the most prime land in the county. As a favor. And he bitches because he's got to do some work. Expected me to come out there and what, put him in his tree stand? Tuck him in? Lead the deer right to him?"

"Unbelievable," Jake said.

"Then some asshole shoots him in the head because he wasn't where he was supposed to be. Where I *told* him to be. I gift-wrapped it for those idiots."

"It's their own fault then," Jake said.

"I hate to say it, but yes," Rif said. It was almost word for word what Sam Stahl had told him Rifkin had been spewing around town for the last year and a half. It had taken all of ten seconds for him to unload on a complete stranger.

"Where were you that morning?" Jake asked.

"Sick," Rif said. "Ate something I shouldn't have. I don't know. Had it coming out of both ends all night."

"Sorry about that," Jake said. "That has to have eaten at you. That you couldn't be there."

"Yeah," Rif said. "I mean, I felt bad. Don't get me wrong. But I really don't know what else I could have done. I idiot-proofed my directions about as well as I could."

"If only they'd listened to you," Jake said. "So how long were you laid up?"

Rif shrugged. "Pretty much all day."

"Stayed at home? I mean ... is that where you were when they called and told you about Cory? Actually, who *did* call you and tell you?"

"I think it was Henry. Yeah. He called me a couple of times. I didn't answer. I was pretty much glued to the can, you know? I wasn't in the mood to talk on the phone. When I wasn't puking, I was sleeping. I think it was late afternoon that day before I even ventured out of the house."

"But you did?"

"Yeah," Rif said. "I was at Loki's. That's a bar downtown. They do dollar pitchers on Thursdays."

"Wouldn't want to miss that," Jake said. Rif didn't notice the sarcasm in his voice.

"Yeah," Rif said. "That's where I heard about Cory for the first time. I walked into Loki's. One of the waitresses told me. She's a friend of Ashley's. Man. Shocked the hell out of me. That's when I started looking at my phone. Henry tried to call. I had a bunch of texts from the guys. Awful, man. Couldn't believe it."

"They ever get your story?" Jake asked. In the span of thirty seconds, Rif had changed his own story. First he said Henry had broken the news about Cory's death. Now he was saying some waitress told him.

"Who, the cops? Nah. I wasn't there. Had nothing to do with me," Rif said. "Look. I gotta get the car back. You wanna drive it? That's fine. But I've got to get back."

Rif's tone had gone from casual bullshitter to borderline anger in a flash. Jake wondered if Andrew Rifkin was finally starting to realize Jake wasn't asking questions on behalf of any insurance company.

"Yeah," Jake said. "I would like to take the wheel of this thing."

"Suit yourself," Rifkin said. He slid out and left the driver's side door open. Jake switched places with him. On the way back to the dealership, all of Rifkin's bluster was gone. He stayed quiet, staring out of the passenger-side window.

"I hope you can help her," he said as Jake handed Rifkin the keys after he pulled into a spot alongside his own car.

"Ashley?" Jake said.

"Yeah," Rif said. "Who else?"

With that, Rifkin waved a dismissive hand and practically stormed back into the dealership, leaving Jake with more questions than answers about the morning Cory Boardman was killed. He pulled a slip of paper out of his pocket and dialed the number. Henry Potter was the final man in Cory Boardman's hunting party. It was time for a conversation.

THIRTY-SIX

Loki's Tavern was easy to find. Coldbrook's only bar, it occupied what was left of the train depot that used to run through town. The train no longer came to Coldbrook. It went away when the last automotive plant did forty years ago.

Jake took a seat at the bar. He checked his phone to reread the text he sent five minutes ago.

The bartender walked up. She was older. Grizzled. She had a toothless smile but when Jake ordered Jim Beam Black neat, she poured a perfect shot without even looking.

"You waiting for him?" she asked. Jake looked up.

"Henry," she said. "He's sitting in the back booth over there. He's been holding court for about an hour. If you're looking for a private conversation, you can tell him to meet you in the pool room. Nobody's in there right now."

"I appreciate that," Jake said, picking up his drink and the cocktail napkin. He turned. Just like the bartender said, Henry

Potter sat in the back booth. He told an off-color joke and his two companions laughed nervously.

"Henry?" Jake said. "I'm Jake. You think we could talk back there?" He pointed over his shoulder.

"Suit yourself," Henry said. When he rose, he met Jake nose to nose. He scooted out of the booth and the two men walked across the sticky floor into the pool room.

"What's this all about anyway?" Henry asked. "Andy Rifkin said you've been asking questions about Cory."

"I have," Jake said. "I'm working on a case in Worthington County that has some similarities to what happened with Cory. I'm just trying to tie up some loose ends."

Henry's face lost a little color as he sat down.

"I don't like to talk about it."

"I can imagine. The case in Worthington County. The victim was a close friend of mine. You were close with Cory, weren't you?"

All bluster and bravado leached out of Henry Potter. His eyes filled with tears.

"He was one of my best friends," Henry said. "We grew up together. His folks lived next door to mine all the way through high school."

"You were all close?" Jake said. "You, Rif, Cory, and Sam Stahl?"

"I was closest with Cory," Henry said. "We'd just met Sam. And Rif? Well, he was mostly Cory's friend. They've been tight for years."

That too contradicted Rifkin's story. He said he and Boardman weren't that close.

"You weren't tight with Rifkin?"

Henry shrugged. "We were closer before Cory died. Since? It's been ... different."

"Sam said Rif's been blaming you guys for what happened to Cory."

Henry nodded.

"He showed me some texts you guys shared the morning Cory died. I just want to be clear. Rif was the one who set up the hunt?"

"Yeah," Henry said. "His grandpa used to own the land we were supposed to hunt on. We'd never had permission to hunt it before but Rif worked it all out."

"Rif thinks the three of you ended up in the wrong place," Jake said. "He seems to think if you'd done what he told you, things might have worked out differently."

"Yeah," Henry said. "Rif's got a big mouth. He's been trying to peddle that story for a year and a half. I don't appreciate it. So if you're here trying to open up that can of worms ... I think I'll just end this conversation right here."

"No," Jake said, lifting a hand. "That's not at all what I'm trying to do. I'm just trying to understand what happened that day."

"If you figure it out, let me know," Henry said.

"Why wasn't Rif with you?" Jake asked.

"What did Sam say?"

"I'd rather you just told me what you remember."

Henry picked up a cardboard coaster off the table and started picking at the edges. "Rif said he was sick."

"You don't believe him?"

"I think it's real curious how he could say he was sick on both ends in the morning, then show up here eating pickled eggs and cheap draft beer by evening."

"You think he was lying?" Jake asked.

"Didn't say that. I'm just telling you what I saw."

"Have you ever asked Rif about that?" Jake said.

"I don't talk to him. Not after he started shooting his mouth off. I don't want to have anything to do with that asshole anymore. And I wish I'd stood up to Cory too. If I had, maybe none of us would have been on that hunt that day."

"Stood up to him about what?" Jake asked.

"Rif's an asshole. He's always been. But Cory? He worshiped the ground Rif walked on. It was always that way. Ever since we were kids. We shouldn't have been out there that day. Cory's the one who pushed it after Rif finked out. I think he wanted to prove something to Rif. Rif used to constantly dog him about how Cory couldn't really shoot the side of a barn. All this macho crap between them. Then Cory ends up dead. And instead of being sad about it. Instead of checking on how me and Sam were dealing with it, Rif's running his mouth trying to get people to believe we're morons at best. At worst, that one of us actually shot Cory."

"People know that's not true," Jake said. "Cory was shot with a rifle, not a twelve-gauge. You had bows, not guns. Detective Mosley ruled it an accident. Are you saying you don't think it was?"

"I'm saying Rif has no business shooting his mouth off. People listen to him. They whisper crap behind my back. I've lost friends over it. That's always how it's been with Rif. People listen to him. He's not a good guy. I tried to tell Cory that."

"But he's got them snowed," Jake said. "I looked him up in your yearbook. Rif was pretty popular."

"He was rich," Henry said. "His daddy had money until he drank it all away. But that dude? Rif? He's a liar."

"You think he had something to do with what happened to Cory?"

"You're the one asking questions. Do you?"

"I'll say it again. I'm just trying to figure out what happened that day. That's all. I find it odd that nobody questioned Rif after Cory's shooting."

Henry let out a bitter laugh. "Yeah, right. Like the cops were going to bother with Rif. He gets away with everything. They look the other way. It's been like that for twenty years."

"What's he gotten away with?" Jake asked. Henry just kept shaking his head.

"Henry. I'm not from here. I don't know Rif. I don't know his family. I don't care who they know or how rich they are. I'm asking you. What do you think happened?"

Henry just kept peeling the corners of the coaster. He wanted to say something. Jake could feel it. Jake took a gamble.

"Henry," Jake said. "I don't think Andrew Rifkin is really your friend. Friends don't go around saying the kinds of things Rif says about you. He thinks you're not telling the truth about what happened out there."

"Is that what he said?"

Jake nodded.

"Unbelievable. He's a prick. He's always been a prick. And he should have gone to prison a long time ago."

Jake let the silence settle between them. Henry had broken out into a sweat.

"Why?" Jake said. "What did Rif do that should have landed him in prison?"

"He's a bully," Henry said.

"Sam hinted at that too. But when I pressed him on it, he clammed up."

"Of course he did. He's scared of Rif."

"But you're not."

"If he did something, you're wasting your time, man. Andrew Rifkin is untouchable around here. Just ask his two ex-wives. He put one of them in the hospital about five years ago. She wouldn't press charges. But he broke her arm. I tried to warn her before they got married. Sally, she was a sweet girl. I knew he was cheating on her even before they got married. I told her she should talk to Chris Tansey about what kind of dude she was about to shack up with."

Henry chugged his beer. His eyes glazed over and Jake realized Henry was on his way to a good drunk.

"Who's Chris Tansey?"

"Never mind," Henry said. "Forget I even mentioned it."

"What did Rif do to Tansey, Henry? Is that why you think he should already be in prison?"

"It's some bad stuff, all right? Cory tried to do the right thing. I could never understand why he stayed friends with him after that. I don't know. Maybe it was because of it."

"What happened, Henry? If you know something ..."

"Tansey was a decent kid. Nerdy. Skinny. Awkward. Weak. But he was a decent kid. He was just easy pickings, you know? And Rif was always a bully. I wasn't there. I wanna make that real clear. I had no part of it."

"What'd he do to Tansey?"

"Before he sold off all that land, Rifkin's place was where it was at, you know? We had bonfires. Parties. It was great. You were *somebody* if you got invited out there. You ever drive by it?"

"No," Jake said.

"It's off Stone Creek Road. Gorgeous. His grandpa shot one of the top trophy bucks in the state out there. That's why he'd never let anybody hunt it when he owned it. Not even Rif when he was a kid. The new owners don't hunt. Man. It was gonna be something to get out there and hunt that land. That's what Rif promised us all. If it were me? Even if I'd been puking my guts out, I'd have gone out and tried to shoot something."

"Tell me about what happened out there, Henry," Jake said, trying to focus him. "What about this Chris Tansey you mentioned?"

"We used to have these big paintball tournaments out there when we were kids. It was like the biggest, coolest thing you can imagine. I told you. You were somebody if you got invited out there. Well, one year, Rif invited Tansey and some other kids after the Homecoming game. It was a big deal. Tansey bragged about it at school all that week. Rif would laugh about it behind his back. We all knew he had something bad planned. But nobody would stand up to him. Tansey should have known better. But he was a kid. He wanted to fit in."

"Why should Tansey have known better?"

"He was a geek. A real loser. Skinny-ass kid who wore friggin' headgear to school. In the 2000s? Who does that?"

"Rif invited Tansey as a joke," Jake said.

"Yeah." Henry got silent. He ripped the coaster in half.

"What happened on Rif's grandpa's land, Henry?"

"I told you, I wasn't there. But I saw Tansey's face. And that was a week after it happened. When he got out of the hospital. He was a mess. Broken cheekbone. They said he had a collapsed lung."

"It wasn't paintball, was it?" Jake asked.

"Oh, it was paintball. But Rif froze them before loading them. He creamed that kid. He could have killed him. Cory swore to me he didn't know the balls were frozen. None of them did. But it was Cory. Rif. This other kid Cory was friends with from one of the Catholic schools. St. Paul's. Schuler. Victor Schuler."

"You're right. They could have killed him," Jake said. "Frozen paintballs are about as lethal as bullets."

"Yeah," Henry said. "I was supposed to be there that day. I got grounded. My dad caught me smoking weed. It was his weed. I think that's what he was mostly angry about."

"They arrested Rif?"

"He was sixteen," Henry said. "They were gonna charge him as an adult. Felony assault. I think it should have been attempted murder. Rif knew what he was doing. He never knew, but Vic Schuler was the one who turned him in. He told me that a few years after it happened. He called the crime stopper line and told the cops what happened."

"They didn't already know? You said everyone knew about paintball at Rif's grandpa's."

"Yeah, well, Rif fed them some line of BS. His daddy bailed him out."

"But he was arrested?" Jake asked.

"Yeah. Spent a night in jail. The whole bit. But then all of a sudden, the charges got dropped. A week or so afterward, Tansey was back in school saying the whole thing was a misunderstanding. He wouldn't talk about it after that. I mean, the kid's face was smashed in."

"Someone got to the prosecutor, you think?" Jake asked. "Do you remember who that was at the time?" If he couldn't, Jake knew it would be easy enough to find out. At a minimum, he had new questions for Mosley. He would have been on the force. If Rif was sixteen during the incident, it was only fifteen years ago.

"I don't know. Tansey's still around. Maybe you should ask him. He's still got a scar on his cheek from it. He lives over on McKinley Street in a brick house painted yellow."

"Maybe I will," Jake said.

"Look," Henry said. "I'm glad you're asking questions. This whole thing. Cory. It just hasn't sat right with me. It's like you said. Nobody's ever asked Rif about that day. They just let him strut around spinning his own version. And people believe him."

"I appreciate this," Jake said. He took out one of his business cards. "If you can think of anything else that might help me. About Cory. About what happened that day."

"Sure," Henry said as he pocketed the card. He shook Jake's hand as Jake rose to leave. "Vic Schuler might be able to tell you

more about what happened with Tansey. I told you. He's the
one who cooperated with the cops. He was scared to death that
Rif was going to find out he was the rat. If you can find him. We
lost touch after high school. He dropped out. I moved away for a
while. I moved back three years ago. I haven't seen Vic in years."

Jake got to his car and sat behind the wheel for a moment. Cory
Boardman. Henry Potter. Andrew Rifkin. Now Victor Schuler.
On a hunch, he called Ed Zender.

"Hey, Ed," Jake said. "I need you to do me a favor if you've got
some time. Can you run down a name for me? Victor Schuler.
Early thirties. Went to St. Paul's in Coldbrook. Can you see if
you can find an address or a phone number?"

"Sure thing, Jake," Ed said. "But you might wanna get on
back here. Landry's been looking for you."

No sooner had he said it before Jake's phone buzzed
with an incoming text. It was from Meg Landry. He checked the
screen then turned off his phone.

She had texted the words, "24 hours."

THIRTY-SEVEN

S even p.m. and Jake could see lights on through the bay window of the little Cape Cod with painted yellow brick. There was a woman inside, clearing plates from the dining room table. She was dancing, or talking to herself, wearing a powder-blue housecoat that reminded him of one Grandma Ava used to have.

Jake took the keys out of the ignition and approached Chris Tansey's house on McKinley Street. He had to ring the doorbell three times before the woman finally came to the door. When she did, she'd changed out of her housecoat and stood before him wearing a bright pink sundress and bare feet. She stared at him, her face crinkling up. She had a mass of white hair held back with a wide blue plastic headband.

"They've already checked the gas meter this month," she said, looking Jake up and down. He couldn't imagine what part of him looked like a meter reader in his dark-gray suit, his detective badge hanging from a chain around his neck.

"My name is Jake Cashen," he said, holding out a business card. "I'm with the Worthington County Sheriff's Office. I was wondering if Christopher Tansey still lives here?"

"Chrissie? Well, of course he does. He's a good boy who takes care of his mama. Where else would he live?"

"You're Mrs. Tansey?" Jake asked.

"You call me Violet," she said. "What do you want with my boy?"

"I'd just like to ask him a few things. I'm doing a background check on someone he knew from high school and might still be acquainted with."

"Well, come on in, officer," Violet Tansey said. "I was just about to put on a pot of tea. It's the herbal kind. Not everyone likes it. Would you like a cup?"

"That would be great," Jake said.

"Well don't just stand there letting all the cold air in. Kick your shoes off right there on the porch. I just mopped."

Jake did as he was told. The pungent scent of vinegar assailed his nostrils as he stepped inside. She must have used it to mop the wood floors. Some of the boards were warped leading into the kitchen.

"Have a seat," Violet said, gesturing to a floral print couch with a plastic cover. Jake thanked her again for her hospitality as Violet went into the kitchen. A moment later, she came out carrying a tray with two teacups on it. She handed one to Jake. It was yellow, the exact color of the house, with a chipped rim.

"You like sugar?"

"No, thank you," Jake said.

"I like you already," Violet said. She took a seat in the recliner opposite him then loudly slurped her tea.

"Do you know where I might be able to find Chris?" Jake asked.

"He works twelve-hour shifts over at Speedy Parcel Service. Four on three off. He won't get back until five or six in the morning. He might be working over today. They've got a big shipment coming in. Sometimes I don't see him for days. Now what's this about a friend of his you're looking into?"

"Mrs. Tansey ..."

"I'm still a Miss. Never had much use for a mister. Except for that one time. Even then he was in and out and on his way," she said, laughing at her own ribald joke.

"Of course," Jake said. "Sorry about that. Miss Tansey. There's actually something you might be able to help me out with. As I said, I'm doing a background check. I'm interested in talking to people who've known Andrew Rifkin for a long time. I understand your son went to school with him."

"Rif?" she said, her eyes going wide. "Why didn't you say that in the first place? You're snooping around on Rif?"

"I wouldn't call it snooping, exactly ..."

"I worked for his mama. Did you know that? When my knees were still good, I cleaned her house two times a week."

"No," Jake said. "I didn't know that. Are you still in touch with her?"

Violet Tansey threw her head back and laughed. "She's been called to the Lord, officer. Seven or eight years ago now."

"I see," Jake said. "How long did you clean for the Rifkins?"

"Close to ten years," she said. "They paid me very well. Treated me pretty good too. Some don't. Always used to give me a bonus at Christmas and on my birthday. I told them they didn't have to. I would take it straight to church and put it in the collection box though. So that was nice."

"What about Rif? How well did you know him?"

"He was a boy," she said. "I might as well have been wallpaper to him. And that's fine."

Jake studied her. Violet Tansey got a far-off look, but nothing registered in her expression that would have led Jake to think she thought ill of Andrew Rifkin. The boy who had put her son in the hospital.

"Miss Tansey, I understand Andrew got into some trouble relating to your son at one point."

She sipped her tea and looked out the bay window. "You think it's going to snow again? Chris was supposed to salt the walk before he left. He got called in early though. I keep a bag of rock salt in the garage. It's too heavy for me to lift now. Do you think …"

"I'd be happy to take care of that before I leave," Jake said.

"Your mama raised a good boy then too," she said, smiling. "She must be proud of you. Look at you in your nice suit and that shiny badge. I'll say a prayer to St. Michael for you tonight. I'll bet she does every day."

"Thank you," Jake said. "My mother passed away a long time ago, though."

"That doesn't mean she's not still praying," Violet said. "It just means her prayers don't have to travel as far. Or maybe she gets to talk to St. Michael directly for you. Wouldn't that be something."

"It's a nice thought," Jake said.

"You've got yourself a guardian angel then."

"Maybe," Jake said, smiling. "Miss Tansey, about Rif and your son. I don't mean to stir up memories that might be difficult, but would you mind telling me what happened to Chris when he was a kid? I understand he was injured. That there was an assault. That Andrew ..."

"Why are you checking into him?" she asked. "Is he trying to get one of those government jobs again?"

"Something like that," Jake lied. "Miss Tansey ..."

"That was a very long time ago," she said. "My Chris is stronger for it."

"Excuse me?"

"Blessed is the one who perseveres under trial. Having stood the test, he will receive the crown of life that the Lord has promised to those who love him. That's James 1:12. He's my favorite."

"He had to be very strong," Jake said. "I understand your son was pretty badly injured."

"Did Rif tell you that?"

"No," Jake said. "Another of the boys who were involved did."

"Chris and Rif are friends now," she said. "We don't talk about ancient history too much around here."

"Andrew Rifkin arranged to have your son shot with frozen paintballs."

"The sons of Israel did just as the Lord commanded Moses," she said.

"Yes," Jake said. "It would have been the equivalent of a stoning. Your son is very lucky to be alive."

"The Lord intervened," she said. "I prayed by his bedside for days. It wasn't his time. And he's a stronger man for it. We are all made to suffer in this life. And forgiveness is the path to God."

"Chris has forgiven Rif?"

"Of course," she said. "Why wouldn't he?"

"He almost died," Jake said. "Your son was shot in the face, the chest. He suffered serious internal injuries."

"He is so strong," she said. "I prayed for him until he was able to pray for himself. They gave him last rites."

"That had to have been very scary for you," Jake said. "I'm sorry you had to go through that."

"But I'm stronger for it too, you see. It is all a part of God's Will."

"Forgiveness had to be hard too," Jake said.

She smiled. "Why should it be easy?"

"Miss Tansey, I understand Andrew Rifkin was arrested. He was charged with felonious assault. At sixteen they were going to prosecute him as an adult. He could have gone to prison for that for a very long time."

She gave Jake a sympathetic smile.

"Do you know why the charges were dropped?" Jake asked. "Was that your idea? Was it your son's?"

"I don't know anything about that," she said. "Render unto Caesar."

"I don't think that's what that verse means, exactly," Jake said. "Did the prosecutor in your son's assault decline to pursue the case? Can you shed some light on how that happened?"

"I told you. My son forgave that boy long ago. He is better for it. We all are better for it. Andrew has turned his life around. He's a youth minister now. Did you know that?"

"No," Jake said. "I didn't. But I've heard other rumors about him. Domestic abuse. That's pretty disturbing. That doesn't sound to me like someone who has turned his life around. Miss Tansey, I know the Rifkins have some influence in this town. Back then, it's understandable that you would have worried about your job. You worked for the Rifkins. Did they threaten you?"

"It's water under the bridge," she said.

"You don't have to be afraid anymore," he said.

"What took your mother so soon?"

"What?"

"Your mother. Was she ill? Was it an accident?"

"No," Jake said. Violet Tansey's face fell as she understood the meaning of his answer before Jake could cover. She reached for him, putting a hand on his knee.

"You were very young then, weren't you?"

"I was young, yes," he said. Violet closed her eyes and began to murmur a prayer.

"So someone took her from you," she said. "Have you forgiven him?"

"I try," he said.

"Good. But you must do more than try. I can see it in you. It's a demon, Mr. Cashen. One that will tear you up from the inside out and keep you from Glory."

"So you're telling me Chris is friends with Andrew Rifkin now?"

"They are both children of God," she said. "Just as the one who took your mother from you was."

He started to rise. "If you could let your son know I'd like to talk to him if he's willing. Please just give him my card."

"I'll pray for your soul," she said.

"You do that," Jake said.

"She'd want you to forgive him, your mother. I'm sure of it."

Jake's whole body tensed. What did Violet Tansey know about what his mother would want?

"Someday," she said. "You'll have to make a choice. Decide if you want to take the path to glory or damnation. I hope you choose the right one."

"Thank you for your time, Miss Tansey," Jake said. As he rose, Violet slid down to her knees. She clasped her hands together and began to pray in earnest.

"If you do not forgive their sins, your Father will not forgive your sins. Oh Lord, help this man to see the path to glory."

The woman began to rock back and forth. She put one hand up toward the heavens and kept the other clutched to her breast.

"I'll take care of that rock salt," Jake said, awkwardly walking backward until he made it to the front door. Violet Tansey shouted an alleluia that practically shook the house as Jake let himself out.

He grabbed his shoes and made it to her garage and found a torn bag of rock salt propped against the side. He could still hear Violet Tansey's prayers as he spread the salt all along her walk.

His phone rang as he made it back to the car. It was the office number. Jake braced himself for another lecture from Sheriff Landry. She'd want answers. Results. And he would need to buy more time.

"Hey, Jake," Ed Zender said as Jake answered. Jake slid behind the wheel and started his car. It took a second for the Bluetooth speaker to kick in. He lost part of what Ed was saying.

"Happened a little over eight years ago," Ed said.

"What?" Jake said. "Ed, you cut out. What happened eight years ago?"

Ed let out a sigh.

"Your guy," he said. "Victor Schuler. The one you asked me to run down. You're right, he doesn't live in Coldbrook County anymore because he doesn't live at all. His death was listed as a homicide. Unsolved."

"Ed," Jake said, feeling the blood drain from his head. "How? When?"

"He was shot, Jake," Ed said. "A drive-by. Guy was sitting in his own driveway. Eight years ago."

It could be a coincidence. Only Jake knew in his bones it wasn't.

THIRTY-EIGHT

"I need to talk to him," Jake said. He sat behind the wheel, his suit crumpled, his teeth feeling fuzzy. He couldn't go home. He couldn't waste a single second of his time in Coldbrook. He was close. He felt it down to his marrow.

"He's not here, Jake," Virgil Adamski said. It was four o'clock in the morning. Jake had caught a few hours of sleep laid out in the backseat of his car. But the fire burned inside of him. The image of Ben's vacant eyes burned a hole in his soul.

"I just need to talk to him, Virgil," Jake said. "There was another murder. Part of Cory Boardman's same friend group. Years ago. I need to know what Mosley remembers about it."

"So you can rip him a new one about that?" Virgil said. "Jake, you gotta cut him some slack. Mosley is sick."

"I need to know what he knows, Virgil. That's all."

"Well, I told you. He's not here. He left after dinner last night. And he was sober. He needs time. I've arranged to get him into rehab but the bed won't open until next week. I tried to talk him into crashing here until then. He wouldn't listen."

"Christ, Virgil. He probably stopped at the liquor store on his way out. I'm heading over to his place."

"Jake, don't!" Virgil shouted. "I'm asking you as a favor. As a friend."

"Save it," Jake said. "Everything I'm doing right now I'm doing for a different friend. Ben Wayne was murdered. He wasn't the only one. I think there's at least an outside chance that this other case might have something to do with what happened to Ben. That's the priority. Not you. Not Mosley's fragile mental state. I'm trying to catch and stop a killer, Virgil. I'm out of time, patience, and sympathy."

Virgil was still talking as Jake hung up. If Mosley wasn't at home, there was a good chance he'd show up at the liquor store. He hoped like hell he was wrong. That he'd find Mosley quietly sleeping instead of passed out with empty beer cans all around him.

He got to Mosley's two-bedroom house on the easternmost edge of Coldbrook County in fifteen minutes. What he found there, he hadn't expected.

Mosley wasn't passed out. He wasn't drunk, and he wasn't sleeping. Instead, he was sitting in his front living room staring at the television set, his gun and badge on a tray beside him.

"This is your solution?" Jake asked. He had knocked once. Mosley yelled out that the door was unlocked.

"What are you talking about?" Mosley said. He didn't turn to face Jake.

"Are you planning on blowing your brains out?"

"You think Ben Wayne is dead because of me. You think Kenny Mihalek is dead because of me."

"No," Jake said. "I think Ben and Kenny are dead because there's a psycho out there picking off hunters. And I think he's been hurting people for a very long time and getting away with it. You can help me put a stop to it."

Mosley finally looked at him. "What are you talking about?"

Jake filled him in on his conversation with Henry Potter and Violet Tansey.

"Rif," Mosley said. "Andy Rifkin. Jesus, Cashen. You're telling me you think Cy Rifkin's kid is a serial killer?"

"I think Cory Boardman might not have been random. Do you remember a case involving Andrew Rifkin, Victor Schuler, and a kid named Chris Tansey? Rifkin assaulted him with frozen paintballs. Put him in the hospital. Fifteen years ago roughly."

"I don't remember that."

"What about Victor Schuler?" Jake said. "Drive-by shooting. Eight years ago. Ring any bells?"

Mosley shrugged. "It wasn't my case," he said. "Sorry. You can't lay that one at my feet."

"Dammit," Jake said. "That isn't what I asked you. Schuler's murder happened in this county. Two of the boys involved in beating up Chris Tansey have now wound up dead. My source says Rif had a beef with at least one of them. Said he's the one who turned Rifkin in. Can you pull Schuler's murder file at least?"

Mosley got up. He brushed past Jake and walked into his bedroom. Jake waited. A moment later, Mosley came out carrying a laptop. He sat at his kitchen table and fired it up.

Within a few minutes, he'd logged into the Coldbrook County Sheriff's Department website. He clicked through until he'd pulled up the digital file on Victor Schuler's murder. He slid the laptop over to Jake.

"There might be more in the physical file," Mosley said. "You'll have to wait until tomorrow morning for that."

He said other things, but his voice was drowned out by the buzzing in Jake's head as he read through the case file. There wasn't much to it. Victor Schuler had been doing yard work in the middle of fall. He lived on a ten-acre property about a mile from where Jake was sitting. A neighbor had found Schuler that evening. His St. Bernard had wandered down the road.

"A single shot to the temple," Jake said. He clicked through until he found the evidence log. They'd found a bullet fragment lodged in the side of Schuler's pole barn.

Jake's stomach churned. It was right there.

"A 7.62," he said. "God. Mosley, Vic Schuler was killed with the same type of bullet as Boardman. Jessup. Mihalek. Ben. That jogger in Fayette County. All of them."

"He wasn't a hunter," Mosley said. "I remember Vic Schuler. Kid weighed about three-hundred and fifty pounds. He had a heart attack when he was in his twenties. Not fit. Not athletic. He doesn't have anything else in common with the other victims."

"Except he might have been the first to die," Jake whispered.

Mosley buried his head in his hands. "Did I miss it? Are they dead because of me?"

It was in Jake to blame Mosley. Yes. He should have seen the similarities between at least Jessup and Boardman's cases. It didn't matter that Victor Schuler's murder wasn't his case. A simple search within his own department's database would have produced the hit. A tragic missed opportunity. So much wasted time. Except now it didn't matter. Neither of them could turn back the clock.

"I need to know why Andrew Rifkin was never prosecuted for the assault on Chris Tansey. Why was he never charged with domestic assault on either of his ex-wives? He's been getting away with awful things his whole life, Mosley. You're telling me it's just because he's got a rich daddy?"

"His father, Cy Rifkin, was a big deal around here. His grandfather, Cy Sr., got rich selling off some of the mineral rights on some of his properties. Cy Jr. started selling off the family acreage. Big tracts. All over the county. The car dealership where Andy Rifkin works now is on land his grandpa owned back in the day.

"I'd always heard rumors he had local politicians in his pockets for years. And they relied on him. He donated big money to their political action committees. He helped keep them in power. Every time Cy needed a zoning variance for a sale, he got it. That's how it works in this county. Good old boys know how to grease the wheels. New guys get frozen out. There was a big stink about the sale of that land where the dealership now sits. It was zoned ag, not commercial. Some neighbors filed a lawsuit. It got ugly. Then all of a sudden, it went away. Cy got what he wanted. Then when Rifkin wanted to put up a trailer park on the other side of town, bam. He got that variance too. That new park over on Crawford Street has his name on it. It's an absolute joke. They took the woods over there and turned it into a strip mall. But good old Cy gets his picture in the paper for making them build a pond with a waterfall and a foot bridge. The damn thing's in the middle of the parking lot right by the road. It's ridiculous."

"Cy pulled strings for his son, Andy," Jake said. "This Tansey kid's mother worked as a house cleaner for the Rifkins. It's not too big a leap to think Cy got to her too. She wouldn't admit it to me."

"We're a small town, Jake," Mosley said. "You know what that's like. I know Violet. She's been dirt poor her whole life. Cy could have paid her off. Or he could have threatened to fire her. A single mom, no education, no prospects. What was she gonna do?"

"Who was the prosecutor back then?" Jake asked. "I'd like to have a conversation at least."

Mosley took a great breath. "That would have been Brad Barnum. He's a Common Pleas judge now. But Jake, you're talking about a fifteen-year-old case where charges were dropped. Barnum might not even remember. And if he did, you're not gonna get him to admit to doing anything shady. Brad and Cy Rifkin were friends. We can look it up without much trouble, but I'd bet my whole pension that Rifkin was a campaign donor. What does any of that matter now?"

Jake pounded a fist on Ray Mosley's table. "It doesn't. Dammit. It doesn't."

"You really think Andrew Rifkin is your guy?"

"My gut's telling me he knows more than he's saying. He knew exactly where Cory Boardman was going to be the morning of that hunt. He set him up. Then he didn't show up. His friends think he was lying about being sick that day. He's got the flimsiest of alibis. He's got a violent past. Now I find out you've got another murder victim in Vic Schuler killed the exact same way as Boardman. A guy who Rifkin may have a known beef with."

"Fine," Mosley said. "So what's Rifkin's beef with Boardman then?"

Jake gritted his teeth. These were all questions Ray Mosley should have asked two years ago when Cory Boardman died.

"Jake," Mosley said. "I know you're pissed at me. I know you blame me for bungling that investigation. I've got a lot to answer for. I get it. But this isn't your problem. It's mine. This was my case. If there's something that needs doing, it's up to me to do it."

"You're in no condition to do anything, Mosley," Jake said, rising. "I need to chase this down one way or another. I need to know if your murders are connected to mine. Everything in me is telling me they are."

"Fine," Mosley said. "What do you want from me?"

"Boardman," Jake said. "Rifkin said he had a pregnant girlfriend."

"Ashley Rollins."

"You know where I can find her?"

"Yep," Mosley said. He looked at his watch. "She ought to just be starting her shift over at Lincoln Rehab. She's a night shift nurse's assistant. We had to put my dad there before he passed a few years ago."

"Thanks," Jake said. "I'll start there. Maybe she'll have more insight into Boardman and Rifkin's relationship just before Boardman was killed. Rifkin didn't have too high an opinion of her."

"Don't know why," Mosley said. "She's a sweet kid. Jake, I gotta do something to start making this right. I want to help."

Mosley focused a pair of Basset Hound eyes on Jake. The man was tired. Worn out. Chewed up. But maybe somewhere in there, he was still the half-decent detective Virgil Adamski swore he was.

"Rifkin," he said. Jake grabbed a piece of paper off the table and wrote down five dates. He slid the paper over to Mosley. "See if you can figure out where he was on those dates. There was a manager over at the dealership when I interviewed Rifkin. He didn't look like he was Rifkin's biggest fan. He should at least be able to confirm whether Rifkin showed up to work on those dates."

"I'll do it," Mosley said.

"Good," he said. "Can I trust you to keep your hands off your gun and your liquor bottles until morning at least?"

Mosley gave Jake a weak smile. "Yeah." Mosley wrote the address for Lincoln Rehab on a separate piece of paper and handed it to Jake.

"Thanks," Jake said. He rapped his knuckles on the table. "Let's plan on touching base in twelve hours."

Mosley nodded. Jake prayed he could trust him to not tip Rifkin off or drink his day away. A leap of faith. In the back of Jake's mind, he knew there could be another victim out there whose life depended on it.

THIRTY-NINE

"I appreciate you taking a few minutes to talk to me," Jake said. Ashley Rollins brought Jake to the break room next to the kitchen at the Lincoln Rehabilitation Hospital on the farthest edge of Coldbrook County. She was pretty. Not yet thirty with smooth skin and overplucked eyebrows. The residents seemed to like her. They shouted hellos as she led Jake down the hall.

"I don't have much time," she said. "I'm taking my break early for this. We're short-staffed. We're always short-staffed."

"This won't take long," he said. "And I'm sorry to have to bother you with all this. This might be an awkward topic for you. But I'm trying to gather some information about your ex, Cory. I understand you were dating when he passed away."

"He wanted to get married," she said. There was sadness in Ashley Rollins's eyes. It aged her in the few seconds since Jake sat down with her.

"You were having a child together," Jake said.

Ashley pulled her phone out of the pocket of her scrubs. She opened it and showed the screen to Jake. It was a picture of a cherub-faced baby with two front teeth and a perfectly round head.

"That's my Petey," she said. "He's one and a half."

"Cutie," Jake said.

"Are you working for the insurance company?" she asked.

"No," Jake said. Though he'd been cagey when asked that by other witnesses, he didn't want to give this woman false hope or outright lies.

"Oh," she said. "Good then, I guess. I don't know what else I could tell them that I haven't already."

"Ashley," he said. "I've got to ask you some tough, personal questions. I'm trying to figure out what really happened to Cory that day. There's a chance it's connected to another case I'm working on in Worthington County. A friend of mine was killed in a very similar way."

"You think Cory was murdered," she said, her expression flat.

"Do you?"

She shrugged. "I don't know what to think anymore. I really don't. Some days, I wish I'd never met Cory Boardman. I loved him. We were going to get married. A bunch of people in this town have said some pretty mean things about me. I don't see them stopping. Cory's family won't let them. Someday, Petey's gonna be old enough to ask his own questions."

"What mean things, Ashley?"

"It's about money," she said. "Cory and I weren't married. Petey's his. So that makes him Cory's heir. He wasn't rich or anything, but he had life insurance. Half a million dollars. Petey deserves to have that. But Cory's mom acts like I'm some kind of slut or gold digger."

"She's trying to keep that money away from your son?"

"She wants it for herself. She never really liked me. I don't know why. It doesn't even matter. But she refuses to accept that her precious Cory had sex out of wedlock. She thinks it means he'll burn in hell. So she's fighting me with the insurance company trying to prove Cory's not his father."

"Wouldn't a DNA test settle that?"

"She's blocked it," Ashley said. "Legally, she's his next of kin. I need a court order to get the test. She knows I can't afford that. The lawyers I've talked to want a cut of any money I'd get for Petey. Half a million sounds like a lot. It really isn't. I was hoping we could just work all this out without lawyers. I know that's dumb."

"It's not dumb," Jake said. "I'm sorry you're having to go through that."

"It is what it is."

"Ashley, what can you remember about the day Cory died? Did he talk to you about his plans?"

"He just said he was going hunting on Andy Rifkin's old land. I knew a couple of other guys were going too. At the time, I didn't even know which ones. I didn't ask. But later, I found out it was Sam Stahl and Henry Potter."

"Did you know those three well?"

"I didn't know Henry at all," she said. "Sam was one of Cory's newer friends. We actually fixed him up with Cory's cousin Sydney. Boy, did that backfire. She's caught hell too from her family over what happened that day."

"What about Rifkin? Do you know him well?"

"I've known him most of my life," she said. "Cory was a couple of years older than me in school. We didn't get together until a year before he died. But I knew Rif. Everybody knows Rif."

"He was popular?"

"Yeah. The rich kid."

"Did you ever go to parties on his family's property? I heard those were a big deal."

She nodded. "My older brother did. But like I said, I was a few years younger."

"Ashley, what's your opinion of Andy Rifkin?"

She looked at her hands, folded in her lap. "What's he saying about me?"

The question surprised him. "I'm not sure ..."

"You don't have to say it. I already know. He thinks I'm some whore. I've heard what he says. He's a liar."

"I'll bet he is."

"I should have known not to trust him. He was so nice to me after Cory died. He was nice to me before that too. Cory used to joke that Rif was interested in me. It was a thing between them. Rif has been divorced a couple of times. He'd give Cory crap about wanting to settle down with me. It used to make me really angry. It was none of his business. But then after Cory died, Rif was just there for me, you know? I was scared out of my mind with the baby coming. And Cory's family turned on me. That was a shock. But Rif was my friend. Or I thought he was."

Jake took a breath and followed a hunch. "Was he ever more than a friend?"

She closed her eyes for a moment, then met Jake's gaze. "Yes. Okay? Yes. I told you. I was scared. Rif was nice. At least, at first he was nice. It was a couple of months after Petey was born. I know what it looked like and what people said. Cory's family worst of all. That gold digger thing. Only Rif doesn't have any money. All he's got is what his family gave him. The house and land where he lives. He didn't have to pay for that. But he makes dick all selling cars. I don't even care about that. But Rif got mean. Scary mean."

"Did he hit you?"

She shook her head but said yes. "Once. I don't even remember what set him off. He grabbed me by the shoulders, put me into a wall, and smacked me around a little bit."

"That had to have been really scary. I'm sorry that happened to you," Jake said. He kept his hands hidden beneath the table. He dug his fists into his thighs. Nearly everything Andrew Rifkin had told him was turning out to be a lie.

"I broke it off," Ashley said. "Right then and there. I packed Rif's stuff and set it out in the front lawn. He left. But then he started going all over town telling people I was a slut. It fed right into everything Cory's family had been saying."

"Had you heard he's been violent with his ex-wives?"

Ashley chewed her bottom lip. "I'd heard rumors. I try not to pay attention, there've been enough false ones about me. But yeah. I'd heard some stuff."

"I've heard rumors too," Jake said. "About things he did when he was a kid too."

"You know what he said to me?" Ashley said, ignoring Jake's words. "He said he knew he could do it."

"Do what?"

"Like it was some final eff you to Cory. He said he'd made a bet with Cory a long time ago that he could get me if he wanted to."

"Do you believe him? That there was a bet?"

"No," she said. "Not for a minute. Cory wouldn't have done that. I can't believe Cory would have done that."

Ashley Rollins started to cry.

Jake reached out and touched her shoulder. Ashley cried even harder.

"I'm sorry," Jake said. "The last thing I wanted to do was upset you."

"Do you have what you need from me?" she asked.

"Almost. Ashley, did Cory ever tell you about an incident when they were kids out at Rif's property? A paintball game where someone got hurt?"

"No," she said. "Cory never talked about that. But I heard rumors on that too. It all got out of hand."

"What did you hear?"

"Just that some kids got hurt for not following the rules. Like shooting too close to other kids or not wearing goggles or something. The Rifkins quit having those tournaments out there."

"I see," Jake said.

"That was a million years ago," she said.

"Do you know who was hurt?"

"You're talking about Chris Tansey?"

"You know him?"

"He was two grades above me. Yeah. I know he was one of the ones who maybe got hurt. You should actually talk to him."

"Why's that?"

"We got to be friends in the last couple of years. I work part time unloading packages at Speedy Parcel Service during holiday rushes. He works there too. He was really upset when I started seeing Rif. He warned me not to get involved."

"What did he say, exactly?" Jake asked.

"He just told me Rif wasn't who I thought he was. And I mean ... Chris was really upset. I should have listened to him."

"Ashley?" A nurse poked his head into the break room. "I'm sorry to bug you. But we could really use you back on the floor."

"Are we done here?" Ashley asked.

"We are," Jake said. "You've been really helpful. Again, I'm sorry to have to dredge all this stuff up.

"Well, if it helps you with your investigation, I'm glad."

"I may have a couple more questions down the road, if that's okay."

Ashley nodded. "Sure. It was nice meeting you."

"You too," Jake said. Ashley walked him back through the winding hallways to the exit. She used her key card to open the door.

"We keep this locked both ways after ten at night," she said.

It was just starting to snow again. She stood with him for a moment under the giant pink awning. She gave him a curious look, as if she wanted to say something else but wasn't sure.

"Detective," she said. "You really don't believe Cory's death was accidental, do you?"

"I believe I have more questions than answers," he said. It was as honest as he could be.

Ashley gave him a sad smile. "Me too, I guess. I hope you find what you're looking for."

He thanked her again and watched her walk back inside.

It was after eleven at night by the time he slid back behind the wheel of his car. For tonight, he had a room at the local Motel 7. It was crappy, but clean. First thing in the morning, he was going to track down Chris Tansey, come hell or high water.

FORTY

It was a good look for him, the killer thought. Watching Jake Cashen through the crosshairs of the rifle scope was electrifying. Cashen shifted his weight. The movement put Ashley in the crosshairs for just a moment.

The killer looked up outside the scope. Anger jolted the killer. What lies had she told? What would Cashen believe?

The killer centered the scope. It would be so easy. One shot. No more Jake.

Was he the hero people wanted to believe? Was it all an act? Probably. Men like Jake played a role but that's all it was. Bravado. Macho bluster.

Unless...

No. The killer put a finger on the trigger. So easy to squeeze. Infinite power. Total domination. The killer was God.

Jake leaned forward. The killer saw. Of course he wanted Ashley. She would go for him too. If Cashen kissed her, it would make her day. He'd take her back to his filthy motel and probably put *another bastard into her. Or maybe she already had one in her. She'd tell Jake it was his. Would he fall for it too?*

One squeeze. Pow. The killer might be doing Jake Cashen a favor. The likes of Ashley Rollins would never get her hooks into him.

"You're welcome, Detective," the killer whispered, laughing.

Then Jake turned and walked back to his car. Do it now!

The voice inside the killer's head was so hard to quiet sometimes The urge nearly overpowering. It could not be controlled. The need. The hunger had to be sated. The beast would be fed.

Tonight. Now. But not here. The killer lowered the rifle and watched Jake Cashen climb into his car.

"You have hours," the killer whispered. "Just hours." The killer put the rifle in the back seat. Then drove out of the shadows to find the next kill.

J ake's phone ripped him from a nightmare. He fumbled for it, forgetting where he was for a moment. Then the acrid, stale motel air reminded him. Coldbrook. Motel 7. The eighties-era clock radio on the nightstand read 7:24 a.m. He answered the phone.

"Cashen," he said.

"Jake!" It was Mosley.

"Mosley." He yawned, sitting upright. His teeth felt furry.

"Put your pants on," he said. "Listen, I just got off the phone with dispatch. Violet Tansey called 911 about twenty minutes ago."

Jake was still groggy. He smelled bad. He threw off the covers and started rooting around for a pair of pants.

"She's hysterical," Mosley said. "She wants to file a missing person's report. She thinks something's happened to Chris Tansey."

"Okay?"

"She said they got into an argument that night after you paid her a visit. He came home for dinner. She kept saying she knew she shouldn't have talked to you about Rif. That he'd get angry if he knew."

"Who? Her son or Rif?"

"Both," Mosley said. "She said Chris told her Rif would lose his temper if he found out Violet was talking to the cops about him again. Jake, she's beside herself. Could barely get her story out. Anyway, Chris left in a huff late last night. He'd calmed down and told his mother not to worry about anything. He was heading over to Rif's to smooth everything over."

"How the hell did Rif even know I was talking to Violet Tansey?" Jake asked.

"I don't know," Mosley said. "But he knew. Tansey told his mother he got a pretty angry phone call from Rif.""

"Christ," Jake said. "This was last night? You're telling me Chris Tansey went over to Andrew Rifkin's last night?"

"That's what I'm telling you. And he hasn't come back home."

"I'm going over there," Jake said.

"To Tansey's?"

"To Rifkin's!" Jake practically shouted. "You go to Tansey's. See what else you can get out of the mother. See if she's ready to change her story about Rifkin. She knows exactly who he is."

"That's what I think too," Mosley said.

"I'm only about five minutes away from Rifkin's. Send a crew over there too, will you?"

"To Tansey's?"

"To Rifkin's!" Jake said, squeezing his phone so tight he thought he might crush it.

"Oh. Yeah. Okay. I'll get right on that."

"While you're at it, you might as well take someone with you to Tansey's house. Just in case."

"You bet," Mosley said. "I'll get you whatever you need." But as he hung up, Jake felt less than confident in Mosley's abilities to find his ass with both hands let alone coordinate an interview with Violet Tansey. He ran a toothbrush over his teeth, found a shirt, and threw his arms into it. Holstering his gun, he slammed the door behind him. The force of it seemed to shake the entire rickety building. Snow had just started to fall again as Jake peeled out of the parking lot headed for what was left of the Rifkin family farm.

FORTY-ONE

The Rifkin farm was one of the premier properties in Coldbrook County. Mosley said it had once taken up hundreds of acres until Cy Rifkin Sr. started selling it off piece by piece, keeping just forty acres for himself. With his parents moved permanently to Florida, Andrew lived there alone. Thanks to an iron-clad trust his father set up for him, Andrew had managed to keep the property out of the clutches of his ex-wives.

Jake checked his HuntStand app as he pulled up and parked on the side of the road. The app wasn't precise, but it showed the basic outline and boundary lines of the property. Roughly rectangular shaped, the lot had a twenty-acre pasture to the east, wooded area to the west with a shallow creek running through. Rifkin had a house and barn at the back of the property. And that was why Grandpa Rifkin's land wasn't worth a damn during deer season.

The main house and barn were barely visible from the road. It was just a small ranch sitting about two hundred yards off the road. He could see part of the pole barn beside it and several outbuildings. Plenty of places for Rif to hide and take cover. Plenty of places to take Tansey.

As he got out of his car, Jake could hear the heavy whir of a diesel engine up toward the house.

Jake checked his service weapon then slid it back into his hip holster. Whatever was going on up there, this wasn't Rif's M.O. Why would he draw Tansey to his own house if he meant him harm?

Jake had parked to the east of the gravel driveway. To the west of it, he saw two other vehicles parked. A small gray sedan, and a blue SUV.

Jake headed for the cars, but by the half inch of snow accumulated on the windows, he knew they'd been parked there for at least a few hours. He approached the sedan. With a gloved hand, he scraped the snow off the driver's side window. There was no one inside of it, but the keys were still in the ignition. Jake scraped off the back window and peered inside. There was nothing there but a bunch of empty Burger King bags and cigarette butts.

Jake straightened and headed to the SUV. It was a dark-blue Ford Explorer. It was fitted with a black roof rack and the left corner of the back hatch was rusted through. As he walked around it, he saw the passenger-side door had a big dent in it. It hit almost the exact level of Jake's right foot as he lifted it. Someone had kicked the thing in. It looked recent. No rust had formed in the crease.

He heard the diesel engine again up toward the house. Still, no outward signs of distress.

He made his way to the driver-side door. Just as he was about to scrape away the snow, his phone rang. It was Mosley.

"What you got?" Jake answered, keeping his own voice low. He doubted whoever was down the driveway could hear him, but he wasn't ready to give Rifkin a heads-up that he was here.

"I'm at Mrs. Tansey's," Mosley said.

"Miss!" Jake could hear Violet yelling in the background.

"I take it she hasn't heard from him," Jake said. "There's a blue Ford Explorer parked on the road just after Rifkin's driveway. Ask her what kind of car he drives."

"A blue Ford Explorer. But Jake," Mosley said. "I think you need to get over here. There's something you have to see."

"Then Tansey's here. I'm heading up to the house."

"Jake!" Mosley barked. "I said I think you need to get over here."

Jake straightened. "Tell me what's going on."

"I asked his mother if I could look around in Tansey's room. Trying to figure out if he maybe packed a bag or something, you know. Anyway, she let me right in. Jake ... this place is a shrine. She opened his walk-in closet and it's covered with posters and news articles. Give me a second. I'm texting you a video."

Jake stepped away from Tansey's car and headed back to his own. He slipped behind the wheel again so he could see his phone screen without the glare of the sunlight.

A moment later, Mosley's video came through. It was herky-jerky at first, as Mosley either pointed the lens at the floor or stuck his thumb over it. But a few seconds in, he managed to point it at something that mattered.

Jake blinked. It took a moment for his heart rate to catch up with what his brain could immediately sense.

Vasily Zaitsev, the Hero of Stalingrad. Tansey had posters of him taped to every spare inch of wall in the closet. Photo after blown-up photo of Zaitsev in his military garb. Getting medals pinned to his chest by Josef Stalin. And there was the Mosin-Nagant. Tansey had at least ten glossy, color posters of it. Promotional shots.

"Christ," Jake said. Without even thinking, he left his car and walked back over to the Ford Explorer.

"Jake?" Mosley called out. Jake didn't have him on speaker, but he could hear him clearly on the other end of the phone.

"Jake?" Mosley called out.

Jake took a hand and wiped the snow off the backseat window of Tansey's car.

"Mosley?" he said as he peered inside and brought the phone back to his ear. "I'm looking in the window of Tansey's Explorer. Can you hear me?"

"I gotcha, Jake," Mosley said.

An empty black rifle case lay across Tansey's backseat.

Jake's heart felt like it leapt straight out of his body. Something Sam Stahl said when he'd interviewed him just days ago. He'd tried to flag down help when he found Cory Boardman's body. No one would stop. But he mentioned an SUV. A blue SUV with a roof rack. At first he'd thought it was a police vehicle. It had slowed, looked at him, then flipped him off and sped away.

My God. "Shit," Jake whispered. On instinct he ducked down below the window of the vehicle.

"Jake?" Mosley yelled through the phone.

Whizz. Crack! The unmistakable sound of a rifle shot. Jake heard a man's scream.

"Shots fired, shots fired!" Jake called into his phone. "Mosley. I need backup. Lots of it. He's here. He's here!"

Another rifle shot. A scream.

Adrenaline took over. Jake pulled out his weapon and began to run toward the sound.

Do you see the threat? Do you see the threat?

Jake ran up the gravel driveway.

Get to cover! Get to cover!

Spotting a small lean-to storage shed about fifty yards up ahead, he stuck to the creek bed and ran toward it, his heart pounding out of his chest.

"Stop!" he heard a man shout. Rifkin. "Stop!"

Another shot rang out, coming from Jake's left up the hill.

Jake dove, pressing his back to the shed wall. He sank down, pulling his weapon up to his chest.

Another rifle shot whizzing through the trees.

"Help!" Rifkin shouted.

The sniper had him pinned down. He had the perfect position, hidden in the trees at the top of that damn hill on the other side of the creek bed. Slowly, carefully, Jake peeked his head around the corner of the shed.

Cover. He needed to advance and find his next cover.

Another rifle shot, this one closer. It hit something metal.

"I give up! I give up!" Rifkin cried out.

"Shut up," Jake whispered. "Stay down and shut up!"

But it was futile. Rifkin kept shouting for help, giving his shooter all the information he needed on his location.

Jake could draw his fire. One shot, straight in the air. But his next cover was too far away. He was outgunned. Outpositioned. He had just one advantage. He prayed Tansey didn't yet know he was there.

He heard movement in the trees. Jake peeked his head out from behind the shed. About seventy-five yards ahead of him, he saw Andrew Rifkin trying to get up and run toward the house.

"No!" Jake whispered, with no hope of Rifkin being able to hear him.

The rifle shot took him in the back of his left calf as he ran. Squealing, Rifkin hit the ground and began to crawl. Three more shots hit in quick succession, cutting a semi-circle in the snow around Andrew Rifkin's head.

Rifkin covered his head with his hands, as if that could stop the bullet from penetrating his skull.

"Whatever you want," Rifkin cried out. "I've got ten grand in a safe inside the house. I'll get it. Just let me get to it."

Then, Rifkin staggered to his feet, holding his hands on top of his head.

"I'll get it for you, man," he cried. "Whatever you want."

Step by step, Rifkin lurched and limped toward the house.

The trees. If Jake could just get to the edge of the trees. He could take cover behind one of them. Try to get a bead on Tansey. Where the hell was his backup?

"Do you know who I am?" Rifkin shouted, his voice cracking. "Do you know who I fucking am? I'll give you whatever you want. But if you kill me? You think you can kill me?"

Jake took a breath. "Keep talking, Rifkin," he whispered. "Keep pissing him off. Keep his attention."

Slowly, Jake slid around the corner of the shed, keeping his back to it. He stepped over broken two-by-fours, an empty gas can, frozen clumps of hay on the ground. He stopped next to a rusted-out shovel, propped against the side of the shed. To get around that he'd have to step out or move the thing.

If Tansey heard ...

Another shot. This one clipped Rifkin in the shoulder. He spun around, jerked backward, then fell to the ground.

Jake felt his phone vibrating in his pocket.

"Christ," he whispered. "Not now, Mosley."

Another shot. This one made Rifkin jerk as he lay face down in the snow. But he didn't cry out. He didn't roll. Andrew Rifkin had passed out.

"Shit," Jake whispered. "Shit. Shit. Shit. Shit."

Rifkin was down. Not mortally wounded yet, but not moving and lying right in the open. Tansey just had to take one more shot.

Jake heard laughter coming from the woods.

"You're worthless!" the man called out. Tansey.

"You're worthless, Rif! Look at you. You think that hurt? How about one to the chest? How about one that breaks the bones in your face? I'll shoot your jaw clean off just to shut you up."

Jake had to move. Draw Tansey's fire until backup arrived or Andrew Rifkin was as good as dead.

"Get up!" Tansey shouted, his voice getting closer. "I want you to dance before you die!"

Movement. A running figure. He was running down the hill toward the frozen creek bed. Jake clocked him at maybe sixty, seventy yards away. Still in the woods. Dressed in camo from head to toe.

Jake pressed his back flat against the shed wall. Tansey was running straight for him. He'd come out of the woods right in front of the hay shed.

Too fast. Too far. The sun shone in Jake's eyes. But he could see Tansey holding his rifle in his right hand as he ran toward him.

Jake looked back. His footprints were clearly visible in the snow leading straight to the shed. If Tansey saw. He would know.

Jake raised his weapon. Tansey was moving too fast. There were too many trees blocking Jake's aim. One shot, and Tansey would know right where he was. The second Tansey came out of the woods, he'd be able to see Jake's tracks. If he looked. If it registered. He had maybe five more seconds for the element of surprise.

Don't look. Don't look. Don't look.

One shot. But it was one in a million. If he missed, Tansey would come out right in front of the shed. Jake had seen with his own eyes how good of a shot Tansey was. With that weapon, he didn't even have to be.

Then, as Tansey broke through the trees and ran at top speed, straight for Jake's position, Jake acted on instinct.

Not a shot. Not a chance. He took a breath, grabbed the shovel from the side of the barn, wrenching it out where it had stuck in the ice.

At that moment, he saw. Tansey's eyes went wide. He started to raised his rifle. He didn't break his stride. Jake swung the shovel with all his might, hitting Christopher Tansey square in the chest. The blow knocked him backward as he got off one last rifle shot.

FORTY-TWO

He was strong. Stronger than he should have been. He was flat on his back, probably still seeing stars, the wind knocked out of him. Then, Chris Tansey reared up, trying to push Jake backward as air started to get into his lungs.

He got a knee in Tansey's chest. Tansey tried to arch his back, gasping for more air. His eyes widened, the whites practically glowing amidst the dark camo greasepaint smeared all over his face.

"Jake," he gasped. Jake pulled his weapon, pointing it squarely between Chris Tansey's eyes. His pulse was a drumbeat between his temples. Jake felt his heart practically leap from his chest. Adrenaline made every nerve ending buzz.

"Jake," Tansey whispered, finally catching his breath. He knew him. Tansey knew him. How did he know him?

"Don't move," Jake said through gritted teeth. "Don't so much as blink, Tansey."

"Help!" Andrew Rifkin's strangled cry came from further up the hill. He was alive. Thank God. But had to be badly bleeding.

"Stay where you are, Rifkin," Jake called out. "Help is on the way."

"He's out of his mind!" Rifkin croaked. "He's trying to kill me. He's still out there."

"I said, stay where you are," Jake called out.

"I'm glad it's you," Tansey said. A smile split his face, showing a row of crooked, yellow teeth. "You know what he is. You know what he's done."

"Yeah," Jake said. "I know."

Tansey's eyes and smile widened. "I knew it. I knew it would be you. I heard what they said about you. You're not like him, are you? You stand up for people like me. You can help me make sure he can't get away with it anymore."

"Don't move," Jake said. He thought of Ben as he pointed his weapon at Tansey's head.

"He's a bully! He beats up women, Jake. He has to pay for that. He has to be stopped. That's your job. You're like me. I'm glad it's you. I know you, Jake. I *know* you!"

"I know what you are," Jake said. "I know what you've done. It's over, Tansey."

Something changed in Chris Tansey's eyes then. For a moment, he seemed almost euphoric. Relieved. Now, as he read something in Jake's tone, his face, all of it changed. A monster settled into his gaze.

"You gonna shoot me," Tansey said. "Right here? Like this? That's not how you like it. Where's the sport in it? This is cheap, Jake."

"Shut up," Jake said. Even his name on Chris Tansey's lips felt like a violation. An evil he almost couldn't bear.

"It's over," Jake said. "You're done hurting people, Tansey."

"Him?" Tansey said. "You think he's worth saving? Come on. I know what you want. I know what you want. You're a hunter, Jake. So hunt."

"Help!" Rifkin shouted. "I'm shot. I'm dying!"

"Shoot me!" Tansey hissed. "You think you're better than me. This is the only way you can win."

Jake knew he should have activated the speaker on his cell phone. Should have called Mosley. Told him he had Tansey neutralized. He couldn't move. He couldn't take his eyes off Tansey. Something snapped inside of him. White hot rage made his blood simmer as he saw Ben Wayne's body lying on the coroner's slab. He heard Travis Wayne's strangled cry as Jake held him that day in Louie Jaffe's woods, when he kept him from ruining the rest of his life.

"Why?" Jake said. It would be easy. One shot. Rifkin was too far away to see him. He'd only hear the shot. He had no idea whether Tansey was still out there.

Tansey smiled.

"Why?" Jake repeated. "Why'd you kill Ben Wayne? Why any of the rest of them?"

"He was weak," Tansey said. "Lazy. Your friend. Almost too easy. He wasn't the prize. I did him a favor. I could have made him dance. Just like Rifkin. I thought about it. He turned toward me. Some predator. Didn't know I was there. I should have taken the first shot and unmanned him. Right between the legs. Let him live with that for a few moments. But then he would have welcomed that second shot. You all would."

Pure, molten hatred poured through Jake's veins. This man. This sniveling coward, miserable human being thought he had taken a piece of Ben Wayne. As if his manner of death could ever touch the way that he'd lived.

"He was better than you," Jake said. "He was a man. What are you? Sitting there. Lying in wait. Hiding. You think that makes you brave? Makes you strong? You're worthless, Tansey. A weakling."

Tansey bucked, trying to shake Jake off of him. "You don't know what I am. You have no idea the power I have. None of you do. He pissed himself. They all do. Weak. Worthless. They all submit. Every single one. The boy did too. Did you know that? Did he tell you? He cried like a little baby. Called out for his mother. No strength there. No courage. Weak. Pathetic. He'll be pathetic his whole life now. I bet he still cries himself to sleep. Do you, Jake? Did you piss yourself when they told you your daddy died?"

"Shut your mouth," Jake said. Just the slightest tremor went through his hand as he kept his gun aimed at Tansey's face.

"Ah," Tansey said. "So you do. Well, now it'll be my face you see in your nightmares. I was so close. That boy's head was in my scope. Pop. Pop. Split his head like a rotted pumpkin."

It would be easy. One shot. Tansey already had gun residue on his hands. His last shot lodged in a half-dead Sycamore tree. They would find the shell casing still in Tansey's rifle and an undamaged chunk of lead in the soft tree trunk. Andrew Rifkin lay just a few yards away, bleeding, maybe even mortally wounded. A clean shot. Justified.

No one would ever know.

Vengeance. Justice. The line had never been so thin.

He warned me. Jake thought. Coach Frank warned me. Someday, there will be a case. A line. It would hurt.

Vengeance. Justice.

No one would ever know.

"Get up!" Jake said. He moved off Tansey's chest.

Smiling, Tansey lay right where he was.

"I said, get up!" Jake demanded. "On your feet!"

Jake saw Travis in his mind. Not as he was now. As a toddler, the last time Jake visited Ben before he came back for good. Before Abby died. Before Travis had lost his mother too.

Slowly, Chris Tansey got to his feet. He kept his hands spread out. He could be armed. His rifle lay on the ground a few feet away, but Jake hadn't checked him for anything else.

Reach for it. He thought. Reach for it. Make it easy.

Justice. Vengeance.

Jake kept his finger on the trigger.

"Do it," Tansey taunted. "Show me who you really are."

And then ... Jake did.

"You have the right to remain silent. Anything you say can and will be used against you in a court of law. You have the right to an attorney. If you cannot afford an attorney, one will be provided for you."

Jake grabbed the cuffs out of his back pocket. He ordered Tansey to turn and put his hands flat on the side of the shed. One by one, Jake cuffed his wrists behind his back. Then he shoved Chris Tansey to his knees and pushed his face against the side of the shed.

Toward the road, he heard the sirens as his backup finally arrived, tearing up the gravel as they lit Andrew Rifkin's driveway with blinding lights of red and blue.

FORTY-THREE

"You're one lucky man," Mosley said as he stood at the foot of Andrew Rifkin's gurney. Rifkin had been shot three times. Once in the shoulder. Once through the calf. Once in the right thigh. But all three bullets left only superficial wounds, digging through soft tissue but no major muscles, no major arteries.

Lucky.

Jake knew better. Rifkin's death was supposed to be slow, painful, not instant lights out like all the others. If Chris Tansey had wanted to kill Rifkin, he'd be dead.

Mosley had just finished taking Rifkin's statement as Jake stood in the corner of the examination room. A nurse came in once or twice to check Rif's vitals.

"They'll get you stitched up," Mosley said. "But the doc says you don't even have to have surgery. Bullets were through and through."

Jake had just finished giving Mosley his statement as well. Christopher Tansey sat in a holding cell in the Coldbrook County Jail facing charges on felonious assault and attempted murder. Each of them carrying a maximum sentence of up to life in prison with possible parole.

"Do you have what you need?" Jake asked Mosley. The two of them walked into the hallway as Rifkin's nurse helped him switch from a gurney to a proper hospital bed. Rifkin howled with pain.

Mosley showed Jake to an empty waiting room just around the corner.

"He admitted to killing Ben Wayne to you," Mosley said.

"He'll say he was under duress," Jake said. "I had a gun pointed at his face. But no. I didn't solicit the confession. He was all too willing to talk."

"Jake," Mosley said. "I haven't had a chance to run through all this with you. But you need to know what we found in Tansey's room after we served the search warrant. You might wanna sit down for this."

Mosley held a tablet in his hands. He set it on the table and pulled up a series of photographs from the inside of Christopher Tansey's bedroom.

"He kept a journal," Mosley said. "Jake, he wrote poems for every victim he killed. Detailed drawings like the one he sent you of your friend's hand. For each crime scene, he's done dozens of them. They're intimate too. Nobody else has seen this stuff. No way this could have been done by anyone who hadn't been there. One of them was in an envelope addressed to you, Jake. Take a look."

Jake looked closely at the drawing. Tansey had drawn a picture of Kenny Mihalek as he lay near the tailgate to his truck, a hole blown through his head.

"Nobody else could have known how they found him, Jake," Mosley said.

Jake kept scrolling. There was Woody Jessup, slumped on the banks of the Giant Oaks River. His fishing pole was still in his hand. Tansey had drawn a closeup of the wound in Jessup's head. His right eye had bulged out.

The next picture was Cory Boardman. Tansey had drawn picture after picture. Cory's hands as they curled into fists after suffering his mortal wound. The blood as it poured out of the wound in Cory's temple. His parted lips, a spot of blood in the corner.

"And here," Mosley said.

Jake looked closer. He didn't recognize the next drawing. The victim lay in a driveway in front of a ranch-style house. Like the Boardman drawings, there were at least fifty of these. A heavy-set man. His eyes bulged. The fatal shot had entered straight through this man's temple too.

"That's Victor Schuler," Mosley said. "His first victim, we think."

"He had a vendetta against him," Jake said. "It was personal. Just like Boardman and Rifkin."

"The first," Mosley said.

Jake kept scrolling. There were other victims. Most were wearing camo. Men he didn't recognize. Then one he did.

Jake tried to turn to steel as he stared down at Ben Wayne's lifeless face again.

"I don't need to see anymore," Jake said.

"He kept newspaper clippings in the same journal," Mosley said. "Reports from every killing. And Jake ... he had a trophy case."

Mosley turned the screen, showing Jake one last photo. It was a long, rectangular piece of wood. Tansey had eight shell casings lined up. Beneath each was a small bronze label with a date engraved.

"My God," Jake whispered.

"Eight victims," Mosley said. "Most in Ohio. But there's one of them up in Alpena, Michigan. Five years ago. Also ruled a hunting accident."

Jake kept the comment he wanted to make to himself. He knew Mosley would bear the guilt of his own mistakes for the rest of his life. So would Jake.

"I've seen enough," Jake said. "I need to get back home. I don't want Ben's family to hear about this on the internet. I want them to hear all this from me. They deserve at least that much."

"Sure. Sure," Mosley said. "Jake ... I don't know how to ..."

Mosley broke. His shoulders racked with sobs, he collapsed into Jake.

Jake put an arm around him. There was nothing he could really do for the man. He felt numb. "Take care of yourself, Mosley. Listen to Virgil. He walks the walk on this stuff. And he's your friend. Do it for yourself, okay, man?"

Sniffling, Mosley nodded. He shook Jake's hand. "Okay," he said. "Okay."

The nurse poked her head out of Rifkin's room. She looked at Jake. "He wants to talk to you."

"I'll see you around, Mosley," Jake said. He shook the detective's hand one more time and walked into Andrew Rifkin's room.

"I just wanted to thank you," Rifkin said. With a morphine drip on board, the man was feeling no pain. "You're a hero. I'll make sure everyone knows. I'll make sure you get some kind of commendation for this. My family ..."

"Keep your plaques," Jake said. "The doc is right. You were lucky, Rifkin. You've always been lucky. But I know you. I know who you are. What you did. To Tansey. To your ex-wives. Your girlfriends. Ashley Rollins."

Rifkin's face fell.

"You're not the good guy here," Jake said. "The victim. This case? It's going to make national news. Your part in it is going to come out. What you did to Tansey is going to come out. People will know. They'll always know now, Rif. So consider this your second chance at life. Use it. You never know. There might be another Tansey out there, coming for you someday. You make amends to those you've wronged. You understand?"

Slowly, Andrew Rifkin nodded. He looked scared. Jake could only hope that was enough.

FORTY-FOUR

"It started out as revenge," Jake said. He was exhausted. Bleary-eyed. Meg Landry sat behind her desk, deep lines of worry in her face.

"He was a time bomb," she said, thumbing through the initial draft of Jake's report.

"Ever since he was a kid," Jake said. "Andrew Rifkin. Cory Boardman. Victor Schuler. They were his bullies, his tormentors."

"Schuler was the first victim?" she asked, still reading.

"Yes," Jake said. "I'm sure the profilers are going to want to get a hold of him, but that's the theory. Tansey started to develop an unhealthy obsession with famous historical snipers. They were like rock stars to him. He taught himself how to shoot. It looks like he tried to join the army at one point but couldn't pass the physical."

"They found an armory in his basement," she said. "What set him off? Why Schuler? Why then?"

"We may never know," Jake said. "Maybe he just got good enough. He shot Schuler in his driveway. Once he got away with it, he probably started to develop a taste for it. Andy Rifkin? The others? They were all hunters. All jocks in high school. All of a type in Tansey's mind."

"Alpha males," she said. "And he was the epitome of an omega."

"Until he learned how to use that rifle," Jake said.

"He let Rifkin and Boardman live though," she said. "It was years between Schuler and Boardman's murders."

"He couldn't risk the connection," Jake said. "He started focusing on random hunters after that. Woody Jessup. That jogger in Fayette County. Then, he saw an opportunity with that hunt on the old Rifkin property. Maybe Rifkin was who he really wanted to kill that day, but he didn't show. So Cory Boardman made a good substitute. Boardman was sleeping with Ashley Rollins. She said Tansey warned her about him. Who knows; in his twisted mind, maybe he thought killing Boardman made him some kind of hero. And he *was* one of the boys to shoot at Tansey."

"And Ben," she said, closing the file. She rubbed her temple. "My God, Jake. He was just prey to Tansey. If he'd known him. Ben Wayne was exactly the kind of guy who would have stuck up for Chris Tansey."

"I think he knew that," Jake said. "After the fact, anyway. He said something to me about it. I think he's been following me. Stalking me. He mentioned the details of a conversation I had with Curtis Barnaby at the gun store. Barney thanked me for sticking up for him against bullies when we were kids. I'm gonna have Barney pull some surveillance footage, but I'll bet my badge Tansey was there. He's been in the county. We've got some initial data from his phone."

"Oh Jake," she said. "I can't even think about it. He could have killed you too."

"Not today," Jake said. "Not anyone. Not anymore."

"What about Mosley?" she asked. "His bungling of Jessup and Boardman's killings is going to get out. I wouldn't be surprised if the attorney general gets involved."

"He's already tendered his resignation," Jake said. "He did step up these last couple of days. Showed what kind of detective he was before he was burned out and drunk. At least he helped give justice to the families of these three victims now. Schuler, Boardman, Jessup. Rick Mosley needs help. Virgil Adamski's going to help him get it. I hope he takes it."

"Me too," she said. "Still, if he'd only ..."

"I can't," Jake said. "If I go down the 'if only' road, I'll lose my mind."

"Well," she said. "This is going to get out. I expect that Dark Side of Blackhand Hills group will run with this. Hopefully, they get their story straight. If it weren't for you ..."

"I can't think about that either," Jake said. "But thank you. You stuck your neck out for me on this case. I know exactly who's out there gunning for my badge. Still."

"You let me deal with the Rob Ardens of the world," she said. "Trust me. I'm going to make sure everyone knows who's responsible for cracking this case. Solely ... responsible."

"That's up to you," he said.

"Tim Brouchard is already running around talking death penalty on Tansey. He thinks it'll look good in a campaign ad."

"Leave him to it," Jake said. "I just want to make sure Travis and Ben's sister don't catch wind of this from the internet. I need to get over there now if you don't mind. I can finalize my report in the morning."

"Of course," she said. "Take all the time you need. Take a couple of days off. You deserve it."

"Thanks."

"When you see Erica Wayne, tell her ..." Landry let her voice trail off. She tilted her head in a curious way. She was smiling.

"What?" Jake asked.

"Nothing," Landry said. "Just tell her. You know, about all of this. You're right. We need to make sure she hears it from you."

"Thanks," he said.

"If I don't see you beforehand, Merry Christmas, Jake."

He paused. He hadn't even thought about what time of year it was.

"You too, boss," he said. Jake left Landry's office and walked straight out of the building. There was one last thing he needed to do for Ben Wayne.

"His name was Chris Tansey," Jake started. Travis Wayne sat on the couch in his father's living room. He'd lost weight. His skin looked gray. He was so small. So young. Jake wished he could take Travis's pain away. He knew it. He lived it. It would shape the man he hadn't yet become. Would it break him? It would. For a while. But that day and every day after, Jake made a vow. To Travis and to Ben.

"I'm not going anywhere," he would tell him. Time and again. He could not replace the father he'd lost. But Jake would stay with him. Watch over him. Jake could feel Ben's presence that day. Giving him the strength to bear the pain in his son's eyes.

"It's over," Jake whispered when he'd told Travis all of it. "He's never getting out."

"Will he get the death penalty?" Travis asked.

"He might," Jake said. He knew someday if it happened, Travis would ask him if he could be there to watch the death of the man who killed his father. And Jake would help him find the strength to face that too or walk away. He knew what the healthier course would be. But Jake wasn't sure if he'd take that path when the time came either. For now, there was just today.

At the end, Travis let Jake hug him. He let himself be a boy in Jake's arms, drawing strength from him. Then he straightened. Jake watched the resolve go through Travis's body. The hardening. And he knew he would not break. Not all the way.

Birdie waited for him on the porch. It was snowing again. Christmas was two days away. She hadn't put a tree up. How could she put a tree up?

"Thank you," she said. "I suppose I owe you an apology."

"For what?"

"For all the names I've been calling you behind your back."

Jake couldn't help himself. He laughed. "I suppose I deserved at least half of them."

"Oh, you deserved all of them," she said. "Still. I'm sorry. I know one thing though. This case? This man? He wouldn't have gotten caught if it weren't for you. You're good at this, aren't you?"

Jake turned to her. It was still so hard to see her for who she was. A woman. Tall. Strong. Maybe even beautiful. She was Birdie. She was Ben's little sister. Again, it was as if he could hear his friend whispering in his ear.

She's going to need you now too. Don't screw it up.

"Have you talked to your parents?" Jake asked. "Decided what you're going to do?"

Birdie stared at the woods across the street. Two cardinals, a bright-red male and his muted-brown mate, landed on the branches of a pine, laden heavy with snow.

"I'm staying," she said, taking a breath. "I've worked it out with the army. I'm eligible for a dependency discharge. As of the first of the year, I'll be honorably discharged."

"Does Travis know?" Jake asked.

Smiling, Birdie turned to him. "We decided together," she said. "He was very insistent that he doesn't need anyone to take care of him."

"He loves you," Jake said.

"I'm going to need help though, Jake," she said. "I know that."

Jake smiled. "How does that feel? Knowing you need help?"

She jammed her shoulder into his. "Shut up."

"I told him. I'm not going anywhere either, Birdie."

Her eyes glistened with tears as she looked up at him. For a moment, it was Jake who thought he might break.

"I loved him," she whispered.

"Me too."

They stayed like that, staring at the cardinals until they finally flew away. They were calling for more snow by morning. They would get a white Christmas this year.

"Gemma's having a thing," Jake said. "Christmas Eve. She makes a big deal out of it. I'd like it if you both came."

Birdie nodded. "Oh, she already insisted. I told her not to make a fuss."

"She's pathologically incapable of not blowing things out of proportion."

"I've noticed."

"I'll help you get settled," Jake said. "Have you made arrangements for your stuff to be sent from Fort Lewis?"

"The army is taking care of all of it," she said.

"Will they help you find a new job?" Jake asked.

"About that," she said. "I've already got one."

"Oh?" The way Birdie looked at him, he knew he wasn't going to like it.

Birdie pulled something out of her back pocket. She held it out in her palm. The silver metal gleamed in the sun.

"Sheriff Landry gave me this yesterday. You're looking at Worthington County's newest deputy. I told her I wanted to tell you myself."

Jake went rigid. He tried to keep his reaction from showing on his face. Once again, he felt Ben's presence. The promise he knew his friend would hold him to.

Look after her.

"You're not going to make this easy on any of us, are you?" He sighed. "Geez, Birdie. Couldn't you get some job down at the mill? Answering phones. I hear they're looking for a new manager at the Dollar Kart. I could put a good word in for you."

She slipped the badge back into her pocket. "Somebody has to keep an eye on you, Jake," she teased. "Might as well be me."

"Birdie ..." he started, then knew it was futile.

"About that," she said. "You don't need to be calling me that down at the station. The first time Ed Zender calls me Birdie, you're getting a throat punch. My name's Erica. You always forget that."

"I don't forget," he said. "Not my fault you've got those stick legs."

"Butt-head," she said. "I can think of a few nicknames I can make stick. Try me."

Jake smiled. "Fine. I'll work on it."

It was his turn to shove her with his shoulder. She shook her head in exasperation as the cardinals reappeared, settling back down on their favorite branch.

"You and Ben were the only two who ever called me Birdie," she said, her voice dropping to a whisper.

"Yep," Jake said.

"I don't know. Maybe when it's just the two of us, I wouldn't hate it."

Jake looked at her, then watched the first flakes of new snow as they began to fall.

One-Click Bones of Echo Lake- Jake Cashen Book 3 so you don't miss out!

Keep reading for a special preview...

Interested in an exclusive extended prologue to the Jake Cashen Series?

Join Declan James's Roll Call Newsletter for a free download.

Special Preview

Bones of Echo Lake
Jake Cashen Book 3

Spring. Five Months Later

"Traffic duty," Jake said.

"Shh." Landry slapped Jake's shoulder.

"Babysitting a DOA."

"Quiet, they're starting soon."

"Seriously, put me on community services. I'll drive the Cops and Cones truck. Anything else."

She turned and looked up at him through her mirrored sunglasses. Jake's scowl reflected back at him. He pushed up his own sunglasses. Sweat made his dress shirt stick to him under his suit coat. The last week in May and the temperature had shot up to eighty. He stood on Landry's right, the sun beating down on both of them.

"Zip it," she said. "If I've gotta be here for this, you've gotta be here for this, hometown hero boy."

Jake rolled his eyes. "Trust me. I can think of at least one person here who'd rather I be out writing speeding tickets today."

They laid tarps down to keep the mud off the VIPs' shoes. The small crowd gathered thirty feet from the eastern shoreline of Echo Lake. Here, the grandest of the luxury homes would go in. The model home. Three thousand square feet of high-end, custom-built home on one hundred feet of hard, sandy-bottom lake frontage. The builder hoped to fetch close to a million for it.

"Thanks for coming," Mayor Devlin said. The wind kicked up, blowing sand everywhere. "I'm gonna hand this over to Commissioner Arden. He's been the true champion and brains behind this project. He's assured me his remarks will be brief."

That got a laugh and a smattering of applause from the crowd. Jake's Uncle Rob Arden wasn't known for brevity at public events. Arden shook a fist at Mayor Devlin and stepped to the front of the crowd.

"This has been a long time coming. Long time. The Arch Hill Estates project is going to bring much needed jobs to the county. This is only the beginning. Over the next five years, we're going to make good on our promises to draw new business and industry to the county. This development is going to draw the most desirable people to our community. Leaders. Innovators. Business owners."

"Good luck keeping the less desirables on their side of the lake," Jake muttered through clenched teeth. Landry smacked his arm again.

Further down the road, a small group of local protesters waved picket signs. Not everyone wanted this part of Arch Hill Township to become a gated community. They'd cut up forty acres of prime buck country and hundred-year-old oaks to break ground today.

"So," Rob Arden said, after droning on for ten minutes. "Without further ado, let's do this right."

A college-aged girl with sky-high blonde hair teetered on a pair of red heels beside Rob Arden. She wore a sash across her chest that read Miss Blackhand Hills. Smiling big, she handed Arden a golden shovel.

"Thanks, honey," Uncle Rob said. He turned back to the crowd. "Ladies and gentlemen, esteemed colleagues, honored guests. It is my supreme honor and pleasure to break ground on this exciting new project."

"Rapists!" A woman's voice drowned out Arden's. Jake turned toward it. Two of the protesters had made their way down to the shoreline. Arden glared at Sheriff Landry.

"You've raped this land!" the woman said. "Save the trees!"

"Jake," Landry said.

Jake broke from the crowd and started to walk toward the protesters. They were just kids. Eighteen at most. They'd probably cut school to come out here.

"I give you Arch Hill Estates!" he heard his Uncle Rob proclaim. From the corner of his eye, he saw Arden plant the golden shovel into the ground. It hit something hard. Uncle Rob jerked backward from the force of it.

The two protesters started running in the other direction before Jake could get to them. He turned back to Landry.

"Let's try that again," Arden said, laughing. He raised the shovel one more time and stabbed it forcefully into the ground. Once again, Jake heard the metal hit something hard. He went back to Landry's side. She was standing in the front row.

"What in the ..." Arden said. He scraped dirt away with his shovel. Whatever he saw made the color drain from his face.

Jake and Landry got closer. Clutching his chest, Rob Arden dropped the shovel.

"Uh ..." Landry said. "Jake?"

He leaned over, peering down at the same time Landry did. Phones clicked through the crowd as people started snapping pictures and taking video. Miss Blackhand Hills screamed.

A human skull poked out of the dirt, right beside Rob Arden's golden shovel.

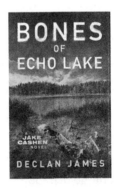

CLICK COVER TO LEARN MORE

Worthington County's coldest case has just come to a boil! Groundbreaking on Blackhand Hills' newest luxury subdivision comes with a grisly surprise. The discovery of human bones sets Detective Jake Cashen on a path that will expose town secrets, long-since buried along with someone from Jake's past.

Don't miss Bones of Echo Lake. Jake Cashen Book 3! https://declanjamesbooks.com/bonesback

About the Author

Before putting pen to paper, Declan James's career in law enforcement spanned twenty-six years. Declan's work as a digital forensics detective has earned him the highest honors from the U.S. Secret Service and F.B.I. For the last sixteen years of his career, Declan served on a nationally recognized task force aimed at protecting children from online predators. Prior to that, Declan spent six years undercover working Vice-Narcotics.

An avid outdoorsman and conservationist, Declan enjoys hunting, fishing, grilling, smoking meats, and his quest for the perfect bottle of bourbon. He lives on a lake in Southern Michigan along with his wife and kids. Declan James is a pseudonym.

For more information follow Declan at one of the links below. If you'd like to receive new release alerts, author news, and a FREE digital bonus prologue to Murder in the Hollows, sign up for Declan's Roll Call Newsletter here: https://declanjamesbooks.com/rollcall/

Also by Declan James

Murder in the Hollows

Kill Season

Bones of Echo Lake

With more to come...

Stay in Touch with Declan James

For more information, visit

https://declanjamesbooks.com

If you'd like to receive a free digital copy of the extended prologue to Murder in the Hollows, sign up for Declan James's Roll Call Newsletter here: https://declanjamesbooks.com/rollcall/

Made in the USA
Coppell, TX
08 April 2024